Replace Me

Book 2

The Kin Series

The story of

Lacey and Shayne

Written By: Jennifer Foor

Copyright © 2013 Jennifer

Foor

All Rights Reserved

**Cover Art By : Wicked Cool Designs –
Robin Harper**

Photography: Toski Covey

I0551651

Check out the other books by Jennifer Foor

(Contemporary Romance)

Letting Go - Mitchell Family Book One

Folding Hearts – Mitchell Family Book Two

Raging Love – Mitchell Family Book Three

Risking Fate – Mitchell Family Book Four

Wrapping Up – Mitchell Family Novella 4.5

Wanting More – Mitchell Book Five

Saving Us – Mitchell Family Book Six

Blinding Trust – Mitchell Family Book Seven

Losing Him – A Mitchell Family Book Eight

Hope's Chance (Contemporary Romance)

The Somnian Series (YA Paranormal)

Books 1-5

Hustle Me (A Bank Shot Romance)

Hustle Him (A Bank Shot Romance)

Diary of a Male Maid

Twinsequences

Repair Me (Erotica)

Beta Readers

Kayla Kennedy, Emma Clifton, Kristy Davidson,
Catherine Roberts, Lara Petterson ,
Jennifer Harried, Mechelle Lovell Jackson, Dorilyn
Harrison

Margo Lomeli, Amy Haigler, Karrie Stewart, Erica
Willis, Sarah Thompson, Kim Eckley,
Kim Person, Milasy Mugnolo and Stephanie Horning,
Lisa Hentz

Web Design and Marketing by: Amy Haigler

Acknowledgements:

Thanks to my kick-ass street team, Foor Players. I love and appreciate you so much!

The Big Tittie Committee

Author: Emily Snow

Author: Michelle Valentine

Author: Michelle Leighton

Holly Malgieri (iloveindiebooks.com)

Thanks to all of my new friends on my FB, Twitter and Goodreads.

Author: Amanda Bennett, Author: Elizabeth Buchanan

Author: Heather Gunter Author: Kim Karr

I adore you and your magical words

Authors Kristen Proby and Kelli Maine from the Naughty Mafia

Thank you for spreading the word and all of the support you give.

Thanks to all of my other Independent Author Friends. (you know who you are)

Thank you to my new street team, Foor Players.

Thank you to all the book bloggers out there spreading the word for me and others who write.

Rockstars of Romance (Milasy and Lisa), iloveindiebooks,

Book Bitches, Maryse Book Blog, Shh Mom's reading, Into the night Reviews, Word, Kindlehooked, , Totally Booked,

Word, Reading is my time out, Stick Girl Book Reviews,
Wolfels World of Books, Dirty Books and Dirty Boys
Book Broads, Book Studs, Books Books Books, Reality
Bites Books, Naughty Mafia, Smutty Book Whores Obesession,
Smexy Girl Book Blog, Just Booked Blog, Book Crazy, BookFri-
ends,
Submit and Devour, Three Girls and a Book
Obsession, The Whispering Pages Book Blog, All Is Read With
Lexipat, Lit Slave, Six Chicks and Their Love For Books, Zee
Books Blog,
Evette Ashby Sexy Girl Reads, Risque Romance Reads,
Nicely Phrased,
Books Coffee and Wine,
S&M Book Obsessions – I love these dirty girls!!
What to read after fifty shades – Summer Daniels
Special Thanks to:
The Mullet Ninjas (You know who you are.)

Everyone who has made this series the success that it
is. I am forever grateful. Thanks to my family and my faith.
With them, all things are possible.

Chapter 1

Shayne

Three rings and the voicemail picked up. After exhausting all other options to get in touch with her, this was my last resort. I'd fucked up and she'd made it clear that we were through, even without hearing my side of the story.

"Lace, It's me again. I'm goin' to keep callin' until you pick up the phone and talk to me. I know I messed up, but you need to know that I was tryin' to protect my brother. What would you have done if you were me?" I scratched my head and couldn't believe that I was leaving the same message as I'd left all week long. "Please call me back."

When I hung up the phone I saw my dad walking in the kitchen. He was going to blow a gasket when he learned what Parker had gotten himself into. Since my cousin Ford knew the truth, it was only a matter of time before his ex Ashley came looking for money and support from us.

I didn't hate keeping things from my dad, considering he could overreact and make my life miserable. The longer he was kept in the dark, the longer I had a roof over my head.

It would have been better if I hadn't just moved back home. Having my own place would have allowed me to avoid him for as long as possible.

My dad wasn't the type of man that you could reason with, and since my brother had a real chance at a professional career in sports, it was going to be even worse. Parker was my father's favorite. He never said it, but it was blatantly obvious. He'd always wanted me to play sports and stay in school, but my eye was always on the prize. I didn't like answering to people and doing what he suggested that I do. My hard-headedness had left me exactly where he said I'd end up. I ran the modification part of his company. Most of the time, he'd come in and yell at me for something that I had nothing to do with. I would have liked my job, if he wasn't my boss. Instead, he repeatedly made me his punching bag and I was a laughing stock. I couldn't complain when I looked at my cousin Ford, who had given up everything to help run his dad's shit-hole of a repair shop. That place was better off burning to the ground.

"What's your problem, Shayne?"

I shrugged and started walking into the other room. "Nothin'. What time is Mom comin' home?"

"She ain't makin' dinner if that's why you're askin'. You can fix somethin' yourself for once."

I rolled my eyes and headed back to my room without saying anything to him. It sucked that the summer was coming to an end, because I really liked being at the beach, away from him.

A few minutes later I heard him yelling. My sister came bursting into my room and leaned her back up against the door. She rolled her eyes. "What a dick!"

"What'd you do now?" My sister Peyton was a little spit-fire. She was mischievous and definitely a handful. I'd had to take care of her messes several times when she was too drunk and fucked up to do it herself.

She came and sat down on the bed, leaning her head on my shoulder. "I should have gone with Parker. Dad would have paid for us to have a little apartment. I hate it here. He's such a jerk. He might as well put a fuckin' chastity belt on me, the way he thinks he can control me. Does he not get that I'm an adult now?"

I kept playing the video game instead of rolling my eyes and pissing her off.

"You're his only daughter, Pey. You know he's just lookin' out for ya."

She threw her hands up as she stood and faced me. "Lookin' out for me is fine. He's like a fuckin' warden at a prison. I hate livin' here."

I thought about our brother and how the truth of his predicament was going to trump anything she could ever complain about. Peyton didn't have a clue. Like all women, she expected to be treated like a princess, without having to live by certain morals.

My phone ringing caught me off guard. Peyton reached over and grabbed it off the bedside table before I could get to it. "It's Lacey."

I reached for it, but she moved her hand out of the way. "Give me the damn phone!"

"Are you two fightin'?"

I couldn't tell her or anyone else why we hadn't been talking. "Just give me the damn phone!"

She tossed it on my bed and started walking out of the room. "You don't have to be so rude!"

I shook my head and hit accept for the call.

"Hello?"

"Please stop calling me, Shayne."

"Lace, don't hang up."

"What now? Are you going to tell me you're sorry again? I heard it a zillion times. We're through, Shayne. You lied straight to my face and almost destroyed my best friend's life. You deceived your cousin's trust. Why should I think that you would be loyal to me?"

"Because, it's completely different!"

"Have you ever cheated on me, Shayne?"

Her question caught me off guard. Since I'd never considered us to have been exclusive, I never thought I had to explain what I was doing every second of the day. I'd gone out a few times with other girls and still talked on the phone occasionally to some of them.

"Shayne? You can't even answer?"

"I...Lace...It's not..."

"Save it! I was a fool to think that you'd changed. Lose my fucking number and don't call me again! I'm not kidding. I'll change my number if I have to."

I heard the click of the phone hanging up and tossed my phone on the bed, before covering my face with my hands.

She was just a woman in a slew of many that wanted my attention. If she was done, then so was I.

End of story!

Lacey

I held the phone up to my ear and listened to it ringing. "Come on, Sky, pick up the damn phone!"

I waited a couple more rings.

"Lace, this isn't a good time," She giggled and I heard Ford in the background saying something to her.

"I need to talk to you. Shayne called me again."

More giggling. "Ford. Stop!"

I rolled my eyes. They'd been making up for days and I was so utterly sick of hearing about their happiness. "Can you two just take a break for a minute and lend me your ears? Damn!"

"Sorry, Lace. I'm here. What happened?"

I plopped down on my bed and looked at the ceiling. "Same as last time. He called and kept leaving messages. I couldn't stand it anymore, so I called him back. Then he proceeded to feed me the same bullshit, and get this, I asked him if he'd ever cheated on me and he couldn't even answer. What the hell?"

Sky was quiet and she got that way when she didn't know what to say.

"Sky, I'm done with Shayne. I'm not being with someone that I can't trust. He isn't worth my time and effort if he can't even man up and admit his wrongdoings. Obviously, he's got too much going on in his life to want to make an effort with me."

"Are you going to be okay?"

I shrugged, even though she couldn't see me. "I love him, you know. It's hard walking away from something that I still want to have. How do people do that?"

"You don't want my opinion on that. I mean, I was supposed to let go of Ford and move on, but we all know I couldn't. I guess it takes time."

I sighed and wondered what I was going to do with my time. "Do you want to go out? We could catch a movie or go shopping? Anything would be better than sitting around here thinking about the amazing sex that I'm never going to have again. I don't even know if I'm more upset about breaking up or not being able to sleep with him again. We were so compatible in that category."

"Right now?" She was whispering something and I could hear him laughing again, through the muffles. "We're kinda in the middle of something."

"Gag! For real, I didn't need to know that." I looked around my room, which was nothing to make a big deal about. Clothes were strewed all over the bed and floor. "I guess I'll clean my room or something. God knows I can't sit around and dwell on being boyfriendless and horny."

"We never told you that you had to break up with Shayne. If you still want him, go for it. I won't love you any less. I hate seeing you miserable."

"I'll love myself less and I don't want that. We're done. I'm hanging up now, to be depressed without having to hear the two of you banging each other and being so happy. Enjoy your night and call me in the morning, when you're dressed and not in a bed."

After we'd hung up, I felt even more depressed over the situation. For months I'd been so happy. Shayne seemed to be the kind of man that I wanted to be serious about. I'd already cried my eyes out several times and felt like they had doubled in size from swelling.

It was easy to say that I wanted nothing more to do with Shayne. Inside, it was destroying me. I wanted to crawl in a hole and disappear. The problem was, I knew I had to stay strong. Sky had been through so much and as sad as I was for myself, I wanted to be happy for her and Ford.

So, I did something drastic. With my phone already in my hand, I called my provider and had my number changed. Then, I erased his number and deleted him from my social networking page.. It was drastic, but needed to be done.

Then I cried some more.

A few hours later, I had changed into a pair of sweat pants and was eating ice cream out of the container. Sure, it was cliché, but I didn't care. I was twenty-one years old, jobless and now alone. I was pathetic!

With my life in such a sudden disarray, I began to think about what I could do to change things. Instead of being negative, I decided that it was a perfect opportunity for me to decide what I wanted to do with the rest of my life. My friends were already starting their careers and fully vested in college, while I'd dropped out and done nothing productive, but filled my closet with sexy outfits to wear for a boyfriend that no longer existed.

Two days later, and a lot of sleepless hours, I was sitting down in front of my mother, letting her know that I'd made the decision to go back to school. This time, I knew exactly what I wanted to do and I was determined that my new goals were going to help me get over Shayne and move on with my life.

Chapter 2
Shayne

A few weeks after the whole episode with my cousin, I got a call from Ashley. I'd wanted to ignore her attempts to contact me, but knew that it would result in her showing up at my door.

My brother, who still didn't have a clue about the pregnancy, was excelling his ass off at college. His coach was impressed, as was my father when he heard all about it. My parents made a huge deal about us making the trip up to his college to see him play in the first game of the season.

During the drive, I thought about a million ways I could break the news to him. No matter how I did, it wasn't going to be easy. In fact, I already knew what he was going to say. Parker didn't want a baby spoiling his dream. He'd beg her to abort, so it wouldn't ruin things for him.

Since I'd managed to keep the truth from my dad, and my uncle hadn't spilled the beans, I felt it was necessary to handle the problem before it escalated. Of course, being that my cousin wanted nothing to do with me, I didn't have anyone to run things by with. The mistake that I'd made had caused my whole life to fall apart.

Where I felt like Lacey was just another girl I was banging, I was beginning to contemplate that maybe she'd been more. I thought about her all of the time and hated that I couldn't have her.

I knew it was a shallow assumption, but I'd never been turned down by any female. As much as it frustrated me I knew it wasn't realistic to think that I could have everything I wanted in life. I still missed her and it pissed me off that I did.

As soon as we pulled up to the college, my mind finally eased from Lacey to all of the fine ass that was walking around the campus. I must have been too obvious with my lingering eyes, because my sister smacked me a couple of times. I laughed it off and kept enjoying the scenery.

My brother was in a co-ed dorm which separated male and female tenants by floor. Since we had been invited, he'd made sure his room was pristine, on account of our mother flipping out over it. She put the t in tidy and hated when things were an inch out of place, at home.

Parker introduced us to his roommate before leading us on a tour of the campus and surrounding areas. We finished up the tour at a local restaurant where he'd gotten a part time job. My stomach turned when I thought about how responsible he was. I'd never studied my brother's actions enough to consider that he always did the right thing, when it came to his life.

Then I knew.

Parker wouldn't want Ashley to terminate the pregnancy. He would want to keep the baby and even possibly do the right thing, by dropping out of school and taking care of her. It was what my father had done when he knocked up my mother with me. Sure, they were still together, but sometimes

I wondered what his life would have been like if he hadn't married my mom.

They bickered a lot and I wondered if it was because deep down they resented each other.

Parker continued telling us how amazing his life was. When he introduced us to his beautiful blonde girlfriend, I felt like my lunch was going to come hurling back out of my mouth. They looked at each other like Sky and Ford, as if nobody else in the world existed. As curious as I was to feel that for myself, I knew that this secret could destroy everything.

My dad would be so disappointed, in not only him, but me. Since we weren't exactly close anyway, I didn't want to picture our relationship once he found out. It would all be blamed on me. That was a definite.

We stayed at a hotel near the campus, and to make it easier on Peyton, I got a room for the two of us to share. I knew she didn't want to be near my parents. Her animosity towards my father was annoying as hell. Them rooming together would have made our weekend, and our ride home, unbearable.

Once inside of our room, she plopped down on the bed. "What's wrong with you today? You haven't said ten words since we got here."

I sat down and played with my phone. "Nothin'! I'm tired."

She flipped over and leaned on her elbow to get a good look at me. "No. It's somethin' else. You still miss Lacey don't you?"

I shook my head. "No! She's just a girl I was fuckin'. Mind your business."

She rolled her eyes. "Whatever! It was more than that and you know it." She sat up and faced me. "It was always more for her, Shayne. If it wasn't, she'd be here with you right now."

I cocked my right eyebrow and sighed. "I ain't talkin' about this with you, Pey. It's between me and my dick."

She threw her hands up, like I was a hopeless cause. "Ugh! You'll never get it!"

I turned off the light between us, so she couldn't judge me for giving her a dirty look. "I'm goin' to bed."

The light came back on and she was standing over me. "Mom and Dad are goin' to bed. I say we sneak out and find a party. Come on. You know you want to."

I ran my hands over my face and thought about the last time I'd partied with my siblings. My brother had knocked up my cousins ex and everything went to shit from there. "That's a bad idea."

She grabbed her bag and started walking into the bathroom. "I'm goin' with or without you. You can either come with me and keep me safe, or lay in bed wonderin' if some stranger is havin' his way with me."

I hated that she knew how to push my buttons. It also sucked that I was obligated to protect her, even when I felt like it was the last place I wanted to be. "You're the worst sister, I tell ya. Do you really think that sayin' shit like that is goin' to make me want to help you? Why would you even put yourself in situations that would endanger your life?"

She jumped on my bed and wrapped her arms around me, while sticking out her bottom lip like a little kid. "Please?"

Knowing that it was a terrible idea, and that I was just adding more reasons to be homeless once my dad found out, I patted her to get off of me. "A couple hours and then we both come back here and sleep. You got it?"

Peyton got up and acted giddy. "It's a deal!"

Lacey

Ford and Sky had found the perfect place to move in together. It was part of a single family home, that had been converted into two apartments. They had two bedrooms, which meant I could come over and stay the night whenever I wanted.

After helping them unpack, we got some movies and vegged out in their living room. I had to admit that they really were cute together. Ford, who gave off this asshole vibe, was like a gentle giant around her. He was so mesmerized when she talked to him and I could tell that she had his whole heart.

As much as I needed to get out of the house, I envied what they had so much that it became almost impossible to be around them without getting jealous. It didn't matter how many days passed. Shayne was the only guy that I'd never been able to get over. Well, that was until Ford's cousin Joey walked in. Then my thoughts of Shayne dissipated.

This guy was gorgeous and I was mad at Sky for not telling me about him sooner. He came right in, without being invited, and threw his keys on the table, before sitting down next to me, so close that our legs were touching. "Thanks for the invite, cuz."

"I didn't invite you, Joey!"

"Mom told me to stop by and see if you needed any furniture. She said she's gettin' rid of some shit and wanted you to have first dibs."

Then he turned his attention to me. "So where were we?"

His cockiness caught me off guard. I should have known that he would be a total douche. Most hot guys were. "We weren't anywhere!"

His raised his brows and smirked. "Not yet!"

Ford caught us off guard when he stood up and headed for the kitchen. "Leave it be, Joey. She doesn't want what you're offerin'."

Joey didn't look away from me. "I think we should let her make that decision."

I was speechless, sitting there watching him fuck me with his mind. His eyes were a hazel shade of brown and his dark hair stubble across his cheeks made me curious as to how old he was. When he smiled, displaying his white teeth and perfect smile, I was taken back.

Sky stood in front of us. "Ignore your cousin. He's being a terrible host. Would you like a beer?"

He still didn't stop looking at me. "Yeah."

I crossed my hands over my chest. "Staring isn't going to get in anywhere near my underwear."

He looked over to make sure they weren't coming back into the room. "You can keep your panties in your dresser. There's no reason to wear them around me."

I was so shocked that he'd said it that I started laughing. "Are you serious? That's the best you can do?"

Ford walked into the room with two bottles, handing us both one. "Give up, Joey. Lacey ain't interested. She just broke up with Shayne."

Joey looked at Ford. "Shayne? Your cousin on your mom's side?" Then he looked at me. "You were with that player?"

My stomach knotted up. "Unfortunately!" I couldn't let anyone in the room know how torn up I was over it. Had I been the only fool to trust someone like him? Did the whole universe know that he was a terrible boyfriend?

"Shit, you let me know when you want to experience what a real man can do to you. I don't need to wear a pair of red lifeguard shorts to get pussy, that's for sure." He took a drink of his beer and didn't crack a smile. For someone that was so flip, he was definitely confident in himself.

Sky walked back into the room and cuddled up next to her man. "Be nice, Joey. She cared about Shayne."

"Aunt Viv could have called me. Why are you really here?"

Joey looked around the room. "Your dad mentioned the place next door is for rent. I was thinkin' about gettin' my own place. In fact, I just came from checkin' it out and meetin' with the landlord. I just stopped by to meet my new neighbors." He looked back and me and winked. "And their sexy ass friends."

Ford reached over and punched Joey in the arm. "Are you fuckin' kiddin' me? You're movin' in next door?"

"As early as tomorrow. You goin' to sit around mopin' or help me move my shit in?"

It wasn't my business, but I had to ask. "Are you two even friends?"

Ford and Joey looked at each other and then back to me. "We're family!" Ford's description made Joey laugh.

"We like to compete, but we're cool." He added.

We forgot all about the movie that was playing. Sky grabbed the remote and turned down the volume. "I think it will be fun."

Ford shook his head and finally seemed to relax. He leaned back on the couch and held his beer out to cheers with his cousin. "Welcome to the neighborhood, bro!"

"That's what I'm talkin' about!" Joey drank to that and then looked back in my direction. "Hey Sky, so do all your friends look like this one?"

It wasn't cool that he was speaking to me like I was some object.

"You're not going to give up are you?" Sky was laughing, leaving me to be the only one in the room that had a problem with the way this jerk was acting towards me.

"I'm not a fucking trophy, you know!"

"Yeah you are. You just don't know it yet." He leaned in and ran his stubbly face against my ear. "Give me one night."

I pulled away and scrunched up my face. "Get a life!"

"Your loss!"

After he finished his beer, Joey got up and left. He said nothing else to me, nor did he even look in my direction. Ford was nice enough to wait until he left to warn me. "Stay away from that one. You think Shayne's bad, well, he's worse!"

It was enough of a warning to let me know that I shouldn't think twice. "Don't worry about that. There's no way I'd ever be with someone like him."

Chapter 3

Shayne

Partying with my little sister wasn't exactly my idea of a fun night. Instead of having fun, I found myself feeling like a babysitter. Peyton was wild and she held nothing back. She was the kind of girl that I'd always gone after and I hated that she acted that way, because I knew exactly what guys thought of her.

I don't even think she cared. Peyton was gorgeous and she didn't need to ask people how she looked, because she already knew it. Parker complained that all of his girlfriends hated her, because she'd either broken up a past relationship of theirs, or one of their friends.

I watched her getting close to one particular guy and had to clench my fists. She was my sister, my flesh and blood. I didn't like thinking about what guys wanted to do to her. My natural instinct to protect her was only heightened in situations like this.

While keeping an eye on Peyton, this hot brunette held up a red cup full of beer. "You look like you could use this."

I grabbed it and smiled. "Yeah, thanks."

She stood with me and spotted what my eyes were focused on. "She your ex?"

I laughed. "Worse. She's my sister."

"Well, it sucks to be you. I mean, she's hot. I'm a girl and I'd get with her, so I can't imagine what the guys think."

All of the sudden my mind did a one-eighty. I felt my beer coming out of my nose as I struggled with what this chick had just admitted to me. "So, are you a lesbian, or somethin'?"

She looked at me with her smoky eyes and bit down on her lip. "I like to keep my options open, depending on what the night brings."

My dick reacted to her words and I knew that the ball was now in my corner. How could I not be curious about a girl who was admitting to my hottest fantasy. "My name's Shayne."

"Amber."

I took another good look at her. Her hair was down to her shoulders and styled wildly over her head, like she'd blown it dry and sprayed it as is. It was hot and with her dark makeup surrounding those gray eyes, I couldn't help myself. "You live here?" The music was loud, so we found ourselves having to yell to hear each other.

"Off campus. How about you?" She leaned into me so I could listen better.

"I live in Maryland. My brother goes to school here. We're just visitin'."

She pulled away and smiled, right before grabbing the waist of my pants and pulling me on the dance floor. She put her arms in the air and turned around, rubbing her ass into my dick. I immediately reciprocated by running my fingers over her tight black t-shirt. Her hands reached back and ran through my hair, so I ducked my head down against her neck.

She smelled like she'd just gotten out of the shower and her shampoo was scented similar to suntan lotion. I felt her fingers trailing across my face right before she turned her body to face me. Her lips were close enough that I could smell the alcohol on her breath. "So my friends over there bet me that I couldn't take you home with me."

I looked in the corner and saw the girls quickly try to look in other directions. Suddenly, the challenge went in a different direction. I looked back at Amber and we slowed our pace, even though the music stayed the same. "And if you win the bet, what's in it for me?" My hands were still around her waist and I played with the edge of her top.

She bit down on her lips again and it made me crazy watching it. "What do you want?"

I leaned into her ear, feeling confident that this was going to be an eventful evening. "That depends."

She backed away and smiled. "On what?"

"If you like being fucked hard." I pulled away from her neck and looked right into her eyes. She kept her stare on me, and I could tell she was considering what her answer was going to be.

She smiled and ran her tongue over her top teeth. "Can my friend come too?" Amber pointed and waved to a petite short haired blonde. When she waved back, already smiling, I knew they were playing me.

I turned to see my sister still grinding on the same guy. "Let me tell my sister I'm leavin' and we can get this party started."

Peyton didn't argue with me. She was all for having a good time and not having me judge her. She was an adult and I needed to trust that she'd be responsible enough to make it back to the room before our parents got us up.

Amber and her friend were waiting for me at the door. They were laughing as I got closer. "What's so funny?"

Amber grabbed my hand and started pulling me outside. "When we're done with you tonight, you may never want to leave."

This was a challenge that I wanted; that I needed. This was going to make me forget all about Lacey.

Lacey

Once Joey left, we settled back in and finished the movie. As much as I tried, I couldn't stop thinking about how cocky he'd been to me. What kind of man thinks he's *that* good? Had it not been for me respecting my friends, I may have slapped him, or punched him right in his dick.

Did he not hear that I'd just had my heart broken?

Joey didn't come at me with sexy banter. He came at me like he knew it was going to happen between us. That pissed me off, considering that I wanted nothing to do with him.

As the credits started rolling, I decided to head out to my car to get my bag and change into my pajamas. Sky and Ford had announced that they were going to head to bed, and I knew they weren't going to go to sleep. For two grown adults, they couldn't take their hands off of one another.

The driveway was dark and I didn't think that Joey had stuck around, but there he was, taking out a bag of trash at the entrance to the other apartment. He had a cigarette dangling from his lips and tossed it in before noticing that I was standing there checking out what he was doing. "You leavin' already?"

"I'm getting my bag, if you must know."

He approached my car and I already felt like we were too close. I grabbed my bag and locked the car door quickly, before I started to walk back toward the house. "I knew your ass was goin' to be sexy."

I turned around and gave him a dirty look. "Will you please stop? Sky is my best friend and I like coming to see her. I really don't feel like having to go through this bullshit every time I come for a visit."

"I don't bullshit. I tell it like it is. Always have and always will. Soon enough, you'll know why."

He flicked his cigarette into the street and started walking toward me again. I walked backwards, afraid of him trying to put his dirty paws on my butt. "You're ridiculous! It's not going to happen."

He walked faster and grabbed my arm. I pulled away and pushed him. "Don't touch me! I don't know where your hands have been."

He began to laugh and crossed his arms over his chest. "It don't matter where they've been. All that matters is where they will be. Just give it some time to sink in. I guarantee I'll have you screamin' my name. They always do."

"You are gross. I'm not some whore that will just jump into bed with a stranger. I have morals and can promise you that," I motioned from me to him, "we will never happen."

He laughed again, this time louder, not caring who heard us. "I don't fuck, whores. I fuck beautiful women cause they ask me to fuck them. Keep playing hard to get. I love the challenge."

I huffed and walked away from him without continuing the argument. He obvious thought he knew what I was thinking.

When I got inside, the lights were turned off and Sky was walking back toward the bedroom. "Goodnight, Lace."

"Have fun!"

She giggled. "We're going to bed. I swear!"

"Yeah right, you lucky bitch. I still can't believe you hooked up with him all because you wrecked your car. Who gets that lucky?"

She played with the bottle of water in her hand. "It's crazy, right?"

"Just remember that I was the one that told you to go for it."

"How can I forget when you remind me once a day?"

I laughed. "Just making sure. You better get going. I wouldn't keep a man like that waiting too long."

"Shut up! He isn't going anywhere. I've got him right where I want him." She giggled and backed herself to the bedroom door. "Later, bitch!"

I shook my head and went into the guest room to change, but the sounds of moaning, not only got louder, so did the banging. I thought that sleeping out on the couch would be better, but from there, I could still hear them grunting.

Knowing that they wouldn't do it all night, or hoping, I decided to go back outside and wait. I knew Joey could still be lingering, so I snuck out and leaned against the corner of the house.

The sound of a motorcycle startled me and the headlights gave away my location. When they turned back out,

I started to make my way back in the house. Unfortunately, Joey was already standing there. "What are you doin' outside this late? Did you come out here to find me?"

He pinned me against the house and I felt uncomfortable and alone. "Please leave me alone. I didn't come out here for you!"

"Why then? It's nearly midnight."

"They are a little loud. I figured I'd wait it out!" Sky was going to kill me for giving him that kind of information.

"How about I give you a ride while you're waitin'?"

I smacked him in the chest and he chuckled. "Fuck off!"

"Doll, I wasn't talkin' about fuckin' you. When it happens, and it will be happenin', I won't be the one askin' for it. Now, do you want a ride or not? You can wear my helmet."

I felt like an idiot when he pointed to his bike. "I think that being that close to you is a bad idea."

I couldn't see his facial expressions, but I knew he was going to challenge my decision. "You scared of a motorcycle, or are you scared of wrappin' those arms around me and feelin' somethin'?"

I crossed my arms. "You're a pig. I'm not scared of anything!"

He walked over and grabbed the helmet, holding it out for me. "It's one fuckin' ride. Instead of bein' bit up by mosquitos, why don't you ride with me. I promise I won't bite, unless you ask me, of course. Besides, Ford would kick my ass if I hurt his woman's B.F.F."

I took the helmet into my hands, not even realizing what I was doing. "One ride?"

"I won't even touch you."

I'd never been on a motorcycle and the fascination of it took away the fact that I hated this guy. It wasn't like I wanted to hear my best friend getting it on. "This is a really bad idea! Maybe I should just drive home."

"You afraid you'll enjoy yourself?"

I put my hands on my hips. "No! I'm afraid I won't!"

He climbed on his bike and started it up. "I'm pullin' out of this driveway in the next ten seconds. Whether you climb on this bike or not is up to you."

He started backing up the bike and I don't know why, but I strut over and swung my leg over the back. Joey waited to let me get the helmet on, then he turned his head so I could hear him. "Hold on tight, woman. This is goin' to be a ride you're never goin' to forget!"

Chapter 4

Shayne

On the way to their room, the girls giggled and talked amongst themselves, almost like I wasn't with them. They held hands, which made me wonder if they were a couple the whole time. I didn't care what they were, or who they were. Ever since my break-up with Lacey, I'd been consumed with the memory of how great she was in bed. Surely, these two vixens could make the memories fade away. I was certain that just one night with them was going to top my list of sexual experiences. Obviously, having two girls at one time was every man's fantasy. It was almost bittersweet considering how I was going to brag about it for the rest of my life.

The girls didn't live on campus, but their place wasn't too far off the grid. We walked about five minutes and came to a three story, old Victorian house. "Come inside and make yourself at home. We're going to go freshen up and get ready."

The living room seemed like it was set up comfortably. Two couches faced one another and the TV was located above the mantle. At first glance, I would have thought that the house belonged to a family instead of a bunch of college girls. It was very tidy and all of the furniture matched. From the apartments that I was used to seeing, everything was usually a disarray of furniture that people had handed down. This was good quality stuff that coordinated.

The girls didn't keep me waiting long. I heard my name being called from the foyer and made my way to the base of the steps. Amber stood there at the top wearing nothing but her bra and panties. I couldn't help but lick my lips just knowing what I was about to get involved in.

Each step felt like it took forever as I made my way up to where she waited for me. I felt like a kid that got a free run inside of a candy store. Amber took my hand and smiled as she led me into one of the rooms. Her friend was sprawled out on the bed and patted the spot beside her. I climbed there, allowing room on the other side for Amber. While laying on my back, I watched the two of them sitting up on their knees on either side of me. Each of them took one of my hands and lifted them to their bras. They giggled when they did it. "This is Leesa. Leesa, this is Shayne."

The bubbly girl smiled and looked right into my eyes. "Nice to meet you, Shayne."

I ran the back of my hand over her ribcage. "Likewise." What else could I say to some hot stranger that was going to let me have my way with her?

Amber climbed on top of me first, straddling me. "Are you ready for the night of your life?"

"Does a bear shit in the woods? Of course I am. I've been waitin' my whole life for a night like this. Why don't you tell me what's off limits so we can get this party goin'?"

She bit down on her lip and looked at her friend before grabbing my shirt and lifting it over my head. I sat up to get it off of my head and then fell back down on the pillow. "You're going to get naked and watch us until you can't stand it anymore. That's when you'll get your turn."

Amber lifted her legs and climbed on top of the bed, away from me. As much as I wanted my turn with these two girls, watching them going at it was going to be equally enjoyable.

I put both of my arms back behind my head and watched them lean closer until their lips pressed together. There was something so hot for a guy, watching two women caressing each other.

They kissed opened mouthed, giving me a view of their tongues playing together. As intriguing as that was, I couldn't help but notice their wandering hands. Amber reached around and unhooked Leesa's bra. She then tossed it right toward me, before leaning down and kissing her friends soft nipples, all the while watching me watch her. I cleared my voice and tried not to let the undeniable lust for them get the best of me.

It was difficult.

Each slip of her tongue hardened Leesa's nipples and left a wet shine as it traveled.

When Amber sat up again, they wasted no time removing her bra. Her friend played with both of her breasts, squishing them together and giggling before kissing each one.

My hands were ready to play and I was fighting the urge to whip out my dick and start stroking it. I know that if I did, I'd be done in seconds and unable to perform for when it was my turn.

Leesa was pushed back to lay on the bed, while Amber slid down between her legs. She ran her fingernails up her thighs and then started kissing up one of them. Leesa closed her eyes and reached down to play in Amber's hair.

Amber was so close to her friend's pussy. I was captivated as my eyes watched, in slow motion, her taking her tongue and licking it over her friend's panties. She repeated the process, and then grabbed the fabric with her teeth, moving it over to be able to get to the main prize.

Her lips puckered and she placed soft kisses over the exposed pussy. My mouth was watering, wondering how her friend tasted. Hell, I wanted to know how both of them tasted and I planned on finding out when I had the chance.

Amber's tongue slid between her friend's folds and she began to devour that pussy in a way that I'd never seen. She licked her bud over and over, making her friend cry out in passion. Even after it appeared that her friend had climaxed, she kept doing it.

The room was on fire and I knew I couldn't wait any longer. Without asking, I leaned over and played with Amber's ass, over her panties. She stuck her ass up higher and moaned something as she continued pleasing her friend's pussy.

With her ass up in the doggy position, I got behind her and ripped down the fabric coming between me and her sweet cunt. With the underwear down to her knees, I ran my fingers against the base of her pussy and felt the moisture. She was hot and bothered from licking off Leesa. I pulled my pants down enough to get my cock out and slapped it against her naked skin. She moved her ass in a shimmy, letting me know she wasn't going to fight.

Amber reached over the bedside table and handed me a rubber. I was glad they were still in the right state of mind, because I was all fucked up in the head. There was nothing responsible about this. This was raw and for the first time in my life, I didn't know what to do. After applying protection, I positioned myself and thrust into her. She lifted her head, looked back at me and licked her lips, before diving back down into that hot muff.

I closed my eyes and pictured what her tongue was doing while I continued to pound into her. Leesa sat up and massaged Amber's head as she looked right at me. "Smack her ass, Shayne." She bit her lip. "Make it hurt!"

I smacked her friend's ass and heard her moan.

"Again. Fucking smack her!"

I smacked her ass again, this time trying my hardest to keep from exploding inside of this girl, but it was too difficult. With one last smack I leaned into her and let myself go. It felt too good to be able to control it any longer.

When I finally was able to pull out of her, she flipped around and started rubbing her pussy, while laying in Leesa's lap. She licked her lips and laughed. "Mmm, that was a good start, but we have much more to do before we're finished with you."

When I dove down between her legs, nothing else was on my mind. I was too caught up to care about anything or anyone. It was fantastic.

Lacey

So what, if I was riding on the back of a motorcycle with one of the biggest jerks I'd ever met. What I needed was to do something ridiculously insane to get my mind off of losing Shayne. Thinking about him, especially when I was supposed to be sleeping, was starting to affect my sense of self. I wanted to feel alive again and not dwell on the fact that I'd wasted my time and energy on a relationship that meant nothing to him.

I needed to feel free, like my old self again.

Then I met *him*; this man that was so bad, in all the right places.

Joey wasn't my type. He was a badass, who thought he was hot shit. I'll give it to him for having good looks. If you could overlook his rude comments and conceitedness, you'd only see how genuinely gorgeous the man was. He didn't have a single flaw that I could find about him physically. As much as I hated the man, I still wondered how sexy he was under that shirt he was wearing.

Climbing on the back of the bike wasn't the hard part. When my arms wrapped around his waist, I could feel heat coming off of him. We made it to the stop sign before I leaned my head against his back and closed my eyes. This was my first time on a motorcycle and as much as it frightened me, it also excited me. I was doing something so dangerous and I loved it.

41

We drove for a while, not having to say a single word to one another. The air was brisk albeit the heat of our close bodies kept me comfortable. After a while, we stopped at a gas station and he hopped off, leaving me straddling the seat. "You want somethin' to drink?" he asked.

"A water would be nice." I smiled, but feared having to hold a full conversation with the man. As much as I was enjoying the distraction, I knew I wanted nothing personal with the guy. Bad boys were no longer on my radar. If I wanted to change my life and find happiness, I needed to be with someone that shared in my beliefs. Not every woman could be as lucky as Sky and get rescued by the man of our dreams, like Ford had done for her.

This was my call and I knew that taking this ride was going to be my first step at moving forward.

Joey came out with two bottles of water and twisted mine open before handing it to me. "You havin' fun?"

I didn't want to admit it to him, since he thought he knew everything already. "It's alright."

He smiled and took another drink. "Yeah, you keep tellin' yourself that when I know you're goin' to be thinkin' about me later."

I cocked an eyebrow and moved the bottle away from my lips. He irked me so much that I wanted to toss the whole thing toward him. "Do you always act like this?"

"Like what?" he chuckled.

"Like you can have anything you want."

He shook his head and kept smiling. "Woman, I *can* have whatever I want, because I don't stop until it's mine. Most people don't have a set of these to push them along." He grabbed his crotch, like his testicles had magical powers, or something.

I pointed towards that area. "You think they give you the ability to be a dick and still get play? You've got to be joking. The only thing I can see coming out of that is a low kick to that precious area of yours."

Joey walked over and got close as he reached behind me and put the helmet back on my head. When our eyes met, he smiled, displaying his bright white teeth. "It's goin' to happen."

"Fat chance," I said as he climbed on the bike in front of me.

When he started the motor I knew he was done talking. It was just enough conversation to have me stewing the rest of the ride home. He was so arrogant that I wondered how anyone could give him the time of day. I'd never met someone like him and I hated it. Part of me wondered if it was all some game he was playing with my head. At any rate, he'd succeeded to get me all roiled up.

When we arrived back at the apartment, he waited for me to climb off of the bike first. He turned off the ignition and followed behind me. Knowing that he had no furniture in his place, I wondered what he was doing. "Are you planning on sleeping on the floor?"

Joey turned me around to face him. He caught me off guard and my hands went slamming into his chest. As I looked up in his eyes, I could sense his intent. His breath was on my face and I was certain that he was going to lean over and try to kiss me. While preparing my hands to react to his boldness, Joey leaned over and kissed me on the cheek. "Thanks for the company. See you around, gorgeous." He turned and walked back down the sidewalk, applying his helmet before he started his bike and pulled away. He didn't wave or wait for me to respond. He just left.

Once inside the finally quiet house, I climbed into the guest bed and stared at the dark ceiling. My heart was still beating fast from the excitement of the ride and I couldn't stop thinking about his tender thank you when it came to an end. It made no sense and seemed out of character, but it was sweet aside from who was giving it to me. I reached up and touched the place where he'd kissed my skin. I got chills when I pictured his lips touching me. As difficult as it was, I finally fell asleep. For the first night in a long time, Shayne wasn't what was on my mind.

Chapter 5

Shayne

After hours of sober euphoria, I was passed out with two fine ladies in my arms. My fantasy had been fulfilled and as much as I thought I'd feel better about being single, I actually felt worse. In fact, I felt so guilty and I couldn't understand why. After much consideration and an emotional fight with my own conscience, I climbed out of bed, leaving the two naked girls, and gathered up my clothes.

What should have been something that I wanted to gloat about had turned into something that I didn't want to admit to doing. By the time I made it back to the hotel room, the sun was starting to come up. Thankfully, my sister was wrapped in the covers of her bed, sound asleep. I plopped down, still in my clothes, on the other bed and put a pillow over my face.

Why couldn't I lay there smiling about what I'd done?

What was causing me to feel so bad?

I knew what it was, but I didn't want to admit it to myself, and especially to anyone else. Doing that would just remind me of how I'd definitely never have it again. I'd fucked that up and with my newest conquest under my belt, and it was undeniably setting the result into stone. I thought I wanted two women and to be able to do what I wanted when I wanted, but what if that wasn't what I needed at all? What if I had that one thing and let it go?

I slept for about an hour before my parents were beating on the door for us to get up and meet downstairs for breakfast. We were taking my brother and his girlfriend out, so my parents could get to know her more. With his big secret leering over my head, I didn't feel that great about starting a relationship with the girl.

My sister said nothing as she walked into the bathroom and jumped in the shower. Since we were used to sharing a bathroom at home, I went in to use the facilities and brush my teeth. Through the fogged up glass, I saw the shower curtain move and her head peek out. "What time did you get in?"

"This morning. What about you?"

She closed the curtain and continued talking. "I guess it was around one. That guy was a total flake. Seriously, he's lucky I hung out that long."

I ran water through my hair and sprayed it to look like I'd showered. My sister took forever and my dad would bitch if we weren't downstairs promptly.

While walking to the elevator, Peyton put her arm through mine and leaned her head on my shoulder. "Thanks for takin' me out last night, Shayne. You're a great big bro."

I leaned my head on hers. "I feel like shit!"

"So which one of those girls did you hook up with?"

I looked at her and shook my head. "Does it matter?"

"Geesh! What's your problem?"

46

I realized that I'd snapped for no apparent reason. She stared at me, wondering why. "Sorry! If you must know, I was with both of them. Happy now? Save the disapprovin' grin, I know I'm an asshole."

She backed away and covered her mouth. "Wow! Have you done that a lot? Do you totally get off on bein' with two at once? You're such a dog."

"Um, no! Don't go tellin' Parker either. I don't feel like his young ass lecturin' me over it."

"Parker isn't a saint you know. He's done that before with these two girls in high school. I think they were just making out and stuff, but he still went there."

Flashes of things that had happened just hours before hit me as the elevator doors opened. Peyton and I put on our fake happy faces and followed our parents out to the car.

Aside from their morning grumbling with each other, they didn't talk much to us, except for the one comment my dad made stating that I looked like Hell. I could always count on him being a total dick first thing in the morning.

When we got to the campus, a few minutes later, Parker was already standing outside of his dorm with his girlfriend in tow. She was blonde, petite and totally his type.

Parker always went for the classy girls.

We got out and stretched while he told my parents where we should go to eat. After a ten-minute discussion, me and Peyton took the liberty of riding with Parker, so that we could avoid being in the car another minute with the parental units.

I was surprised when he offered me the front seat and told her to sit in the back, but didn't argue since I wanted the extra legroom anyway.

"How was the hotel?"

"Fine for the few hours we were there. Shayne took me out to that party you told me about."

I saw him look in the rear view mirror at his twin. "Really? Am I going to be hearin' stories about some out of town chick getting all crazy, cause that really ain't cool, Pey?"

Leave it to Parker to act like a parent. Too bad the king of responsibility was a soon-to-be father himself.

"Spare me the lectures. Shayne was the one who stayed out all night with two girls."

I turned around and gave her a dirty look. "Way to keep a secret."

"He's our brother, for Christ sakes! Get over it."

She didn't understand that as much as I enjoyed myself, I felt equally shitty about what I'd done. The more people that knew, the easier it would be for Lacey to find out. Then my fate would be sealed.

It was all too much to think about with such little sleep. I wanted to be able to admit that I had enjoyed myself, a part of me had, but not the part that wanted to feel what only Lacey had made me feel.

How could I have been so blind?

"Dude, you need to watch who you stick your dick in at this school. There are some nasty bitches around here." He looked back at his girlfriend. "I'm glad I found my girl when I did."

I smiled when I saw how happy my little brother was when he looked at her. It was a damn shame that it was all going to blow up on him. "I was safe, man. You don't need to worry about me. It was a one-time thing. Nothin' to write home about."

"I can't believe how many chicks are bi-sexual now. It's crazy." Peyton had to add her two-cents, which I was sure made Parker's girlfriend completely uncomfortable.

She shocked us when she spoke. "Most of my friends are. Sometimes I wonder if they do it because they think it's cool. They were never like that when we were younger."

The car got quiet. That was the reaction from each of us.

Finally parker broke the silence. "That's why we were meant to meet. You know what you want and don't care what anyone else thinks." Then he turned to me and his words stabbed me right in the gut. "You never should have ended things with that chick, Lacey. She was real cool."

And there it was...

Even my younger siblings were in agreement that I was a total loser for messing things up with Lacey. I had to find a way to get her back, because if two bi-sexual women couldn't fill that void, than nobody else could either.

49

Lacey

I woke up to Sky jumping on the bed. "Wake up sleepy head."

I pulled the covers over my face and rolled in the other direction. "I wouldn't be tired if you two didn't keep me up all night with your panting."

She giggled. "We tried to be quiet. I swear."

"Yeah, that wasn't quiet, Sky."

She tugged on the blanket pulling it off of my head. "It's not like you were here all night anyway. We heard the motorcycle leave and then come back. When Ford went to make sure the place was locked up, we found out you weren't even here. So, I'm guessing you went somewhere with Joey. Save me the argument and get to the details, you little ho."

I rolled my eyes and finally turned to face her. "We went for a ride. That's it. Nothing else happened."

"You're talking about Joey. I mean, I love my boyfriend, but you have to admit that Joey is equally hot. You can tell he's part Cooper, that's for sure."

"I'm not even going there. You heard how rude he was. He's a fool if he thinks I'd even consider being with someone like that."

I thought about how blatant he had been with me and it pissed me off again.

"I hear you saying the words, but I don't believe you. You went for a ride with the guy, alone and in the dark. How did it feel when your arms wrapped around him on that bike?"

She was sitting Indian style on my bed, waiting for some juicy details that I really didn't have. "Seriously? The ride was exciting. He never asked for a thing and brought me back here. It wasn't a big deal."

Sky laughed at me. "Well, even if you aren't going to tell me everything, I just want you to know that Ford says he's a real ladies man. He'd be good to help you forget, but don't count on it ever being more."

As she stood up and walked toward the door, I had to reiterate. "Nothing is happening anyway. I'm not interested in him at all."

She laughed again and closed the door behind her. I knew she didn't believe me and it made me crazy. I was certain that he was a total douche. Why would she even think I'd want someone that could potentially treat me worse than Shayne?

Just thinking of him made me feel sad. I loathed admitting it, but I missed him. I missed his sweet smile and his bright blue eyes. I missed the way his hands glided against my skin and gave my chills.

I was pathetic for not being able to get over a liar like he was.

Once I got up and made it out into the living room, I noticed that Ford wasn't around. "Is he working on a weekend again?"

Sky sipped at her coffee before answering. "Yeah. He and my dad are working on some new contract for a French company."

"Wow, I can't believe he was just a shitty mechanic when you met him. Isn't it weird, almost like he's someone different now?"

She shrugged. "Not really. He's the same guy. I mean, sure, he's determined and has goals, but I'm proud of him for wanting to succeed. He strives for it and my parents adore him, almost as much as I do."

I held up my hand for her to stop. "Please, save me the details. I heard how much you adore each other last night through these thin ass walls. I don't need the visuals too."

"We really didn't mean to wake you."

"Whatever!"

Sky got quiet as I sat down across from her. She looked down and then back up at me. I knew that look she was giving me and I didn't want her two-cents, but she was giving it to me anyway. "You know, I heard that Shayne really misses you."

"I know you didn't hear that from Ford." Ever since the big lie, Ford hadn't been speaking to his cousin.

"I heard it from Peyton. She came over to beg us to buy her alcohol one night. You know, it's crazy the things we do for a six-pack when we're her age. She literally drove a good thirty-minutes for a chance of getting beer."

"Peyton exaggerates, not to mention that Shayne still lied. We didn't break up because I fell out of love with him. I miss him like crazy, but I refuse to be with someone who can't commit, and can't be honest. End of story."

She dropped the subject, probably noticing my animosity. It was a good thing, because I was trying my hardest to forget about Shayne. I didn't need reminders that would linger in my mind. I needed distractions with hot guys that wore leather jackets and rode motorcycles. As long as I didn't have to put out, I knew Joey would be a great distraction. Maybe he was just what the doctor ordered.

No strings.

No heartbreak.

The perfect medicine.

Chapter 6

Shayne

After breakfast, my parents decided to go sightseeing and give us 'kids' time to hang out. I knew it was going to be the time where I told Parker about the pregnancy. He needed to know the truth.

It would have been so easy to just have come out and say it, but I hesitated when I saw him loving on his girlfriend. It wasn't just the way he held her, or the fact that they seemed so genuinely happy. I felt that emptiness in the pit of my stomach and knew that I'd had the chance at that kind of feeling and fucked it up. That saying, where they say something like you don't know what you've got until it's gone, well it's the truth.

Parker was going to have to walk away from something he cared about too, all because of something he could have never imagined happening.

Knowing that this could be something real for him, I hated that one night could change everything for him.

The boy had a chance, not just with love, but with a career in sports and a future of success.

Peyton made it easier for me to get our brother alone. She saw some hot guy that the girl knew and drug her over to introduce them. Parker crossed his arms and leaned against a cinderblock wall. "What do you think? She's great ain't she? I tell ya, I never imagined meeting someone like her, so soon in my life, but I swear to ya, she's the one. I just know it. I can feel it in every inch of my body, bro." He brought his hand up to my shoulder and looked over where his girlfriend and Peyton stood. "I'm not messin' this up. She's too good to lose."

"There's somethin' I need to tell you."

He gave me a weird look. "I think Peyton beat you to it. Look, man, Dad can't find out. My life will be over. I don't want a kid right now and I especially don't want one with her. It was a mistake, Shayne; a mistake that I never wanted to get out. Now this shit happened."

What was I supposed to say to my brother? "When did she tell you?"

"A couple weeks ago, when she talked to Lacey. Apparently she called her and asked why you guys broke up. Lacey told her that Ford wasn't the father. I didn't tell Peyton that it was mine. She doesn't have a clue that I slept with Ashley that night."

"Damn. Why didn't you call me? I'm the one person who knew about it."

"Because I'm fuckin' scared to death. How would you feel if you had the opportunity to make your dreams come true and then somethin' like this happens? I don't want a fuckin' kid." Parker had tears in his eyes and I could tell he was petrified. He looked over to make sure the girls weren't walking in our direction yet. "What am I goin' to do?"

"Have you called Ashley?"

"I don't have her damn number, man. Before that night, I'd barely said two words to her. Can't we just give her money for an abortion? I mean, the shit with Ford is over, so she doesn't have a reason to keep it, right?"

I put my hand on his shoulder, realizing that I was his only hope. "We'll figure it out. Give me a couple days to talk to Ash. I think since she's had some time for it all to sink in, she'll change her mind about keepin' the baby."

Parker, in front of the whole courtyard, pulled me in for a hug. "Thank you."

"I'm proud of you. You're goin' after your dreams and I envy that. We'll figure things out. I promise."

Parker's face remained the same. "What if she won't change her mind?"

"I'll handle it. You stay here and focus on school. I'll do whatever I have to. It's all goin' to work out for you."

He smiled quickly and then shook his head. "I hope you're right, bro. I can't lose everythin' that I've worked so hard for. Dad would fuckin' kill me and I'd hate myself."

"Just don't tell anyone, especially Peyton." We shook hands as I put on a fake smile and pretended that his life wasn't about to change.

I couldn't guarantee that, though. In fact, I had no idea how this was all going to play out. By putting my foot in my mouth, I was setting things into stone before I could even

56

gather what was coming next. In order to protect my brother, I was digging myself into a deeper hole with my father.

I feared that this couldn't possibly end well.

My family stayed and watched Parker play in his first college football game that weekend. I avoided my parents and pretended that everything was okay in the world, when inside I felt like it was all falling apart. This was no longer about me losing Lacey, or making mistakes.

I had to get Ashley to abort the pregnancy. Neither of them were capable of being parents at this point in their lives. Without Ford, I figured she wouldn't want to continue with it anyway.

There was still a chance that she did, though. In that case, things would become even more complicated.

I waited until I got home to meet up with Ash. Instead of being in public, where people could see us, we met at an old abandoned farm on the outside of her town, since she wasn't willing to come anywhere near where I lived.

I climbed into her passenger side and closed the door. "Thanks for meetin' me."

"What do you want, Shayne?"

"Clearly, I think we need to talk."

"About what?"

I pulled an envelope of money out of my pocket. "This is enough for you to have an abortion. Take it and do the right thing. You know you don't want this baby and neither does my brother."

She shoved the envelope out of the way. "Screw you! I'm not gettin' rid of my baby."

I covered my face with one of my hands and rubbed my temples. "Ash, please reconsider. My brother can't be there for you. He has a real chance at getting somewhere with his life. I won't let you or that baby stand in his way."

I was determined to protect Parker. She wasn't going to use his accomplishments to her advantage. My brother wasn't going to be her way out of town.

I looked over at her, almost pleading without saying another word. She raised her brow. "I'm keepin' the baby, Shayne. There's nothin' you can do to change my mind."

I had a decision to make and a brother that I clearly needed to protect. With little options, I knew what had to be done next and I hated that it had come down to this. I was the one who was strong enough to live with this problem. I could handle the judging the disappointment from my parents. I could deal with the scrutiny of sleeping with someone that my cousin had been with, because it was what everyone expected out of me anyway. I was the fuck-up.

No matter how old I was, or what I'd done to make things right, I was clearly the one that couldn't get things right. Nobody would even question this, because it was what they said would happen all along.

Ashley had been a part of the family, since she'd dated Ford for years. There was a time when we were all pretty close. She knew she could trust me.

"Fine, you want to keep the baby, then you're going to do it my way. From this day forward, as far as everyone is concerned, that's my baby you're havin'."

She looked shocked. "What? You're crazy!"

"I'm serious, Ash. I can't let this destroy Parker and I sure as Hell don't want my father findin' out later. This is the only way I see things workin' out."

"Your plan will never work. Ford knows the truth."

"I'll handle Ford. Honestly, he'll probably be happy that my life is so miserable after keepin' your secret from him."

"I'm not sleepin' with you and we're definitely not gettin' married, if that's what you're thinkin'. I don't need your help."

"Save your drama. I wouldn't marry your ass if my life depended on it. At some point you're goin' to want someone to take responsibility for that child and I'm offering to be that person. The child will grow up right. For someone that's so sure of what she wants, I think that my offer would put your mind at ease. You've known me for years, Ash. I'll help you."

"Why would you do something like that? I know you hate me."

I was realizing just what I was signing on to. I hated myself for it, but out of panic I'd sealed my fate. "I might not like you, but I love my brother. I promised my dad that I'd look out for him that night and I didn't. You may not understand, but this is the only way I can make sure he never finds out what Parker did."

"You'd rather take the blame for sleepin' with me? As close as you were to Ford, do you honestly think anyone would believe it?"

I laughed. "My father thinks I'm a fuckin' loser. Of course, he will believe it. Besides, Ford isn't speakin' to me, so it makes perfect sense to assume that I fucked his woman and knocked her up."

"What about your girlfriend?"

"We're through. She wants nothin' to do with me."

"You really want to be a father to a child that ain't even yours?"

"No. I'm not goin' to lie to you. I don't, at all, but I'm goin' to do it because like it or not, that baby is my blood. I may not have knocked you up, but he or she is my family and I will take care of it, because it's the right thing to do."

"What do you want from me?"

"I want you to promise that you'll never go to Parker. If you need somethin', you come to me. From now on, that baby is ours. The truth can never come out."

She stared out at the barn for a few minutes, I guess to consider that she had no other options. "Fine. As long as the baby is loved, I don't care if you want to be some hero. I'm not the one who has to live with themselves for the lie. You do. I never should have slept with your brother that night. I guess it doesn't matter who the father is now, since it won't ever be Ford."

"Yeah, I know that upsets you. Look Ash, I'm not goin' to lie and tell you that I'm goin' to be great at this, but I will make sure the child wants for nothin'."

"I hope you do, Shayne."

When I got out of her car, I felt like I was going to puke. There wasn't a bone in my body that wasn't shaking. How could I have made such a serious decision without thinking it through? I'd just signed over my life to raise a child that wasn't mine.

My entire future had changed in the blink of an eye. Having a child was going to change everything. Knowing that she didn't want marriage or any sort of commitment I couldn't give her, I'd still be free to date, but who would want to marry a loser with a kid?

Before I went through with it, I had to talk to Lacey one last time. I needed her to know that I was wrong for what I'd done to her and this time I needed her to listen. She needed to hear that I was sorry, before I told the rest of the family, including Ford.

Lacey

"I saw you talking to Joey last night. Don't tell me that there's nothing going on between the two of you. You can lie to Ford about it, but not me, so start spilling." Sky wasn't going to let up, even when there was nothing to tell. A couple weeks had passed and he was hitting on me every chance he got.

He wasn't giving up on trying to get me into his bed. Following his moving in, he made a point to pop in to Ford and Sky's place every weekend, making sure I knew where I could find him, if I was ever ready to admit that I wanted him.

His cockiness never let up, nor did my relentless attitude to prove that he was wrong.

"I have nothing to hide, I swear. Yeah, he's sexy as Hell, but I can't get passed how much of an asshole he is. It's not just that. I know you think it's pathetic, but I'm still not over Shayne. I miss the little things, you know?"

She shrugged and took some finger food out of the oven. "I guess. It's been a while, though. Do you remember telling me that I should hook up with some strange guy to help get over Mack? Maybe you should do the same. It doesn't have to mean something with Joey. He's not a stranger and has made it clear that you would enjoy it."

"Ford said he gets around." I didn't want to be some whore. Friends having an arrangement was different than random hookups. Sure, I'd spent time with him, but all I knew was that he thought he was this great prize. As curious as I was, I also wasn't about to stoop to that level yet. I needed another reason to go and sleep with someone like him. It couldn't just be because he said it was going to happen.

"Lace, I'm not saying you should ask him to go steady, but you could at least live a little."

"You're asking me to spread my legs for someone. That thing with Mack was different. You needed to get over him cheating. You didn't want to break up with Mack, but his actions set it into motion. I broke up with Shayne, because I wanted to."

"No you didn't!" She shook her head and leaned on the counter, giving me that look like I couldn't fool her. "You broke up with him because he kept things from you. You didn't do it because you wanted to end things. You loved him. Shit, you still do. Look, I'm not saying that you should jump into bed with Joey. Maybe that's a terrible idea, but it, at least, helps you move forward. How long do you plan on moping around, wishing you could turn back time?"

I look down, unable to admit that she was right. We both knew it though. Sky walked into the other room and started straightening up to prepare for her guests to arrive. She wasn't expecting many, but the apartment would be filled for sure.

Ford walked in with a bag full of groceries and met her for a kiss before coming into the kitchen. "What's up, Lace?"

"Hey." I walked out of the kitchen, passing Sky as I made my way to the door. I needed air.

Sky was right. Even if I didn't sleep with Joey, I still needed to move forward.

Joey's voice caught me off guard. He was inside of his place, with the door cracked. "Lace, you think you could help me for a sec?" All I could see was that he was standing there, shirtless and his jeans were undone.

My mouth dropped when I stared at the small patch of hair that started at his belly button and trailed down below his underwear line. He cleared his throat, causing me to look up at his smiling face. I tried to play it off; by playing the same role that I'd gotten accustomed to using. "I'm not coming in there so you get me in your bed, Joey. How many times are we going to go over this?"

He leaned against the doorframe and traced the wood with his fingers. "I need someone with small hands to reach behind the couch and get my remote. When I try to move the couch, it bunched up the carpet and I don't want to risk tearin' it, but thanks for reminding me how we're never goin' to hook up."

Okay...I felt like a moron.

I threw up my hands and walked toward his door without commenting. When I got inside and he'd closed the door, he pointed to where the remote had fallen behind the couch. "I guess I need to stop putting it on the back of the headrest."

I got down on my knees and went to reach for it. "Why didn't you just use a broom or something to pull it out?"

"Because the broom wouldn't look as good as your ass does stickin' up in the air."

I swung my body around and tossed him the remote. "You're such a dick!"

He was already laughing. "Thanks for your help, and for the show."

I got up in his face. "This is why you'll never have me."

He grabbed my arms and pulled me close to him as I was trying to pull away. I fought him, with no result. "I will have you, Lace." He put his lips up to my ear and I tried so hard not to like the heat that was igniting from his touch. "It's only a matter of time before you come beggin'."

I slapped him hard across the face and he grabbed my arm again, shoving his lips onto mine. I pulled away, backing up while still facing him. "Don't you ever do that again!"

"Why?" He laughed. "You've been dreamin' of that for weeks."

"Screw you and you're sloppy ass attempt. If you touch me again, I swear you'll be sorry. You're the last person I'd ever consider sleeping with."

He cocked his eyebrow, but remained smiling. "Your loss, not mine. I don't beg for pussy, never had to and never will."

I didn't get how he was still being such a dick. I refused to say anything more to him. This day was for Sky and Ford. I didn't have to even look at Joey, not that I wanted to. "Ugh, you're hopeless!"

His smile, the one that made me want to walk up and jump into his arms, forsaking the fact that I loathed him, flashed at me. "You look real nice today, by the way."

I noticed him staring at my breasts. "Seriously? Get a life and leave me alone. If you can get so much pussy, how come you never have anyone here?"

He leaned against the doorframe and cleared his voice. "I didn't want you gettin' jealous."

"Paleease. You are the last man that would ever make me jealous. Screw whoever you want."

"I do. They come by durin' the week, when I know you're not around. If you want, I can give you some numbers so that you can hear about me from them. I'm sure they'd concede that I'm the best they've ever had. In case you're doubting me."

I tossed my hands up. "I'm out of here. You're hopeless."

Arguing with him, over his skills was the last thing that I wanted to do. I'd rather sit in my best friends kitchen and watch her swooning over her boyfriend. Both were torture, but one worse than the other, in so many ways.

Chapter 7

Shayne

Two weeks went by before I had a chance to talk to her. Ford and his cousin Joey had moved into the same apartment building. Ford's mother and his aunt Viv were throwing them a joint house warming party. It was low key, but since I was family, we'd been invited. Okay, maybe I wasn't invited, per se, but I was going anyway, because I knew she'd be there for her best friend.

The day of the party, I paced around my room, thinking of the best way to tell her what I was planning on doing. No way would have worked to my advantage, so I was forced to just be honest, for once. It was going to hurt, but I had to go through with it. There was a baby out there that was going to need a father in its life. I'd promised Ashley that I would take full responsibility and that was what I was going to do.

Lacey was my only concern, though. It wasn't about telling my family, or even Ford. She was the one I was worried about having to face again.

Knowing that this was going to hurt more this time around, I prepared myself the best I could. I wore her favorite cologne she'd bought me and a shirt that I hated, but she loved. My efforts would be for nothing, but at least I could go out remembering that I'd tried.

This was all about sacrifice for me.

I'd lied to my family, my girlfriend and myself for too long.

I'd done crazy things without regard for the people that I hurt, including me.

I deserved this fate as much as my brother deserved to be happy.

Ford had made it clear that he wanted nothing to do with me, but I was willing to bet that when he found out my plan, he'd reconsider. The most important thing to Ford was family. He knew it and I had to at least try to make things right with everyone. It was the only way I'd be able to live with myself and my decisions.

I had to ring his phone twice before he answered and it wasn't a pleasant introduction. "What do you want, Shayne?"

"We need to talk."

"No we don't!"

"I can't let this mistake ruin Parker's life."

"What are you tellin' me for? I don't give a shit about her or that baby."

"That baby is our blood, whether you like it or not. That's why I'm goin' to take responsibility for it. I'm goin' to tell the family it's mine, so Parker can have a chance."

"You're insane."

"I need to know that you'll keep the secret. I'm comin' to you first, cuz. I know you're pissed at me. Hell, I'm pissed at myself, but it's been weeks and I don't want to fight anymore. Lacey refuses to talk to me and I have nothin' else to lose."

He got quiet and I wondered if he'd hung up on me.

"You sure this is what you want to do? It's a big commitment. Your life will never be the same."

"Yeah, I get it."

"I ain't ready to forgive you for lyin' yet. We're kin, so I got your back. This is your problem, Shayne. Keep me and Sky out of it."

"You have my word. Is Lacey there?"

"Yep."

"You mind if I come by later to tell the family? I'm going to tell them that I slept with Ash that night. There can't be any question as to me being the father."

"Are you fuckin' kiddin' me right now? You're goin' to be a couple with that lyin' whore? You've lost your damn mind, Shayne. This plan of yours is insane, you know that right?"

"What would you do if you were me? He's got a chance to do something great. He's so fuckin' talented. I can't sit back knowing that I could do this for him. Ash agreed to keep it a secret as long as the baby was taken care of. I gave her my word. Besides, you don't have to be a couple to raise a kid. When the time is right, Parker can step up and be a father. For right now, I need to do this, for my brother."

"Do what you gotta do. Good luck with that. I know one person here that may tie your balls up and burn you alive. Have you considered what this is goin' to do to Lacey when you announce that you cheated on her and made a kid, then tried to blame it on your brother? She's going to flip."

"Make sure Sky knows, Ford. When the shock has died down and I've gone, she can pull Lace aside and tell her the truth. I don't expect her to take me back, but I want her to know the truth."

"You're a damn fool. That chick is crazy about your ass. She's done cried every time she's been here. You didn't know what you had there."

"I know. It's too late now. I can't change the past."

"Whatever, man. This is your life you're fuckin' up."

"Wait, you think I have a chance at bein' with Lacey again? You think she'd take me back?"

"I think that when you're ready to admit your mistakes and grow a set of balls, she'll consider it. Although, I'm goin' to warn ya, she's been gettin' to know Joey. I can't say for sure, but you may have lost your opportunity, while you were dickin' around your convoluted ideas to save Parker."

"What the hell are you talkin' about? Joey is a dog. Why would she want to be with him?"

"I need to go."

He hung up before I could ask him anything else. Immediately, my blood began to boil, just imagining her being cozy with that douche. She thought I was bad, but this guy cared about nobody except for himself.

Right away, my priorities changed as I considered ways to get Lacey back in my good graces. Even if she didn't want me, I had to save her from being with him.

Then I thought about the baby.

I felt sick again. Ford may not have argued with me, but he didn't have a choice either. After all, the baby was a part of our family. Like it or not, we were all going to have to live with the result of that one drunken night, no matter which one of us donated the sperm.

My drive to his new place was difficult. There were so many times that I wanted to turn around, instead of having to look into Lacey's eyes.

Lacey

"Your cousin is the biggest dick I've ever met." My comment made Ford smile.

"What did he do now, and are we talkin' about Joey or Shayne?"

I leaned my elbows on the counter. "Joey, of course. He thinks he can just get me to drop my pants and bend over. Who does that?"

Ford laughed as he placed small items on a baking sheet and then shoved them in the oven. "I hate to burst your bubble, but Joey usually gets what he wants. I'm just tellin' it like it is, though. Maybe you'll be the first person to set him straight with the world."

I rubbed my temple, unable to take yet another man driving me bonkers. "I'm going to just write off men in general. If they aren't out cheating, they are thinking about who they can bang next."

Ford gave me a funny look. "Lace, not all men are like that. I certainly don't go lookin' for a piece of ass every time I walk out the door."

"Obviously, because you have someone spreading her legs every chance she gets." I said it as a joke, but Sky came in the room with her hands on her hips.

She looked from me to Ford. "I'll have you know that I don't lay around waiting with my legs spread."

I rolled my eyes and decided not to argue with them. They took offense to something that wasn't meant to be. "Forget it. All I was saying is that Joey needs to back off. I don't want him now and I'm not going to want him in the future. In fact, I am steering clear of anyone that Ford is related to, from now on."

Ford pulled Sky into his arms and kissed her neck before adding his two-cents. "I have a lot of cousins, Lace. I wouldn't go makin' promises that you won't be able to keep."

I tossed a washrag at him. "This isn't the dating game. I'm not interested. End of story."

They both started to laugh at my comment and I decided that it was best to walk out of the room. I'd gotten to be so bitter towards anyone that was in a happy and stable relationship. It wasn't fair for me to pull them into my miserable existence. They deserved to be happy and in love.

If I could stop picking assholes, my life would be a lot better as well. Just thinking about Joey and his lame attempts at getting me to bend over made me cringe. He knew how to push my buttons, that's for sure.

After people started arriving, it was easier to be able to avoid Joey. The two apartments weren't combined from the inside, so the guest would walk around and probably congregate on the back patio. As long as I stayed at Sky and Ford's place, it was unlikely I'd run into him at all.

For the most part, I kept myself busy. Like Sky, I'd been around Ford's family enough to know most of them. I'd met several at Ford's mother's party, except for Joey. I was so hung up on Shayne that I didn't even know if he'd been there. I suppose he could have been working at the diner for his mother, since it was the weekend. Here lately, he only worked in the mornings, since he was doing so well at his other job.

I realized that while trying to stay occupied, my mind kept going back to Joey. Unconsciously, I was thinking about him and I hated it.

Then Shayne walked through the door. He had a card in his hand and walked right over to Ford. I could sense the animosity between them, but they shook hands anyway. Ford said something that I couldn't make out, before Shayne walked away disappointed. He spotted me immediately. Maybe I should have ran out the door as fast as I could, but I just stood there watching him approach me.

"Hi, Lace." He placed his hands in his pockets and gave me a half smile. He was so handsome and I imagined myself being in his arms, for only a brief second.

"Hi." I tried to avoid eye contact. "I didn't think you'd be here."

"I'm not stayin'. I came to talk to you."

"So talk." Right away I felt like it was going to be bad.

"I'm about to do something and I know you won't understand. I just want you to know that I was wrong to hurt you. I don't expect you to forgive me for this, but I hope one day you'll be able to."

I shoved him away from me. "Save me the details. I don't care anymore. Shayne, you're not the guy that I waited forever to be with. Do you have any idea how long I waited for you to be able to settle down? I thought you'd changed."

"I have. I'm tryin' to make things right." Out of the corner of my eye, I watched Joey walk into the room. He was carrying a case of beer and handing it to Ford to put in his refrigerator. He winked when our eyes met and when I looked back at Shayne he was aware of what had caught my gaze. "You've got a lot of room to talk about me not bein' what you thought, seein' as you're fuckin' someone that's worse than I've ever been."

Hearing him accuse me of being with Joey added fuel to the fire. It didn't even matter that I wasn't with him, or had no intention to be. "I can see who I want."

"I highly doubt that you would call it 'seein'." He crossed his arms and waited for my response, like I was the guilty one.

I felt like I needed to defend myself. "Screw you. I can be with whoever I want. You lost your say in what I did the day you lied to me."

Joey started to walk out of the apartment again, but Shayne grabbed his arm. "So it's true? You're doin' my girlfriend?"

Joey looked from Shayne then back to me. He pulled his arm out of Shayne's grasp. "Back off, Shayne. Last I heard, she wasn't your anything."

People were starting to watch them and I felt uncomfortable. I had to do something and siding with Shayne wasn't an option, so I threw myself in between them and put my arms around Joey's waist. He looked at me with a puzzled look. I took a deep breath and said words to Joey that I never wanted to say. "Let's just go back to your place."

He motioned to the two of us and I could tell he was at a loss for words. "I don't believe you, Lace. You wouldn't be with someone like him. This is all an act, isn't it?"

I felt Joey's dirty hands wrapping around my back. "It's true. She's with me, Shayne. Sorry you had to find out about it here, man. No hard feelin's."

Shayne said nothing as I was being pulled out of the door by Joey's hand. He looked devastated and a part of me ached for him. Not only had I just lied, but was being groped by someone I hated.

He pulled me all the way into his apartment, past his family and into his bedroom, kicking the door with his boot. "Don't you dare do somethin' like that without warnin' me. I ain't havin' my mother upset because I had to beat the shit out of Shayne in the middle of this party, you got it?"

I nodded. "Sorry. It just happened. I didn't think about what I was doing. Can I leave now?"

I put my hand on the doorknob and felt him pulling me back by the elastic of my pants. "Not so fast."

We were face-to-face, so close that I could lean over and touch his nose with mine. I hated being so close to him.

"You have ten seconds to get your hands off of me, before I ruin any chance of you ever having children again."

Joey did as I asked and let go of his hold on me. "I thought you wanted to play house."

"The game is over. I could see how hurt he was and now I feel like shit."

"He should feel like shit."

I looked down and sat on his bed. "Maybe, but it doesn't solve anything."

"You want to be with him, don't you?"

I looked over at Joey, and for the first time, I realized he was being sincere. "I can't help it. Maybe I'm glutton for punishment, but I still love him. I've liked him since we were younger. My summers were spent chasing him around when we were teenagers. He didn't even know my name back then, and all I knew was that he was the hot guy that had a place close to ours. Then one party changed everything. I never looked back, because I thought he felt the same way I did. I was wrong."

He cleared his throat and knelt down in front of me. "If you want him so bad, then why did you tell him you were with me? That was a game endin' blow, you know that right?"

I shrugged. "I wanted to hurt him, like he'd hurt me. It was stupid."

"I can help you, but you're not goin' to like the idea."

I looked right at him and laughed. "Does it involve me sleeping with you?"

"In theory, maybe. Look, if you want Shayne back, maybe you need to show him what he lost. We got a rise out of him back there. I think it's an option you should consider."

I rolled my eyes. "And I would want you to help me with that?"

"It's just a suggestion."

"What's in it for you? Obviously you want to sleep with me. I'm not trading my vagina for your help."

He chuckled and shook his head at me. "Look, we both need to get out there and mingle. Meet me down here when everyone leaves. I promise that I won't lay a hand on you, unless you ask me to."

"I won't."

"I'll still be nice and help you. I'll pretend we're a couple and play fair. If I can't have you then I'd want you to be happy anyway."

"Are you drunk?" I couldn't understand why he was being so kind.

"Not drunk enough, that's' for sure." Joey stood up and walked out of the room, leaving me to pout alone.

I waited a while before I made my way back to Sky and Ford's. Shayne wasn't anywhere to be found, but Peyton located me right away. "Is it true? You're seein' Joey now?"

I couldn't believe that he'd told her that already. Then I knew that if I told her the truth, she'd run back to him. "Yeah, it's true."

"Don't tell Shayne, but he's really hot. I mean, I wish you were still with my brother, but Joey is a lot of man. What's he like in bed?"

I slapped her. "Peyton, I'm not discussing that with you."

"I bet he's amazing. I can tell from the way his jeans fit him. That man is hung like a racehorse. One night with him and you probably forgot all about Shayne."

She was so wrong. Little did she know that I could never forget about her brother. That's what happens when you let yourself fall in love. "I would have stayed with your brother, had he not done what he did.

She froze and looked right at me. "After what just happened, I don't blame you for movin' on."

"What are you talkin' about? I was only gone for about thirty minutes. What did I miss?"

"Shayne's the father of Ashley's baby. I guess you knew that already. It was probably why you two really broke up. Anyway, he told the family just now. My dad is pissed. He told him he has to move out and get his own place before he brings a child into the world. Shayne left right after and then my dad got mad and they left too."

I was at a complete loss for words.

Shayne had come to tell me that he was taking the responsibility of Ashley's baby. Was he crazy?

I burst into tears and felt Peyton's arms wrapping around me. "I'm so sorry, Lace. I thought you knew. I didn't know he cheated with her. That's just wrong. Ashley was with Ford. That goes against the guy-code, big time. My aunt wouldn't even look at Shayne, and Ford looked like he was in disbelief. It all makes sense though. Ashley called him all the time and he was being sneaky right before you guys broke up. This sucks."

I kept crying, not really taking in anything that she was saying to me. "Yeah, it really does."

I didn't care about making Shayne jealous anymore. All I wanted to do was crawl in a dark cave and die. I thought his brother was the father of the baby, but what if it was Shayne all along? Had he said it was his brother to keep me hanging on? It made no sense. He acted like he hated Ashley. Now they were having a child?

I pulled away from Peyton and went running out of the apartment. Joey was standing there, putting out his cigarette. I slammed into his chest and didn't pull away. His hands reached around my back and I looked up at him with tear filled eyes. "What's wrong? What happened?"

I don't know why I did it, or even if I had control over my actions at all. "Please, just get me out of here."

Chapter 8

Shayne

After making the announcement, which went over as well as could be expected, I was left having to move out of my parent's house. It wasn't that I didn't expect that outcome, but I also hadn't planned on having to look for a new place to live.

Another thing I hadn't considered was that my parents would expect me to get a place with Ashley. They were out of their minds if they assumed I was going to have a relationship with someone like her.

Still, I had to remember that I was doing this as a favor for my brother. As crazy as it seemed, I was giving him the opportunity to get his life together. When the time was right, I would step aside and let him do what he needed to do. For the time being, the baby would be welcomed into our family, as he or she should. Whether he was mine or Parker's he was still our blood.

I drove around for a while, thinking about everything that had taken place after I'd sat them all down and made my announcement. After the initial shock, my father just started yelling at me. I think he expected Ford, who was the only person that knew the real truth, to haul off and hit me. Instead, he and Sky stayed in the kitchen and out of the drama. Maybe they would have been easier on me if he'd given his opinion, but I expected nothing from my cousin, after I'd put him through hell, even if I had come clean in the end.

Then there was Lacey. After she ripped out my heart by showing me that she had moved on, I didn't care about the ramifications of my decision. The destruction was done and now damage control was all I could do to salvage my reputation, especially with her.

I pulled back down the road to the apartment a little later. I needed to apologize and tell her the truth; that the baby wasn't mine, like I wanted everyone to believe. Thinking that Sky and Ford telling her the truth was a bad idea, I set out to clear the air. Sure, she'd still be pissed about what I was doing, but it beat her thinking that I'd lied to her again.

It was becoming more obvious that my chances of ever being with her were in the past. Lacey had moved on, even before she'd heard that I'd slept with someone else. How could I blame her for wanting something new? My only problem was that I didn't want it to be Joey.

Maybe my problem was more than him having a reputation. It was possible that my biggest hurdle was the fact that every time Ford and Sky would have a get-together, we'd both be invited. The last thing I wanted was to have to see the two of them swooning over each other.

I knew the party was over when I pulled into the driveway and the cars were all gone. Lacey's was still parked on the side, so I knew she was around. I walked up and knocked on Ford's door, hoping he wasn't going to punch me in the face. Instead, Sky answered. "Shayne. What are you doing here?"

I cleared my voice and leaned on the doorframe. "I need to talk to Lace. Can you get her for me?"

Ford walked to the door. He'd changed his clothes and looked like he'd just got up off of the couch, after fooling around. "She ain't here, man. We haven't seen her for a while. I think she left after your argument."

"Her car is still here, though."

The couple looked at each other and I could tell they were thinking the same thing.

"What?"

"She's at Joey's," Sky replied.

There was nothing more I could say, so I walked away from them.

Sky came running after me. "Shayne, wait! Why do you care where Lacey is? Forgive me for being blunt, but she's not someone that I want to see hurt. Everything you've done here lately has been hard on her. Now you are trying to pass off a child as being yours, when it would mean you conceived it while with Lacey. Do you have any idea what you've done to her? Her heart is broken. I've been where she's at and it sucks."

"You act like none of this is botherin' me. I care about Lacey."

"She was in love with you, Shayne."

I could sense that I wasn't going to get anywhere. "We never talked about bein' exclusive. How was I to know that she felt that way? She never told me."

Sky threw her hands up like talking to me was hopeless. "Never mind. Do us all a favor and leave Lace alone. Let her get over you so she can be happy. If you care about her at all, you'll at least be decent and give her that." She walked back into her apartment and closed the door, before I could say anything else.

While walking back out to my car, I saw the light on at Joey's. I'd like to say that I tried not to look, but when I saw Lacey sitting with that asshole, and him touching her face, it was like a kick in the balls. I stood there for a few minutes, watching him console her. Anger filled me and all I wanted to do was break down his door and hurt him.

Then I saw him lean over and kiss the top of her head. That tender moment made me feel like maybe she wasn't just sex for Joey. If he cared enough to comfort her, maybe it was enough for her to get over me and actually be happy.

As heart wrenching as it was, I knew I had to walk away from Lacey. Our time together was over and I needed to learn to be a better person, who was responsible for his actions and decisions. I needed to be able to stand by something or someone and feel what it was like to have them trust me again.

As bad as I felt, I knew I was all alone.

For the first time, not even my family had my back.

This was what I deserved.

Lacey

I couldn't believe that this was all happening to me. Why I'd thought that Shayne and I could work things out made no sense now. He clearly had no idea how to be in a committed relationship.

Joey was the last person that I thought would comfort me, but that's exactly what he was doing. After the crowd of people cleared out, he sat with me in his living room. As rough as his appearance seemed, he had decorated his apartment in style. Joey had painted the walls a gray color. His furniture was black leather and he had pictures on his wall with red gray and black hues. His electronics were organized and the place looked spotless all of the time. I couldn't get over it.

Even his bedroom, that I never expected to walk in, was decorated in the same colors. There weren't any clothes laying on the floor and his bed was made. Of course, maybe it was because he was expecting company, but Sky had commented about it before, too.

Joey sat down next to me and wiped another set of tears off of my cheeks. "Do you want my opinion?"

I sniffled. "Not really."

"Fair enough."

He handed me a bottle of beer and pointed to a coaster. I took a sip and sat it down. "Thanks for saving me."

"Which time?"

"Don't be a dick, Joey. I can't take anymore sarcasm tonight."

Joey picked up his phone, looked at the time, and sat it back down. "Listen, I have somewhere I need to be. I think everyone's gone, but you're welcome to stay here. I won't be back until later."

I don't know what made me ask, but the words blurted out of my mouth. "Are you coming home alone?"

A smiled formed in the crease of his lips. "Why do you want to know?"

I shrugged. "I...I don't want to mess up your opportunity to get laid."

He laughed at me. "You could always wait for me in my bed, but that's up to you, of course."

When he got up, started walking in the bedroom, and pulled off his shirt, I couldn't help but stare at him. Joey had a tattoo of a dragon on his back. It looked sexy as hell and for just a second, I wasn't thinking about my broken heart. He turned and looked at me. I pretended to be offended that he was shirtless. "No thanks. I'll probably just go back upstairs, once I know Sky and Ford are in bed."

He tapped on the door. "My door is always open if you change your mind."

When he walked into the bathroom and shut the door, I covered my face and let the real tears pour out. His mind games were not what I needed. I wanted the empty feeling in the pit of my stomach to go away.

A few minutes later, he came out wearing only a towel. Our eyes met and he smiled before going into his bedroom and shutting the door behind him. I wasn't used to Joey being so nice. In all of the times that we'd been around each other, he'd only tried to get me in his bed. This new side of him scared me, because I found myself becoming curious. Curiosity meant that I was interested and I couldn't want someone like Joey. He had nothing to offer me but the same fate I was under at the moment.

I was so sick of meaningless relationships and longed to have something real, except I always fell for the wrong guys.

He came out smelling fantastic and looking even better than earlier. I tried to hide the attraction that I felt toward him, albeit I'm certain he could see me blushing. "So, I'll be back later. Like I said before, you're welcome to stay. I've got ways to take your mind off of him, you know."

I shook my head. "I'll be gone when you get back. Don't worry, I will lock up."

"Suit yourself, Lace." He leaned over and kissed me on the top of the head. "I bet you're awesome to wake up next to."

"Too bad you won't ever find out," I said as he walked out the door.

I waited until I heard him pull out to get up and head back to Sky's. The one thing I hadn't considered was that they'd already be in bed, with the doors locked. Because of the fight, I'd left without grabbing any of my things, including my keys. I couldn't get into their house to get my phone or anything else. I knocked twice on the door, but knew they couldn't hear me from their room, especially if they had the television on. Knowing that I was stuck, I went out to the back porch and sat in the dark.

I have no idea how long I'd been outside, or when exactly that I'd fallen asleep, but I felt someone picking me up. I recognized the smell of his cologne and knew it was Joey. From crying, I was too tired to fight him. I was cold and had to use the bathroom. He led me inside of the house, but carried me to his bedroom. When he sat me down, I sat up quickly. "I'm not sleeping in here with you."

Joey kicked off his shoes and closed his closet door. "I'll sleep on the couch." He grabbed a pillow and walked out of the room.

"What about the spare bedroom?"

"The mattress sucks. I prefer the couch."

Since I had to use the bathroom, I walked out into the hallway and saw him trying to get comfortable . He didn't have a blanket and his legs hung off the arm of the couch.

When I came back out, he was flipping through the television channels. "Can I borrow a t-shirt?"

He stood up and walked into the bedroom. "First my bed and now my clothes. For someone that won't get naked with me, you sure do expect a lot," he joked.

"I got locked out. Don't worry, though. I won't make this a habit."

"I don't mind." He handed me a shirt and a pair of boxers. "Is this good?"

I smiled. "Thanks for bringing me inside. How did you know I was out back?"

"Ford text me and asked if you were staying with me. When I got back and you weren't here, I text him. He said you weren't there either, so I checked out back. I figured you'd locked yourself out of both places, bein' as you were so upset earlier."

"You've been a good fake boyfriend today. Thanks for that."

He stood there, looking right at me, smiling. "How about I keep up the lie and sleep in here with you?"

I crossed my arms. "I'm not sleeping with you, Joey."

"I didn't want to sleep."

I tossed another pillow at him. "Stop!"

He walked out of the room again, leaving me alone. I climbed in under the covers and got comfortable, but I couldn't stop thinking about him being out on the couch. He'd been so nice to me, and jokes aside, we were both adults. It wasn't like he was going to force me to do anything. Besides, I didn't want to be alone, because I couldn't stop thinking about losing Shayne.

I yelled his name. "JOEY."

He came running in the room. "What's wrong?"

I patted the side of the bed next to me. "If you promise not to try anything, we can share."

"So glad you get to make the rules in my apartment." He climbed in beside me and tried to get comfortable. I rolled to face the opposite direction and tried to close my eyes.

Just as I was falling asleep I felt his hand wrapping around me and pulling me close. He brought his lips down to the back of my shoulders and kissed me tenderly. "Goodnight Lace."

I reached my hand up and intertwined it with his. "Don't let go."

And he didn't.

This soft side of Joey was his deep dark secret and it was helping me cope. I didn't want some kind of revenge sex to try to make me feel better. I wanted a friend to help me see that I was going to get through this. Unbeknownst to me, Joey was being that friend.

Chapter 9

Shayne

The bridges were burned and I had to keep moving forward, no matter how bad I felt about it. After sleeping in a hotel, I couldn't get my mind off of Lacey. It was like nothing else mattered; not finding a place to live or figuring out what I was going to do until all of this blew over.

Parker called me first thing in the morning and when I saw his name displayed on the caller I.D., I almost didn't want to answer.

"Are you callin' to say you're sorry?"

"I feel real bad about what you did, Shayne. It's wrong. They need to know the truth."

"It's fine. I'd rather them be disappointed in me than you."

"I can't focus on school while my brother is takin' Hell from the whole family. It ain't right."

I appreciated that he understood the ramifications of what I was doing for him, but he didn't need to worry. I had things under control. "Listen, Park, I need you to stay focused. Dad is being a dick as usual, but he'll come around. Just keep your cool and let me handle it."

"Peyton told me Lacey was there last night. How did she take it?"

"She's with someone else, so apparently she didn't care much. She already thinks I'm a lyin' cheater, so it's nothin' new."

"Dude, I can tell you like her. If there's a chance to get back with her, you should do it. I can handle my own messes, you know."

"She's done with me."

"Thanks for havin' my back, Shayne. I owe you my life."

"If you say you owe me your first born child I might need to reach through the phone and kick your ass."

"I wasn't goin' to say that. Damn. I better go. I don't want to be late for class."

"See ya."

It sucked that I had nobody to talk to about my predicament. In the time that I'd been seeing Lacey, she'd become my go-to. My attempts at rebuilding a relationship with Ford had blown up in my face, so I couldn't count on him to have my back either.

Without even thinking, I started heading back to the apartments. I needed to talk to Lacey and set things straight. She needed to know how I felt about her, even if she didn't feel the same way about me anymore. I felt like I couldn't move forward until I had some kind of closure.

Her car was in the same place as when I left. Figuring that she'd be back at Ford's place, I knocked on their door. After waiting five minutes, Ford answered the door, shirtless, with a spatula in his hand. "It's too early for visitors."

I could smell the bacon cooking from inside and saw Sky walking past. "Sorry, I just wanted to talk to Lace."

He sighed and looked back inside before turning his attention to me. "She ain't here, man."

Feeling defeated, I turned around and started to walk away. Sky came to the door. "Shayne, wait."

"You don't have to be nice to me, Sky. I know where she's at."

She grabbed my arm and looked at me like she felt sorry for me. "I know what you did for me and Ford. He may still be mad at you, but I don't blame you for the other stuff. You were protecting your brother, just like you're doing right now. Lacey needs to know the truth, though."

"I came here to tell her, but she's clearly busy with other things." I shook my head. "So, she really spent the night with him?"

She put her hands up. "I guess. I mean, she never came back and she left her phone here. Joey text Ford and said she was staying the night. Honestly, Lacey didn't tell me that she was into him. In fact, she said she didn't want anything to do with him. It makes no sense."

"You think she's lyin'?"

As much as I hoped for it to be true, I couldn't help what I'd already seen. "I don't know. You're going to have to ask her yourself."

It was chilly outside and she crossed her arms over her chest. "Thanks for the advice, Sky. I'm just goin' to knock on the door and see if she'll come out."

She walked back inside before I got the nerve to knock on Joey's door. I couldn't be mad at him for being with Lacey. She was stunning and had a great personality, not to mention, she was a tiger in the bed. If anything, Joey was going to be the one who had a problem with what I was about to ask.

Lacey

I rolled over and saw the spot next to me was empty. I could smell coffee and the sound of the television playing in the other room. After going into the bathroom and gargling with mouthwash, I walked out to see where Joey was and to thank him for being kind to me.

I found him in the kitchen, cooking up a storm. He smiled when I walked in and leaned my head on the opening to the room. "Hey."

"Thanks for letting me stay."

"No big deal, Lace. I'm not a monster, like you assume. I could tell you needed a friend."

I pulled out a chair and sat down at his small table. "Yeah, is that what we are? Are we friends?"

He shrugged and turned his food around in the pan. "I guess we are, until you tell me otherwise."

I snorted at his comment. "You don't give up do you?"

"I know what I want. Is that a bad thing?"

"It is when you know you're never going to have it." I said it with a bit of sarcasm, but he continued to smile like my words meant nothing.

Joey poured a cup of coffee and sat it down in front of me. "You want milk?"

"Yeah, I can get it." I stood up and our hands reached for the refrigerator at the same time. When we touched, I felt a shock between us. He looked at me and I couldn't take my eyes off of his. "Sorry." I tried to pull away, but he grabbed it and held it in between us.

With his other hand, he reached up and brushed the hair back away from my eyes. "You're just as sexy in the morning, as before you went to sleep."

"Friends don't talk like that to each other."

He bit down on his lip and leaned closer to me. I could feel his breath on my face. "I need to kiss you."

It was that moment where our chemistry was undeniable. I'd spent the night holding hands with this man, who had done nothing but try to get in my pants from the day we'd met. I knew he was attracted to the idea of having sex with me, but this was different. I wanted him to kiss me too. In fact, I needed to feel his lips covering mine. "Friends don't kiss."

He drug his lips over mine slowly and pulled away. "Maybe we shouldn't be friends, then."

I couldn't answer him, because his wet lips were pressed against mine. This wasn't an ordinary first kiss that was awkward and short. This kiss was filled with hot passion. His sultry tongue caressed mine, making me forget about how much I hated him. His fingers traced down one of my arms until he reached my fingers, where he intertwined them together.

I ran my other hand up his chest and felt his warm, smooth skin against my palm. Joey pressed me harder against the refrigerator. I was too afraid to open my eyes, so I kept them shut, as my entire body became overwhelmed with new sensations. When our kiss finally stopped, he kept his lips over mine and opened his eyes, looking right at me. I leaned in to place a small kiss on him, but he backed away and smiled. "Don't get too carried away, Lace."

When he pulled away, I couldn't help but grab his arm and make him stop.

He cocked his eyebrow and gave me another half smile. "I told you that I wouldn't beg."

I sighed and watched him making his way back to the pan. Without arguing with him, I walked up and tapped him on the back. No words could have explained things more than me grabbing the waist of his pants and pulling him back into another kiss.

Joey drug his tongue over mine once and then pulled away. He took my hand and kissed it, before dropping it, picking me up and sitting me on the counter. He pushed his body in between my legs and teased the bottom of the t-shirt that I had on with his thumbs. With one swift tug, my shirt came over my head. I crossed my arms over my chest and he pulled them away. "Don't hide from me. I'm a grown man and you have nothin' to be ashamed of."

I wasn't used to being treated like an adult, or acting modest, but Joey intimidated me. He was so cocky and I completely believed that he was as good as he claimed to be. Maybe that's what scared me so much about him in the first place.

I wrapped my arms around his neck and leaned in to kiss him, but he pulled away. "Once you cross this line, there ain't no goin' back, Lace. When I get you naked and take you to my bed, it's my rules, so you need to decide if that's somethin' you want. I've played this cat and mouse game with you, just waitin' for you to admit that there's somethin' between us. I can wait longer, if I need to." He leaned in, pecked me, and went back to cooking.

I sat there for a second hot and bothered. "You couldn't have known that when we first met, because I thought you were an asshole."

He laughed. "You thought I was sexy."

"Stop doing that. Don't put words into my mouth."

He looked over. "Admit it. You were just as curious as I was. You can hide behind your broken heart, but this never had anything to do with feelin's. We have sexual chemistry. I could tell from that first night. Like I told you before, though, I won't beg. When you're ready to give your body to me, you know where to find me."

His words gave me chills again. "What does that entail; me giving my body to you?"

He turned off the burner and moved the food to the side, before separating my legs and wedging himself between them. I felt his hands touching the strap to my bra, then it falling loose. He pulled it off and tossed it on the table behind him. "First I get you naked." His tongue slid down the base of my neck and over my collarbone. "Then I carry you to my bed."

I ran my hands through his dark hair, while feeling him sucking on one of my nipples. I had butterflies everywhere and I was burning for him to touch me in all the right places.

While reaching my hand down into the front of his shorts, we heard someone knocking on the door. Joey licked my nipple again. "Just ignore it."

They kept knocking.

He stood up and kissed me one more time before walking into the living room to open the door. "What do you want now?"

"Don't act like I'm interupptin' somethin'. I know this is all some show to piss me off."

Hearing Shayne's voice was shocker, but hearing him calling me a liar pissed me off, so much that I stood up, covered myself up with my hands and walked out into the living room topless. "Just a show?"

Chapter 10

Shayne

I couldn't believe my eyes. Lacey was standing there, in nothing but a pair of boxer shorts. Joey crossed his arms and had a cocky smile on his face that I wanted to rip off. It felt like someone was kicking me repeatedly in the gut, albeit I couldn't take my eyes off of Lacey. "I...came to talk to you."

"We were in the middle of something, obviously." She wasn't giving me an inch of respect, not that I could blame her.

"Please. It's important."

Joey motioned for me to sit down. "Have a seat, man. I'll give you two some privacy." He walked past Lacey and headed into the kitchen. She backed up and followed him, then seconds later came out with a large t-shirt on. She sat down on the other end of the couch, pulled her knees up to her chest and sipped on her coffee. "What do you want, Shayne?"

I covered my face with my hands. "I saw this goin' differently."

"Sorry that I ruined it for you."

"Lace, please. Just hear me out."

"If you're going to tell me not to see Joey, I'm afraid that's not going to happen." She was adamant about me knowing that they were an item. I hated it so much.

"This is about me. I mean, I don't like you bein' with him, but I get that my opinion doesn't matter to you." I hesitated before I could begin talking again. It was hard for me to look at her, when inside I was dying because she was sleeping with Joey. "The baby ain't mine, Lace. I never slept with Ashley and I never will. The reason I took responsibility was for Parker's sake. He's got a real chance at goin' somewhere. I can't let this keep him from that. I know in time, he'll be ready to step up, but for now, it's the least I can do to make amends with myself for what I did to Ford, Sky and even you."

The coffee cup left her lips and her eyes widened. "I never asked you to punish yourself."

"No, but I'm sure you wished worse for me."

Lacey's eyes started to tear up. "I may have said things, but I didn't mean them. You hurt me so much, Shayne. I thought we had something special, but to you I was just a piece of ass."

I moved closer to her and touched her foot. "You're wrong, babe. I may not have admitted it, but you were so much more than that. I was stupid for takin' you for granted. If I had a second chance, I do so much differently. I'd start by makin' sure everyone knows that you belonged to me and I belonged to you, but it's too late now. You've moved on and it's clear to me that I lost my chance."

Tears rolled down her cheeks and when she began to sniffle, I knew she was breaking down even more. "All I ever wanted was for you to love me, Shayne."

I had knots in my gut and could feel myself getting emotional when she said those words. They were words that I'd never said to a single girl and meant. "I do."

Lacey wiped her tears away and looked down at her cup of coffee. "I want to believe that, Shayne. I swear I do. It's just that I don't think I'm ready to be able to trust you."

I nodded and faked a half smile. "Yeah, I get it."

Lacey put her legs down on the floor and reached for my hand. She traced my fingers with hers, while little sniffles escaped her. "But I don't want to let you go, either."

I could feel my heartbeat picking up. For once, I had hope. I intertwined our fingers and looked right at her. "What are you sayin', Lace?"

She shrugged. "Can I meet you at your house later so we can talk?"

"No. My dad kicked me out last night. Apparently, havin' a kid is against the rules, even if it ain't really mine."

"Where will you go?" Her concern was reassuring. I appreciated that she still worried about me.

"I reckon I need to look for a place. I was plannin' on buyin' a paper and callin' some places today. It ain't like I'm goin' to show up for work. My dad needs a couple days to cool off before I get anywhere near him."

"I bet." She looked toward the kitchen and I knew she was thinking about Joey. That uncomfortable feeling was immediately noticeable in the pit of my stomach again. "Do you want some company when you're looking?"

I raise my brow and looked at her, wondering what she was implying. "Won't he be mad?"

She squinted and looked at the kitchen again. "I think it's best if we don't talk about relationships today. I'll go with you as a friend."

"I'll take whatever I can get." She had no idea how happy I was to be able to spend time with her. I didn't care that I'd interrupted her and Joey. I didn't even care that he was patiently waiting in the kitchen for me to leave. All I cared about was spending the day with Lacey, even if it was just on a friend's pretense.

Lacey

My head was spinning when I thought about almost having sex with Joey. Had Shayne not come looking for me, I would have been in his bed, letting him have me.

How could I have been so stupid?

Shayne left promptly, with a smile on his face as he walked out the door. I didn't want to give him false hope, but I couldn't let go like I thought I could. As much as I wanted to be able to move on and no longer hurt, I found myself consumed with guilt, over Joey. He'd been right about the chemistry between us. It was there and also electrifying. When Joey touched me I could feel every emotion possible. My senses were heightened and I knew that if I let him take me to bed, it would be something I would never forget.

When he heard the door close, he walked back into the living room and stood there looking at me. "You're leavin' aren't ya?"

"It's not like that, Joey. Please don't make this any harder than it already is."

He walked into his bedroom without saying anything. Feeling like I needed to be fair to him, I followed. He was gathering clothes out of his dresser to change in to. "You don't need to explain, Lace. I'm a big boy. I get it. Shayne wants another chance and you're goin' to give it to him."

I walked up behind him and touched his arm. "It's not like that, but I'm not going to lie to you. I still love him."

He looked down into my eyes and smiled. "I told you, no explainin' necessary."

He was being standoffish and it led me to believe that he was upset I was leaving. It made me consider that maybe he was more interested in me than I'd thought. Why else would he have been so broken up about it? "You were right earlier, when you said the attraction was mutual. I feel it too. I just couldn't bring myself to admit it, out loud."

He pulled a clean shirt over his head. "What do you want me to say, Lace? You want me to beg you to stay? You want me to tell you all the reasons that you should end up in my bed tonight instead of his, because I'm not goin' to do that."

The more salty he acted, the more it made me want him. Shayne was waiting for me and all I could think about was feeling Joey's kisses all over me again. Just imagining them made a rush of heat form between my legs.

Without regard for the repercussions, I pulled the shirt over my head and tossed it at his face. When he removed the article of clothing from his view, I backed up and bit down on my lip as I came to the edge of his bed. "How about you give me a reason to come back?"

I backed myself up onto his bed and watched him approaching me. He climbed up and removed his shirt before making it to where he could reach down and kiss me again. Right away, the tingling began and I knew that even though I was going to regret it, I needed to know what was happening between us.

Joey teased me with his tongue then pulled away. "Tell me, Lace. Say the words."

I felt like I couldn't catch my breath. Since I'd never put myself in this type of situation, it was hard to be able to admit that I wanted what was about to happen. Yet, imagining walking out of his bedroom wasn't an option. This man had me so worked up that I would never be able to forgive myself if I didn't see where it led. The passion between us was so clear and all I wanted was to feel what it was like for us to come together.

"I want you to fuck me. No. I need you to."

He smiled and drug his bottom lip over one of my breasts. "You say one thing, but you mean somethin' entirely different." He lifted my hand and placed tiny kisses over the back of my fingers. "I'll be gentle with you; making sure I kiss every inch of your skin. After that I'm goin' to make you cum and when you scream out my name, it will be because you don't want me to stop touchin' you."

His words were making me pant, just imagining him being able to do what he was promising. I could barely speak, I was so turned on. "Take off my shorts and get started then." Pretending to be subtle was difficult.

Joey stared into my eyes and he slowly removed the shorts off of my legs. He took pride in watching me squirm around as he removed my panties. "Don't get shy on me. I've waited too long to see you naked."

I ran my fingers over my right breasts. "Was it worth the wait?"

He put his hand up to his chin and looked me up and down. "Roll over and give me the full show."

I rolled over, sticking my ass up and rubbing one of the cheeks. "Is this what you like?"

He fell down on top of my back. "I like it all." I could feel his erection hitting my leg as he grabbed my hair and yanked it slowly, while being positioned like he was going to take me from behind. "Oh yeah, I'm going to fuck you so good."

He rolled me over and backed off the bed, taking my foot into his hands and kissing my ankle. I pointed my toes and watched him watching my reaction. His tongue led the way as he kissed his way, inch by inch, up to my thigh. When his eyes left mine and went to my pussy, I wanted to inexplicably scream with anticipation. He was doing all that he could to avoid touching me there. The more he kissed the more I mentally pleaded with him to take me.

Joey's face went lower, close enough to be able to touch me there, but he kissed my opposite thigh instead. He laughed, knowing how crazy it was making me. "You want me to touch you, don't you Lace?"

I nodded.

"Flip over, you're not ready for me yet."

He was crazy if he thought that I could handle much more. His kisses were bad enough on my thighs, but when he leaned down and started kissing the cheeks of my ass, I thought I was going to collapse on the bed. The back of my thighs had never been a sensitive part, so I thought. Joey's tongue trailed over my skin and my body began to tremble as I felt his hand sliding between my legs. I knew I was wet; so wet and prepared for him, but I couldn't have prepared myself for the way his fingers slid right inside. He'd done that to me; making me so horny that I was dripping with desire.

"Exactly how I want your pussy; wet and ready." He took the moisture and spread it over my clit, allowing the slipperiness to work to his advantage. I was lingering on my knees, but shaking so much that I became too weak to hold myself up. The jolts of my orgasm had consumed my limbs, causing me to lose control. I put my face into the pillow as he inserted fingers in me, while using his other hand to roughly rub my throbbing clit. My ass bucked and I felt my body reacting to the movement of his touching me.

I thought that when he pulled his fingers out, he'd be ready to go, but once again I was wrong. "Turn over and hold up your legs. This time I'm going to watch you cum."

He sat up on his knees and allowed me room to twist around. Our eyes met as I lifted up my legs, spreading my pussy open for him. My nipples tingled and I wanted to touch them, except I was busy holding my ankles. Joey licked his lips and sank down low in the bed. He smacked my pussy lightly, getting a reaction out of me immediately. He blew on it and I threw my head back on the pillow, unable to keep my eyes open any longer. He pinched my clit between his fingers and blew on it. I could feel it throbbing, like a heartbeat. This time, when his fingers penetrated me, I really did cry out. My hands let go of my legs and they fell down on either side of him. My body bucked and I dug my nails into my own skin.

Finally, I calmed and a very pleased man slid up beside me, kissing me gently on the lips. "You're so sexy when you cum, Lace."

I went to say something, but he stood up, fully erect under his shorts, and put his shirt back on. I sat up. "Wait! Where are you going?"

"You've got somewhere to be and I need to reheat your breakfast."

"Joey, wait. We aren't done here."

He climbed back on the bed and met me in a kiss full of tongue and angst. "You're right, we're not, but I'm not about to give you everything so you can walk away and never look back. This way, I know you'll return."

"So, you're just going to walk out of the room, even with me here, sprawled out and naked?"

He kissed my neck and ran his hand up between my breasts. "It's very difficult."

I pointed to the teepee in his pants. "Are you planning on icing that down?"

"Nah, it will be waiting for when you get back."

"What if I don't come back?"

He stood up and laughed. "Then I will be icin' it."

"Do I have to beg?" I wanted more and it was making me crazy that he could be alright with leaving me hanging.

"Patience is a virtue." He crossed his arms and leaned on the doorframe. "It's goin' to happen, so I'm not worried about waiting. Your head is too messed up today."

"I know what I want." He kept walking out of the room, even though I was embarrassing myself by pleading. All bets were off when it came to restraining. I wanted him, even more than before. He'd given me a taste and I was craving for us to continue, with no regard for what could come out of it.

Chapter 11

Shayne

Lacey met me two hours later. When I'd left, she was a crying mess, but in that short amount of time, she seemed calm but withdrawn. In fact, she didn't say much as we drove to the first address. "Are you alright?"

"Yeah, sorry."

I couldn't help but ask. "Did you have a fight with Joey? I won't apologize for that, you know."

"We didn't fight."

"What's with the silence?"

She shrugged. "Shayne, I'm not going to lie you, because lies are the reason that we broke up in the first place. This isn't easy for me, but you need to know."

I cut her off. "You're sleepin' with him, aren't you?"

I looked over and she was looking out the window. "No. I mean, sort of."

"Sort of. You either fucked him or you didn't."

"We've never had sex, well, not all the way."

"I don't want to hear about this, Lace."

"So you'd rather me lie? Do you want me to pretend everything is okay?"

"No, but I want you for myself. I don't want to share you with that asshole or anyone else."

"I didn't want to share you, but clearly you thought it was okay to hook up with other people." I could tell from the way she was being defensive that he'd gotten under her skin.

111

I reached over and tried to touch her hand, but she pulled away. "Do you have feelin's for him?"

"I like him."

"What about me?"

She looked at me as I pulled over and put the car into park. "I still love you."

Lacey wouldn't look at me and I could tell she was conflicted. I'd never considered what it was like for the other person in a relationship to have to share affections. I felt like shit. "I can be faithful. I'll change."

She turned and finally peered at me, but the look on her face was different. "Have you been with anyone since we broke up?"

I could feel the bile rising to my throat. Why had she asked me that? Was it really important? "Of course not." The lie lingered on my lips. I knew it was wrong, but telling her the truth would of sent her right back to Joey. Knowing that she still loved me meant I had a chance. I needed a clean slate to make things right. I couldn't add fuel to the open fire and expect to not get burned.

Lacey smiled, seeming pleased of my faithfulness, even though it was a load of crap. "Did you really miss me?"

I ran my hand through her hair and leaned against the headrest. The sun came in the window, showing off the natural highlights of her blonde hair. "Like a crazy person."

"Yeah. I know what you mean."

We stared at each other for a few moments, saying nothing. We were together, maybe not as a couple, but she was still with me and she loved me. It was enough for me to be happy about. Lacey was worth fighting for and I just needed to prove it to her.

We saw three apartments, all about thirty minutes from where I worked. Provided that my dad would have me back, I'd be able to pay for it easily. Of course, if I had a roommate, someone to share my expenses and my bed, it would make things even better.

Lacey was great for the rest of the day, giving me her opinions like she'd be around to help me decorate. I took her out for a late lunch and she even agreed to go with me to get things from my parent's house. I knew he'd be at work, so it was be easy to gather my things without him getting in my face again.

Peyton was in the kitchen when we entered. She gave me a look and shook her head at me. "Save it, sis. I've heard enough from Dad."

I pulled Lacey in my room and shut the door before I could hear my sister respond. We were alone and in private, where no one could interfere. Taking advantage of the situation, I pulled her into my arms and held her there. She didn't reciprocate at first, albeit it didn't take her long to put her arms around my back and lay her head into my chest. "If I could go back, I would."

She looked up and smiled. "Do you really love me, Shayne."

I nodded. "I do."

Our lips met and it felt so good to kiss her. After a few moments, she pulled away. "I'm going to go out and wait with Peyton. You better hurry in case he comes home early."

I started packing up all my things in duffle bags. Twenty minutes later, I realized that Peyton could blow everything up in my face. I grabbed the rest of my shit and ran out toward the kitchen.

Lacey's face told me I was too late.

Lacey

It was good to see Peyton and I wanted to chat with her while Shayne was packing. He was starting to push for more from me and I wasn't ready for that, especially after being intimate with Joey earlier in the day. Not to mention the fact that my body tingled every time I thought of him touching me. It wasn't right to be with Shayne when I was thinking of someone else.

Peyton hugged me right away. "I missed you."

"I missed you, too. How are you?"

She shrugged. "I didn't think I'd miss Parker, but I do. Dad is being even more ridiculous with this whole baby situation. I can't believe you're standin' here when Shayne got another girl pregnant. What are you doin' with him?"

"We're trying to be friends. He's told me the truth about everything. There's no more secrets between us. It doesn't solve things, but it gives us a clean slate."

"Shew, you're a brave woman. If my boyfriend slept with two girls at once, I don't think I could get over that." She was calm and serious.

My mouth literally dropped open and I saw him walking into the kitchen. He put his head down and started shaking his head. "Take me back to the car, right now!"

Shayne waited until we got into the car to talk to me. He called his sister a few choice words before the kitchen door shut. After realizing she'd stuck her foot in her mouth, she didn't offer a goodbye to me.

I refused to look at him as he drove us back to my car. All I wanted to do was get away from him. I'd asked him to be honest and he couldn't do it, again. How was I supposed to move forward or start over when he couldn't tell the truth. Our relationship depended on trust and I had none.

When he pulled up to my car, he hit the lock button so I couldn't jump right out. "Lacey, please wait. Hear me out, at least."

"Screw you!" I slapped him on the arm. "I can't even look at you, right now. Two girls, Shayne? My god, I thought that cheating was bad enough, but now I get why you had to do it. One woman will never be enough for you, I guess. Save your speeches. We're done and I'm not playing around anymore. I refuse to forgive you this time. Call one of your whores when you need pussy. I'd tell you to lose my number, but I've already taken care of that problem, when you crushed my heart the first time."

I climbed out of the car and got into mine as fast as I could. Shayne laid his head on his steering wheel as I pulled away. He had me so worked up that I didn't even realize I'd driven back to Joey's, until I pulled in the driveway. I'd cried away all my makeup and looked like Hell, so I figured I go talk to Sky. She always knew how to make me feel better.

Unfortunately, they'd gone out with her parents and weren't home. I sat in my car crying for the longest time, until a motorcycle pulled in, catching my attention. Joey knocked on my window and I wouldn't look up. He opened my car door and crouched down in front of me. "I'm not goin' to ask you what happened, but my doors open if it's where you want to go."

He walked away, never forcing me to reply. I didn't understand why he was so nice to me, but I didn't want to be alone. Once I wiped my eyes and grabbed my bag of clothes from the backseat, I headed into Joey's. He was in the kitchen and I could smell garlic. I leaned on the wall in between the rooms. "Do you care if I get a shower?"

"My shampoo smells like a man."

I smiled. "I don't even care."

As I entered his bathroom, I could already smell the scent of his shampoo. It reminded me of the way his skin smelled when we kissed. I stripped out of my clothes and let them lay on the bathroom floor. It was pathetic, but I didn't even have the energy to pick them up. The hot water fell over my head and I wrapped my arms around my body, unable to control my emotions any longer. I began to sob in the shower, thinking about Shayne and everything we'd never have. I don't know why it hurt more than the first time. I guess I'd built up so much hope of us having a second chance. I wasn't going to jump into bed with him, but I considered starting off slow. It was definitely over this time. I felt insignificant, like nothing I could do would ever be good enough to make a man want *only* me. I never considered myself bad at sex, albeit it was possible that I was awful and just didn't know it.

Why else would every boyfriend cheat on me?

I don't know how long I'd been crying, but I heard the bathroom door open and froze in place. Through the sheer curtain, I could see him standing there, looking at me. He started undressing and it frightened me, because being intimate was the last thing on my mind, especially with him.

He climbed in behind me and pulled my back against his chest. His hands traced my arms until he brought them up across my chest. Joey kissed my shoulder and let his jaw sit there. "I hate hearin' you cry."

I closed my eyes. "I'm sorry. I feel like I'm drowning in pain."

"I won't ask what happened, but I'm not goin' to let you cry anymore." He turned me around and kissed the top of my head. Our eyes met and I couldn't look anywhere else. He had me completely captivated again.

"I'm sorry I showed up without asking."

He smiled. "You're not sorry, Lace. You came to the one place where you knew you could make it all go away."

Normally, when Joey said things like that, he was being cocky, except this time it was the absolute truth. "I'm not supposed to want you, Joey."

He smiled and let his lips trace over mine. "I'm not supposed to do a lot of things that I do."

"I liked it better when you were an asshole. At least then, I knew what to expect from you."

"I'm still an asshole. Ask anyone."

"I hate to break it to you, but I think we're becoming friends."

"That's what this is?" He laughed and held me closer. "I'm kiddin'."

"Just make me forget I ever left your bed this morning. That's all I want from you."

He raised his eyebrow. "So, you want to use me?"

"Isn't that what you want from me? Isn't it about being able to say you had me?" Even in the shower, I could feel the heat building between my legs again. "Havin' you was never a question." His wet hands ran down my arms as the conflicted look on his face remained.

"Why are you looking at me like that?"

His face changed as he spun me around again. With my back to him, I couldn't read him, which was exactly what he wanted. He picked up the bar of soap and ran it over my back, creating a lather, as he massaged it into my skin. As his hand made its way to my ass, I heard him groan. He put the soap down and kissed me on the shoulder, while the water rinsed off the remaining soaps suds. I was shocked when he began to climb back out of the shower, so shocked that I pulled the curtain and looked out at him.

"What just happened?"

He wrapped a towel around his waist, before I could look down at his package that I'd yet to see. "Nothin. Take your time, Lace. I'll be out here when you're done."

I was puzzled and didn't know what I could have done to make him want to get out and leave me hanging. One minute he had his hands all over me and the next he was walking away. I couldn't help but wonder if it was something that I'd done wrong.

Still, I did as he said and let the water wash away my tears. Once Joey walked away, my mind went right to Shayne. I was so overwhelmed with sadness knowing that we'd never be together again. My mind had been made up and there was no way that I could allow him back into my life, when it was clear he couldn't be honest, or even faithful.

When the water started to run cold, I knew I'd been in the shower too long. My skin was beginning to prune up and soften. I climbed out and wrapped myself in a towel, noticing that a clean folded t-shirt was sitting on the sink waiting for me.

I shook off a smile, knowing that Joey had come into the bathroom to give me something comfortable to wear, even though I had a bag of things that I'd brought with me.

Maybe he did it because he got off seeing a woman in his clothes. Either way, I pulled his shirt over my head and smelled the fabric. His cologne still lingered faintly and it gave me comfort knowing that I wasn't going to be alone.

Even though I was still confused about his intentions, Joey was being nice to me. He wasn't pushing me to do anything.

I found him on the couch with a plate of food on his lap. He was sucking up a noodle in his mouth as I walked into the room. "Do you like pasta?"

"I love it." Even with my mind focused on so many other things, I knew I needed to force myself to eat. Besides, I knew it was going to taste fantastic.

"I made homemade sauce the other night. It's sweeter than the jar." He stood up and went into the kitchen, coming back out with a plate full of noodles and red sauce.

I sat down on the other side of him and wrapped a bunch of noodles around my fork. Joey watched as I took a bite. The sudden burst of flavor was like an orgasm in my mouth, and from the look on his face, he knew I was in love with his cooking." Ain't it good?"

"It's delicious. I'm impressed. Did you always want to be a cook?"

He shrugged and took another bite before answering. "My mom has ran that diner my whole life. I guess it's in my blood. I think I started working there when I was twelve. Since it was all I ever learned to do, she sent me to culinary school and the rest is history."

"Sky made it seem like you and Ford bickered about everything. I couldn't believe you moved in to this place."

"He's my cousin, but we like to compete, that's no secret. Since we've gotten older it doesn't happen so much. We have more in common than he likes to admit, like fast cars and sexy women."

"Are you saying he isn't faithful?" That was how his comment came out.

"No! He's whipped. Ford won't screw up what he's got. He went too long in misery to let anything bad happen to him and Sky. She's a great girl."

I took another bite and answer with a full mouth. "Yeah, she's awesome."

"That is not ladylike." He pointed to my full mouth.

I opened it, showing him my chewed up food. "Ahhhh."

Joey took a large bite, chewed it up, and did the same thing. Then he looked down and let it fall back onto his plate.

I pretended to gag. "Sick!"

We both laughed.

He quickly changed the subject. "What about you? Do you have a job besides school?"

"Nope, I'm just in school full time. Eventually I'd like to have my own accounting firm, but that's just wishful thinking."

He looked shocked. "Wow, I never would have pegged you for a math nerd."

I lifted up my foot and kicked him. "Shut up! I never would have pegged you for someone who was nice enough to be decent to me like you've been. Besides, there's nothing wrong with being smart."

Joey sat his plate down on the coffee table and leaned back on the couch. "True. So, do you live on campus?"

"I did for a bit, but now I'm more like a nomad. I stay between here and my parent's house. Since Sky's back from her other school, we've been able to spend more time together. I really missed her being away."

"Did you just call yourself a nomad?"

I smiled. "I did. It seems fitting. I don't buy groceries or clean. My clothes are in duffle bags or laundry baskets."

"You know I have an extra room, with a bed in it. You can stay here whenever you want. Shit, I don't even care if you use the closet in there."

He really threw me a loop by saying that. "Are you asking me to move in here? Do I look like live in pussy to you?"

Joey was taking a sip of a beer and it went flying out of his mouth. "Jesus Christ, woman. I didn't say that at all. I said you could crash here , in my guest room. My mom brought over an old set. It ain't much, but it's a bed" Then he smiled. "Unless you're offerin' somethin' else."

I kicked him again. "I'm not!"

"I'm just sayin'. This is my first place. It's great, but I'm not used to livin' alone. Aside from you fightin' me every ten seconds, we get along. I wouldn't mind if you stayed every once in a while. Of course, if we had that kind of arrangement, we would have to discuss this new friendship."

"You don't get sex because I sleep in your guest room."

"Nah, it would be the opposite. If you stayed here that much, we could only be friends; the kind that doesn't sleep together."

I was shocked. Joey had fought so hard to sleep with me and now he was saying that he didn't want to. I sat my plate down and scooted over toward him, grabbing the waist of his shorts and pulling them out. "You mean to tell me that even if I begged you to fuck me, you wouldn't do it?"

He nodded. "Yep. Relationships complicate things. I like my life and don't want drama. You're fun to be around and if we took things there, it would change. If I slept with you last night, or today, I probably wouldn't have offered for you to sleep here when you wanted to. In fact, I know I wouldn't have. It's a big boundary that I don't like crossin'."

I wasn't willing to take that for an answer, so I climbed on top of him, straddling his legs. He kept his arms at his sides, not responding to my body. When he refused to react, I rocked my hips forward and then backward.

He still didn't react.

The more Joey fought me, the more determined I was to be with him, which was ironic, since I'd fought him for so long. I climbed off of him and removed my panties, stepping out of them before climbing back on his lap. I ran the back of my hand up his bare chest and brought my lips to his ear. "This doesn't make you want me?"

His hands remained flat on the sofa, but I could feel something hard protruding against me. I brought my lips to his and grazed over them. "What about kissing?"

He grumbled and tried to readjust without touching me. "You're playin' with fire."

I grazed his lips again. "I know you want this to happen. Are you afraid you won't be as good as you say you are?"

His hands immediately grabbed onto either side of my ass. "Trust me, that's not what I'm worried about."

I pulled back and looked right at him. "What then?"

He patted me and lifted my weight off of him. I felt rejected again, but in a concerned way this time. Something was off with Joey and I didn't understand it. "We need to just be friends. If you sleep with me, right now, you'll hate yourself in the mornin'. This ain't about you wantin' me, it's about Shayne. If you were someone else, I'd already have you in bed, givin' you all I have to offer, but I can't do it with you."

I hated that he'd brought up Shayne. "Why? What's wrong with me? Why am I different? Am I all used up or something?"

Joey leaned back and wiped his face with his hands. "This is why I don't get serious." He finally turned to look at me and I couldn't help notice that he seemed conflicted again. "You think we met for the first time in Ford's apartment upstairs, don't you?"

I nodded.

He shook his head. "That ain't when I first noticed you. I saw you with Shayne several times and knew I wanted you even then, but also knew it was wrong. You were taken and seemingly happy." He looked down, like he was ashamed to continue. "When I found out you'd broke up, I was happy, because I knew I could make a play at you. The more I got around you, the more I realized you were different. I'd never seen someone that made my dick hard with just a smile. Those deep dimples of yours make me fuckin' crazy. When you're sad, I find myself carin' and wantin' to make you forget. It scares the shit out of me knowin' that I can't fuck you, because I know I'd get lost in you, Lacey. I'm too damn stubborn to do it to myself. I'm happy where I am in life. I don't want complicated."

My body was shaking and I wasn't sure what to say to his confession. He'd noticed me before I knew he existed. He'd wanted me even back then and the reason that we weren't in his bed was because he actually cared about me and it scared him.

I was speechless.

"You need to put on them panties and stop messin' with me, because we both know what's goin' to happen if you don't."

So, I did what my heart and my body told me to do.

I stood up and walked in front of him, lifted off the shirt I was wearing, and walked into his bedroom. When I turned around he was staring at me in shock. "This isn't about

Shayne anymore and you know it. You think I could leave this morning and not think about how it makes me feel to touch you. When you kiss me, my body reacts like it never has before. I should be crying about a failed relationship, but at the end of the day, being with you is all I can think about. I'm tired of fighting myself and lying to you. I won't be in the guest room, although I appreciate that offer. I'll be waiting in your bed. When you're ready to face me and get lost in whatever this is going on between us, you know where to find me."

I walked in his bedroom in shock from my plea to him. I didn't know if he'd listen, but I was tired of the back and forth. Joey made me crazy, albeit I wanted him more every second. I'd lied when I said I just wanted him to forget about my problems. I wanted him because I knew he was going to be fantastic. I wanted him because when he looked into my eyes, no other woman existed and I'd never felt that type of connection with any man, ever before.

Chapter 12

Shayne

Peyton tried to call my phone six times before I finally answered. I was so pissed at her, but knew I only had myself to blame.

"It's not a good time."

"Shayne, I'm so sorry. She said you told her everything. I'm so stupid."

"I shouldn't have lied about it."

"You must think I'm the worst sister in the world. Do you want me to talk to her? I'll do anything to make things better."

I thought about the possibility of Lacey listening to Peyton. As much as she liked my sister, I was pretty sure she was done with my bullshit. "Don't worry about it. I'm just goin' to move forward and let it go. Even if she forgave me, how long do you think she's goin' to stick around through everything else?"

"But you love her."

"I care deeply for Lacey. As much as I feel like it could be love, I just don't know. She deserves more than that."

"Are you okay? Where are you going to crash?"

"I'm goin' to drive to the beach and stay with some friends for a few days until Dad chills the fuck out."

"Call me if you need anything. I won't tell him where you went."

"Thanks, sis. Talk to you later."

I had a good drive to think about everything that had landed me in the situation I was in. The only person to blame was myself. I had a great girl and I let her slip through my fingertips. Like them all before her, I'd move on, because it was what I did best. My time with Lacey would be something I wouldn't soon forget. She was special, more than any other before her. Knowing that nothing lasts forever, I had to move on.

My priority would be Parker and the baby. I'd get him through this mess and everything was going to work out. It had to.

Lacey

I climbed in his bed expecting him to continue to be hardheaded. Instead, there he was standing shirtless in the doorway. His brows were creased as he watched me positioning myself.

I was petrified about being with him, not because I knew he was going to be amazing. Somehow that didn't even matter. I was scared because as much as I should have been a miserable desperate mess from losing Shayne, it had all faded away. I trembled at the thought of giving myself to someone like Joey.

Sure, his body was amazing and he knew how to touch me in all the right places, but it was something else, something much deeper.

He slowly walked over to the bed and shook his head before climbing on it. "This is bad."

I leaned up on my elbow and watched him. He mimicked me and we stared at each other. He took my hand, bringing it up to his lips, "We don't have to do this. I can wait until you're over him."

I shook my head. "Shut up and kiss me." While climbing on top of him, I felt his arms wrapping around my back. His lips met mine and that instant spark had ignited. Our tongues met and as they brushed together, my eyes closed, unable to stay open for another second as I became consumed with a burst of heat between my legs. I was so ready for this;

for him. "I want you." I opened my eyes as he pulled his lips from mine.

His thumb rubbed over my lips and I leaned into him doing it. "I want you, too."

I kissed his fingers as they moved against my mouth and eventually ran through my hair. He held it out of the way to lean in and pleasure my neck with his lips and tongue. When he reached my ears, I leaned in the opposite direction, giving him room to do whatever he wanted.

Joey's hand reached down and grabbed onto mine. Our fingers laced together and he kept them tight as our tongues met again. As if it were in slow motion, He pulled me up to straddle him. We were both sitting up, me naked and him in a pair of loose shorts. He was hard and ready and I needed to finally discover what had been hiding from me this whole time.

With my free hand, I slid it up his shorts, letting my fingers glide over the smooth skin on the tip of his shaft. A low sound escaped his lips as my hand grasped ahold of the thickness. That fire between my legs intensified when I realized that his girth alone would send me straight into sexual bliss. Knowing it wasn't always about size, and more of how a man knew how to work it, I felt confident Joey hadn't been lying to me. In fact, everything he'd said thus far had been the truth.

Considering that I'd been with a liar for so long, I had to grasp the goodness in him, even when I knew how much of an asshole he could be when he wanted to.

Joey took my hand and pulled it out from inside of his shorts. He flipped me on my back and hovered over my naked body, looking at all of my assets while biting his lip. "You're so God damn beautiful." I could feel my cheeks heating up in reaction to his statement. He continued to look at every inch of me, like he was planning on eating me alive. Joey licked his lips before he leaned down and kissed me full on the mouth.

I dug my hand into his hair while our tongues mingled together. Like the times before, his mouth matched my movements. After removing my hand from his hair, I slid it down to his bicep. Since he was holding himself up with it, the muscle was hard and defined. I tickled his skin with my fingernails, while he used his free hand to cup and massage one of my breasts.

Joey kissed me one more time and jumped off the bed. I felt confused until I saw him coming back in the room. He had something behind his back and I had no idea what it was. Had it not been for the giant smile he was wearing, I would have been afraid of what to expect.

He climbed back on the bed at the foot. "Close your eyes, Lacey."

"You're scaring me."

"Just close your eyes. I swear I won't hurt you."

I listened and did as he requested. For a few seconds, I heard plastic moving, but nothing else. Even the bed didn't move. As I began to say something, I felt something touching my right nipple.

It was cold and completely unexpected. I opened my eyes immediately.

Something red caught my attention as it was making contact with my nipple again. Upon further observation, I realized it was a frozen strawberry. Leave it to the chef to get creative with frozen foods on the first night of us having sex. I bit down on my lip and tried to prepare myself for the reaction to the coldness. "Close your eyes."

"It's cold."

He reached down and sucked on my nipple. His saliva felt hot and my body reacted, making it harden. He pulled away and blew on the sensitive area, before taking the melting fruit and rubbing it over my other nipple. I gasped, even though I knew what to expect. I could literally feel it in my toes as it soaked my breasts. Once again, his mouth sucked away the coldness.

I opened my eyes and watched Joey bringing the strawberry up to my lips. My mouth opened and I let him feed me. When I began to chew, he leaned down and kissed me there. He pulled away and smiled. "Your pussy's next."

My nipples tingled, and it traveled down to my pussy, that eagerly awaited the idea of being touched again by Joey.

He'd already showed me how easy it was for him to pleasure a woman.

He pulled another strawberry out of the bag and showed it to me as he focused on my pussy. I knew it was going to be intense, so I clenched the sheets beneath me as it made contact with my clit. My body bucked feeling the immediate, almost sting of the frozen fruit hitting my sensitive bud.

Joey rolled it around in circular motions, and the friction from the texture of it, combined with the sting of the coldness, was incredible. My hips thrust and the butterflies came, followed by my screaming out into the bedroom. He didn't give me any time to settle either, as I watched him going down on me, determined and eagerly.

The warm heat of his tongue made contact with my clit and I lost total control of myself. I dug my hand into his dark hair and shoved his head back down over my pussy, not willing to lose the euphoric sensations that were filling every inch of my sensitive skin.

Joey fought me, pulling away enough that he could look right at me as his tongue separated the lips of my sex. I was panting as I watched him kissing my clit and then sucking it into his mouth. The pinching pleasure traveled up to my nipples and I couldn't help but run my fingers over them, circling my own hardened nubs and pinching them.

When I watched him eat that strawberry, I thought I was about to scream out his name. It was so erotic and in seconds, he was back at my pussy, licking up my clit, like a battery-operated machine.

I kept squeezing my nipples as my body reacted. Joey's head bobbed, but he never stopped lapping me up, even when I began to shake. He sat up and took my hand, bringing it down to my pussy and moving my finger over my own clit. After showing me what he wanted to see, he stopped guiding me and watched me touching myself.

I almost couldn't stand the pleasure as it jolted through my body again. Joey kissed my inner thigh, then the back of my hand, while it circled over my clit. He grabbed it and moved it out of the way to kiss my pussy again, then he smiled. "That's two."

I moaned and watched him making his way up to kiss me. I could taste my essence on his lips "How many do you expect to give me?"

"That's for me to know and you to find out. Prepare yourself for a long night. I can cum twice before I need a sandwich break."

I smiled and teased his lips with my tongue. "Prove it!"

"Are you challengin' me? You do realize that I've made you cum four times now and never even fucked you?"

Of course I knew that. The anticipation was killing me, especially knowing how thick he was and how good it was going to feel when he was inside of me. "Give me what I want, Joey."

He shook his head and started tugging down his shorts. I was too excited to look down, just knowing we were one step closer to it finally happening. The anticipation alone was making me want him more than I thought it was humanly possible.

Joey grabbed protection out of his dresser and rolled over to apply. I appreciated that even in my irrational thinking, he was responsible. At least one of us was. When he rolled back over he kissed me tenderly, like we had all the time in the world. It was so personal, the way he touched me, like I was the only woman he'd ever been with. He stared me in the eye, before looking down at my body. While holding his body up with one arm, He ran his erection over my entrance. His dick was hot and my tiny bud hadn't recovered fully from the last orgasm, so the smallest contact made me react to him, exactly like he wanted me to.

I kept my eyes focused on him, concentrating on his olive skin and the way he had begun to sweat.

Joey leaned down and kissed me repeatedly, sucking on my bottom lip and pulling it. I reached for his mouth, but fell back on the pillow when I realized he was in position and ready to penetrate me.

We looked into each other's eyes and I reached up and touched his face. It was right there, slowly entering me. He was purposely taking his time, allowing me to feel every single inch of him filling me. Our lips met and before he'd gotten all the way there, we were caught up in a mind-blowing connection.

Little cries escaped me the first few thrusts, but Joey never stopped kissing my skin. His hands explored while every move was geared to give me the most pleasure. I wrapped my legs around his back and clung to him as our bodies rocked together. Maybe I should have known better, but I found myself experiencing something that neither of us was ready to admit. We stared into each other's eyes once more while I came another time; this time because he was inside of me, finally.

Moments later, our pace picked back up again. Joey's focused face scrunched up and I knew he was fighting the inevitable.

However, he was much stronger than I'd imagined. He pulled out of me and rolled over on his back, breathing heavily. "Ride me."

I climbed on top of him, grabbing his cock and letting it slide right inside of me. Then Joey grabbed both of my hands and held them as I began to ride him, like he wanted. He didn't try to finish early, so he could get off and go to bed. He wasn't trying to rush me out of his bed, or make promises to satisfy me that never were kept. He fulfilled me over and over, sending me to places that my body had never been before.

He never took his eyes off of me and that's when I knew that he'd been right all along. Our intense connection was scary and that meant that when we came down off of the high, we'd created a mess that neither of us knew how to handle. His tough facade wasn't in this bedroom. This man I was with was someone else completely and I wanted to know everything about him.

We'd crossed a line, acting on pure lust, and nothing was going to come out of it except heartache, because all along it was about sex and nothing else.

Joey erupted and finally let himself release nearly an hour later. Not only was I surprised about his ability to last, but also that he'd never been selfish, not even for a minute. When I felt him ejaculating, I got off again, tightening my walls and almost squeezing him out. He clung to my ass and held me still, until he could open his eyes and move around again. I fell down over his chest, sweating and out of breath. Instead of rolling me off of him, he held me and kissed the top of my head. "You weren't lying," I managed to announce.

"Woman, we're just gettin' started."

Chapter 13

Shayne

My friends place at the beach wasn't anything to write home about. Aside from it looking like a pig sty, it could have probably been condemned at any moment due to the structure being in such poor condition.

Chris Bono, also known as Boner, had been a friend since we both were lifeguards. We trained together and partied together.

Even though we still kept in touch, Boner hadn't changed and still lived his life drinking and hooking up with random girls, even the small amount that came around in the winter.

He greeted me with a half hug and a smile, before shoving a bong in my face. "I missed you, brother. What's goin' on, man?"

Boner had a lot going for him. Aside from his parents paying for him to live at the beach year round, his father was a huge part of the Ocean City community. He'd grown up there and only moved recently, when tourism got too much to handle.

Living only ten miles outside of Ocean City, he frequently paid his son visits where he would press him about growing up and finishing school.

Boner didn't care. He said he was happy and didn't need anything more to feel adequate. He was a beach bum in every way and a part of me envied his easy going lifestyle.

"Shit hit the fan this week at my place. I had to get the fuck out of there." He was going to want details and I didn't know where to begin.

After an hour of explaining, several beers, and then my having to re-explain, he finally got it. "Dude, you really fucked up this time. Lacey, she was a fine piece of ass."

"Yeah, I know. The thing is, as much as I want to be able to say that I could try to be with one person, I don't know if I could. I care about the girl, that's not a lie, but it wasn't like I wanted to get married and shit."

"I hear ya, dude. You're better off just lettin' her go. Girls like that will mess with your mojo, big-time."

"Tell me about it." I popped open a beer, that he happened to keep in a cooler next to the couch, so he didn't have to get up to grab them.

"You need to get laid?"

"Nah. I just want to get drunk. This one has gotten into my head."

"You sure you're over it?"

That was a good question. "It doesn't matter. She's moved on already." I moved my head around, disappointed. "She's seein' someone who's related through marriage. I think I'm just pissed that I still have to see her."

He looked shocked. "She's seein' a relative? Holy shit, dude, that's lame."

"We share a mutual cousin. It don't matter."

Boner took a hit from his bong and offered it to me, but I held up my hand to pass. While still holding in the smoke, he began to speak. "I'd show up at every function with a hot ass bitch on my arm."

Hurting Lacey wasn't part of some diabolical plan to make me feel better. I'd put myself here and I needed to live with it, without hurting her. "I don't want to do that. She's a nice girl. I just wish she wasn't with that prick."

When Boner sat his bong on the table he checked his phone before leaning back. "Annie and her friend are comin' over."

Annie was another local. She was raised by her grandparents and had a wild side that they had no idea about. Not only did she have tremendous tits, but she had an amazing body, skinny in all the right places and stacked in the others. We'd hooked up several times, including right before I got with Lacey and once when we were together. In fact, Lacey always seemed threatened by Annie, so I didn't tell her that we still talked frequently.

When she arrived, her hair was done and she was dressed nice, as opposed to her usual bummy look. Her long brown hair was rarely down, and especially not straightened and styled like it was. She saw me and smiled, walking over and climbing on my lap without even looking around the room for who else might be there. Her lips pressed against mine before she spoke. "Mmm, I missed you, Shayne."

My hands traveled back to her ass and I pulled her closer to me, ignoring the fact that her friend had sat down and was waiting to be introduced. Annie finally turned around and began giggling as she pointed to her friend. "Shayne, this is Megan. She's my new roommate."

I motioned to wave to the girl, but when I got a good look at her, everything in the room disappeared except for us. Not only was she blonde, beautiful and totally my type, but she reminded me of Lacey. When I said nothing, Boner added his two-cents. "Excuse my friend. You sort of look like his ex."

"Shut up! It's nice to meet you."

She smiled and looked down like she was shy. It was different than I was used to. Most girls came on to me without me having to do anything at all.

Annie climbed off of me and walked into the kitchen like she owned the place. She came out with a bottle of rum and four shot glasses. "Before you decide to hit on my friend and take her innocence away, I think we should get drunk."

I took a shot glass, but never looked away from the girl. She grabbed one and smiled, but I could tell she was uneasy. "Where are you from?"

"St. Michaels."

In the midst of throwing back my shot, I began to gag. St. Michaels was ten minutes from where Lacey grew up. Realizing the millions of people in the world, I didn't want to even ask if they knew each other. It wasn't possible. Lacey had never mentioned a girl named Megan that I could remember. "Is your dad a waterman?"

She gave me a funny look, like I had offended her. "No. My dad owns the Inn on the Island. He also owns a fishing tour business here at the beach. That's kind of why I'm here. We got a new office and it needs a lot of work. Plus people book their excursions in the winter for next summer. I work Monday through Friday in the office and go to school at Salisbury State at night."

Annie leaned on her friend's seat and pointed to me with the glass still in her hand. "You need to stay away from this one. He can be charming until he gets you naked."

I gave her a dirty look and wondered if she'd made the announcement because she didn't want to share. It would have been fine if this new chick wasn't so intriguing to me. Annie was a great lay, but maybe it was time for me to slow things down. This girl was too nice to fuck and walk away from. I could tell that she was uncomfortable and hated that I was pegged as some douchey man whore. "Let the girl decide that herself." I winked at Megan but she didn't respond.

Annie walked back over and sat next me, putting one leg over mine. She put one arm behind me and looked back at her friend. "Or, I could just tell her all your dirty little secrets."

I looked at Annie and clenched my jaw. She knew she was pissing me off and I think she was doing it on purpose.

143

Boner cut in before I could say something that would make her leave and never come back. "Are ya'll staying the night? We need to get more liquor before the store closes."

Megan stood up and grabbed her purse. "I'll go."

I practically pushed Annie off of me as I stood up, too. "I'll go with you, since I know he doesn't have any money."

Boner put his hands up. "Hey, I supply the place, you're in charge of the booze."

Annie remained sitting, but added, "Don't do anything I wouldn't do."

As we walked outside, I finally felt like I was going to have a chance to get to know this girl. Then she turned around and stuck her finger to my chest. "I know who you are, Shayne. Don't get any ideas of trying to sleep with me, because it's never going to happen."

Lacey

I woke to the sunlight coming in through a cracked curtain. Upon turning over, and discovering that the spot on the bed next to me was empty, I sat up. On top of Joey's pillow was a note.

Lace:

Had something to do this morning. Help yourself to anything in the kitchen. I'll be back around 3pm.

J

I traced over the words that he'd written in cursive and thought about how he'd made me feel, even after the horrible day I'd had. Joey's touch made me forget about all of it, especially Shayne.

Then the guilt hit me and I began to cry.

A knock at the door startled me, and before I could get up out of bed and find my clothes, I heard Sky calling my name.

"Lace, you need to open this door, right now. I know you're in there hiding. Ford called Joey and made sure."

I grabbed the blanket, wrapped it around my naked body and went to unlock the door. Sky was standing there with her hands on her hips. I held the door open for her to come inside. She plopped down on the couch and I followed. "I wasn't hiding. I just woke up."

She motioned to the blanket I had around me. "I guess you lost your clothes? Do you usually sleep naked when you're hiding from your ex in another man's home?"

"Shut up!" I shook my head and covered my face. "I slept with Joey. Are you happy now?"

"You said it was never going to happen. How long has this been going on? I knew you two were hiding something." I hated that she assumed I was sneaking around.

"It just happened. You weren't home and I didn't know where else to go. Joey's different when it's just us. He's nice to me."

"Of course he's nice. He wants to screw you."

I had to know what she knew that she wasn't telling me. "You think I'm stupid?"

"No! Of course I don't. Joey's a perfect one-night-stand, forget about Shayne kind of guy, but don't expect anything else. Ford says that Joey doesn't have girlfriends."

"What do you mean? I know he's not gay." After last night and the way he devoured my pussy, I knew that was impossible.

"I didn't say he was. It's just, he doesn't get involved. Joey likes casual sex and that's as far as he goes. Ford told me that he's never had a real girlfriend. In the time we've lived here, he's had several girls come over and they're gone by morning. I just don't want you thinking that it could be more. I don't want to see you hurt."

"I'm fine and I don't expect anything from Joey. We're friends, who had one hot night together. It's no big deal." I was lying through my teeth.

"Are you planning on sticking around or do you want to go out with me and my mom for lunch?"

I shrugged and ran my hand through my tangled hair. "I don't know. I didn't sleep much last night and I think I need to go home and take in all that's happened. I mean, I pretty much told Shayne to go to Hell then jumped right into bed with Joey. I need to clear my head before I do something even more irrational."

Sky stood up and leaned in to hug me. "I love you. I'm here for you. We would have come home to be with you last night. Why didn't you call?"

"I don't know. Joey was just there. It wasn't a big deal."

"Sleeping with Joey is a big deal. Ford is flipping out. He said he told Joey to back off. Last night when we saw your car was back, I thought he was going to beat down the door. Joey text Ford and said you were going to sleep in his guest room, but we both know that's not what happened."

"He said I was different."

"He probably says that to every girl he brings home. Look, I'm not trying to hurt you, Lace, but someone needs to look out for you. I can see you falling for him and it would be another Shayne all over again."

I faked a smile. "Why do I always make the worst decisions?"

"Get dressed and come over to our place. You can sleep all day for all I care. All I know is that I don't want you here when Joey gets back. He needs to know that last night meant nothing to you either. Don't give him the benefit of the doubt."

I was shaking as I grabbed my clothes and got dressed while Sky waited for me. For someone that was pushing me to move on, she didn't seem happy that I'd been with Joey. I knew it was because she knew me better than I knew myself. Sky was fully aware that I liked Joey more than I should have.

Once we got to her place and I got in her guest bed, it all hit me. I'd slept with someone who would never be anything more than sex. He'd made that clear and even offered me a chance to just be friends, probably because he knew that if we slept together it would sever any type of friendship that we'd made.

I felt worse. Considering how amazing he'd made me feel, caused me to crave him more. I wasn't going to be okay watching him with someone else, knowing the things that he was able to do. Hate filled me when I imagined him being with different women and telling them the same things that he'd said to me. Maybe that was his game all along.

Suddenly Joey and Shayne seemed like the same person. Leave it to me to find someone else to drag my heart into the dirt and destroy me again.

I cried myself to sleep, but woke up when I heard men talking with raised voices.

"I said you're not comin' in here and fillin' her head with lies."

"Back off with that. I just want to talk to her."

"Is that what you told her to get her into bed with you, Joey?"

When I heard his voice and then his name, I jumped out of bed and ran into the living room. "Stop!"

Joey looked right at me. "This fool won't let me talk to you. Tell him we're cool, Lace."

I just stood there, thinking about where he'd went all day. I knew he didn't have to work at the Country Club where he worked as head chef during the week, and he'd been gone all day. I shook my head. "I'm going to stay here tonight."

He looked confused and even hurt. "What did I do?"

"I'm sure you can call someone else to keep you company. Do you keep a black book or do they just show up on certain days of the week?"

Joey took a step forward, but Ford made him stop. "Lace, I don't know what you're talkin' about."

"I think you should go, Joey."

He shook his head and even smiled. "This is bullshit and the reason I don't get involved. See ya'll later." He backed himself out of the door and we heard his motorcycle starting up and pulling out of the driveway. I didn't understand why'd he'd care anyway. Didn't Ford and Sky say he had plenty of women? Why had he even come looking for me?

More importantly, why was I such a mess over it?

Chapter 14

Shayne

I'd spent the night getting to know someone that wanted nothing to do with me. After six shots and a five hour conversation, Megan fell asleep against my chest on the couch. It was the first time that I'd not tried to sleep with someone.

Annie passed out in my bed and I refused to go in there with her, knowing what would happen if I did. One look at her naked body and my dick would fight me until I was inside of her.

I slid off the couch and checked my phone out of habit. There were messages from my sister and even Parker, but none from an odd number that could have been Lacey. It drove me crazy that we were really over with and I couldn't, for the life of me, understand why it was bothering me so much. She was just a girl, who'd been a friend and then something a little more. I didn't deserve another chance and I didn't even know if I wanted one.

The only thing that bothered me was that she was with Joey.

It made no sense how someone *like him* could get Lacey. She left me for being with other people and lying. Joey was going to do the exact same thing.

After sending a text back to my sister to let her know I was alive, I headed into the bathroom. My phone started ringing and I didn't recognize the number, but I answered it anyway, thinking it was someone about an apartment.

"Hello?"

"Shayne, it's me." Lacey's voice shocked me. She was crying and I felt like shit for hurting her the day before.

"What's wrong?"

"Nothing. I got your number from Ford's phone, because I need to tell you something, even though it's not going to make a difference. I just can't lie about it, because it's what ripped us apart in the first place. I lied to you the other night when I said I was with Joey. He went along with it, because I asked him to. I just wanted to hurt you, because I thought it would make me feel better."

My stomach was aching. I hurt for her and for the fact that she cared what I thought, after everything I'd done. "Lace, I lied to you yesterday, because I wanted another chance. I knew you'd freak out about the other girls."

"It doesn't matter now, Shayne. Even if I wanted to forgive you, and even try to be friends, it's never going to happen now; not after what I've done."

"Lace, you're not makin' any sense, babe."

"I slept with Joey last night."

I was shocked and confused. "You just told me you were lyin'."

"I was at first, but we've been hanging out and it happened anyway."

I clenched my fists thinking about him swooning her. "What did he have to do to get you in his bed?"

She was quiet and cried more. "That's just it, Shayne. I came onto him." More sobbing filled the phone.

"What do you expect me to say here? I can't be that kind of friend to you about him, Lace. I know I owe you for breakin' your heart, but you need to call Sky or someone else. You think I never cared, but hearing this hurts. I feel like you're slappin' me in the face. Is that why you're callin'? Is this another way of makin' me pay for what I've done?"

"No. I don't know why I called. I'm so confused."

"Did he hurt you? If he hurt you I'll kill him."

She got quiet. "He didn't hurt me. Joey was kind to me."

"Then why are you callin' me, cryin' about it? Why aren't you with him now?"

"Because...I want the pain to go away."

"You're scaring me, Lace."

"I need to go. I'm sorry I bothered you, Shayne. Forget I ever called you."

"Lace?" She'd already hung up.

I dialed the number back and she wouldn't answer, so I called Ford.

"Shayne, it ain't a good time."

"The Hell with that. Where's Sky? I need to talk to her."

"For what?"

"Lacey just called me. She wanted to apologize for sleepin' with Joey and then she wasn't makin' sense. I'm worried about her."

"She's fine, man. I think she's just beatin' herself up over all of this bullshit. Look, I'm not doin' it for you, but I'm keepin' her away from Joey. A failed relationship has already cost us our friendship, I don't want to lose another cousin over the same thing."

"Do me a favor, Ford. Let me know if she's not alright. I care about her, even if she doesn't believe it."

"Will do."

I felt a little better when we'd hung up, but not completely sure that Lacey was okay. I knew I was to blame for all of it, but couldn't get past her sleeping with Joey and the fact that she'd run right back to him, after I'd hurt her again.

A knock on the bathroom door broke my train of thought. "Yeah, hang on."

Megan was standing at the door as I walked out. "Is everything okay?"

"Yeah. Family drama, that's all."

"I just wanted to say goodbye before I left. I needed to be in by twelve, so I need to head home."

I shouldn't have done it, and looking back, I don't know what made me think that I could take on anything else in my already fucked up life, but I asked for her number anyway.

After walking her out to her car, I got in my own. It wasn't like I could go back to sleep, and even if I could, my postponing the inevitable with my father was stupid. I was at the end of my rope and needed to get as much worked out as I could. He was going to expect me to be with Ashley, so I had to prepare us both for what that may entail. I needed a place to live, because I couldn't stay with Boner or any of my other friends without owing them something.

About thirty minutes later, I was pulling up at my parent's house. I knew they'd both be at work, which gave me time to go inside and shower. Peyton was still sleeping when I walked past her room. She called my name when I hit the bathroom. "Shayne, is that you?"

"Yeah. I came to get cleaned up before I go and talk to Dad."

"He's meetin' Ashley's dad at the shop. I heard him talkin' to Mom about it. They argued and he said that he had to be responsible since you couldn't get your shit together."

I ran my hand through my hair. "Jesus Christ, are you fuckin' kiddin' me? What else can go wrong today?"

"Why, what happened?"

"Lacey called to tell me she slept with Joey."

"That bitch!"

"Don't call her that. If I would have been good to her, none of this would be happenin'. Besides, she can be with whoever she wants."

"Still, calling to brag ain't cool." Peyton leaned against the wall across from me. "What did you say to her?"

"What could I say without soundin' like an asshole? The only thing I know about Joey is that he likes women and doesn't want to be tied down."

"Sounds familiar."

I shot her a dirty look. "Maybe I'm ready to settle down."

Peyton shook her head and started laughing at my comment. "I'd like to see that happen. Now that you have a kid on the way, it's probably good you want to change."

"About that." I wanted to tell my sister the truth. She was always around when I needed someone on my side, but she also didn't know how to keep her mouth shut. I couldn't risk her going right to Parker about it. "I don't think Ashley and I will ever have anything between us. That one night we were together was a mistake. We don't even get along, especially since the Ford thing."

Peyton changed the subject without me asking her to. "Are you going to go interrupt Dad?"

"Hell yes, I am. He's got no right to get in my business. He thinks because I work for him that he still has reign over what I do with my life. I'm so fuckin' tired of it."

"He's just worried about you. You're the last person we thought would be havin' a kid."

Apparently the whole world thought I was nothing more than a fuck-up. I was getting sick of everyone's opinions.

Just because I didn't live by their standards didn't mean I wasn't happy with my life. If they only knew that their precious Parker had fathered the kid, they wouldn't be saying shit.

"I better get a shower. Thanks for the info."

I closed the bathroom door before she could say anything else. After the Lacey drama this morning, the hot water felt good falling down on my body. I wished that I was able to wash away all of the stress that I'd been putting on myself, but more was surely going to show up and take it's place. I couldn't catch a break to save my life.

Even with a dark cloud hanging over my head, I knew I needed to move forward. There was a baby involved, so nothing in my life was going to come before that issue. I was going to have to face both my father and Ashley's. By the end of the day they'd know that I was serious about being a parent, even if it was temporary as a favor to my brother.

Lacey

"Why in the hell would you call Shayne? Are you crazy?"

I shrugged and refused to look at a very pissed, Sky. She had her hands on the edge of the bed as she scolded me.

"Lace, you need to talk to me. What is going on in that head of yours?"

I put a pillow over my face. "I don't know. One minute I feel terrible for sleeping with Joey and then next I want to knock on his door and do it all over again."

"What happened between the two of you? I've never seen you act like this. Is it Shayne or Joey that's getting you so worked up?"

I removed the pillow and finally looked at Sky. "It doesn't matter. Neither of them are any good for me, you said it yourself. They both lie and cheat, so either way I'm screwed."

She sat down on the edge of the bed. "There's nice guys out there. If you wouldn't have been so determined to have Shayne, you'd probably have met a few by now."

"I thought he'd grown up and wanted to be with me. He acted like it every time we were together. How could I have known he was messing around on me?"

Knowing she wasn't going to give up driving me insane, I got up and grabbed my things. I kissed her on the cheek. "I love you, Sky, but I need to get home and get some rest. I've got class in the morning and need to pass or my dad's going to skin me alive. I still have to finish an assignment."

We said our goodbyes and minutes later I was pulling out of the driveway, but not without noticing Joey had returned. Both his bike and his car were parked in the driveway and his light was on in his place. I wondered what he was doing, or if he'd already started coming on to someone new that would take my place. I wondered if I was just a simple game to him.

My parents hadn't seen me in days, and after ten minutes, they went back to acting like I wasn't in the house with them. That was my key to leave. I headed up to my room and turned on my laptop. My assignment was easy and I kept flipping from a social media site then back to my school work. When it chimed that I had a new friend request, I curiously flipped back to see who it was. Joey's name popped up and I was quick to deny it.

Moments later a private message came through.

Lace, if I said something or did something to piss you off, I don't know what it was.

I stared at his words and tried three times to write a response.

He must have gotten tired of waiting. *You came on to me last night. I didn't make you take off your clothes and seduce me.*

It was a mistake.

You didn't act like it last night, when I was making you cum over and over. What happened? Did you like it too much? Are you afraid to admit that it was even better than I said it would be? Is that what's gotten you in such a tizzy?

Leave me alone, Joey!

I can't do that. You see, ever since I tasted your sweet pussy, it's all I can think about. I fucked up four orders today at the diner because I couldn't stop thinking of how good it felt to wake up next to you.

He was pushing my buttons and turning me on at the same time. The sex had been phenomenal from start to finish.

I bet you tell that to all of the girls.

A few moments went by and he said nothing. Just as I was ready to flip back to my homework a message came through.

I've never lied to you, Lacey. I've also never let a woman stay the night, because it made things personal. You're the first woman to spend the night in my arms.

I don't believe you.

I don't believe you either. You act like last night wasn't great for you. I woke up wanting more and I know you did too. Now, I don't know what happened while I was gone, but something got you spooked. I'll leave you alone, but you know where to find me when you're ready to admit that you want more.

I hate to burst your bubble, but you aren't as good as you think you are.

When I hit send, I had a smile on my face knowing that was going to floor him.

Does it bother you more that you enjoyed it, or the fact that I was right all along? Tell me, Lacey, when you're naked in that bed, will you close your eyes and picture me eating that sweet pussy? Did you memorize how I fucked you and made you cum with my tongue?

Don't you have someone else to annoy?

The messages stopped, but I wasn't able to get back to my assignment. Instead, I stared at the screen, like his words gave me some kind of reassurance. I didn't understand how someone that was supposed to have so many women at his beck and call would be trying so hard to get me to talk to him.

After trying to eat an apple, and still feeling sick over everything, I lay down and stared at the ceiling. So many things were going through my mind, especially every moment of my time with Joey.

My phone rang and I saw it was Sky. Figuring she was calling to check on me, I picked up and just started talking.

"I'm fine. I even ignored Joey when he tried to talk to me. Are you proud of me?"

A masculine laugh caught me off guard. I looked at the phone to make sure it was really Sky's number.

Then he started to talk.

"You're sexy when you're playin' hard to get."

"Joey? Seriously, how did you get Sky's phone? I know she wouldn't just give it to you."

"I told her I couldn't find mine, so I needed to borrow hers to call it. I knew she wouldn't just let me call you and I knew you wouldn't answer if I tried from my phone. We need to talk, Lace. I gave you what you wanted last night, even after tellin' you that it was goin' to change things between us. Don't give me that bullshit that I need to leave you alone. You and I were the only people in that bed last night and I know you weren't thinkin' about anyone else but me."

I opened my mouth to argue, but no words came. He was right. Just hearing his voice was giving me butterflies. I think that's why I called and told Shayne what I'd done. I felt guilty for wanting Joey. I felt like a slut for wanting to be with him when I'd just gone out with Shayne.

"Say something, Lacey."

"What do you want me to say? Do you want to hear that last night was amazing? Do you want me to say that I can't get you out of my head? Is that how you get off? Do you like stringing women on?"

"What the fuck? Who has been puttin' this bullshit in your head? Did I ever make you feel like you were one of many? I told you that you were different and I meant that shit. If you were just some other woman, I would have fucked you and sent you on your way. That ain't what happened and you know it. You can believe everyone else, but it's a lie. I didn't just want to fuck you, Lacey. I thought you knew that."

"Maybe I'm more mad at myself."

"For what?"

"For thinking you could make me forget about Shayne. I'm sorry I used you, Joey. I'll stay away from Sky's place so you won't have to be around me."

"Lace…"

I hung up before he could say anything else. I knew what I'd done was the right thing, but it felt so wrong. In seconds, I'd collapsed down on my bed and started bawling. I shouldn't have been so torn up over Joey, but I was.

I liked him, no matter how wrong it was, or what everyone else said about him. It killed me that we couldn't be together again, because when I was in his arms, nothing else mattered.

Chapter 15

Shayne

When I walked into the door of my dad's office, he was sitting there with Ashley and her father. She smiled as I came in.

"What are you doin?"

My dad folded his hands across his desk. "We're tryin' to do what's right for you two kids."

"That's not your business."

"It's important that you think about your future. Neither of you is ready to raise a child. How are you going to support my daughter now after the fiasco you pulled with your cousin? Were you really goin' to let him raise your child?" Ashley's dad and mine were too much alike.

"Dad, please. It was a mistake. Shayne didn't know it was his." I appreciated her trying to help, even if she was lying.

"Look." I stood my ground. "I get that you both are worried about us, but we're going to have this baby."

"It's best if we terminate the pregnancy, son." My dad's words ripped me in two, considering this was Parker's life also. If only he knew what he was saying and what it would do to the one son he still loved with his whole heart.

"That's not an option. Ashley and I have discussed it. We're adults. You don't get a say in this decision. I get that you think you do, but you're both wrong. I found us a nice apartment and there's plenty of room for the baby."

I didn't realize what was happening until the words were coming out of my mouth. I hadn't found us a place and I certainly wasn't about to live happily ever after with Ashley.

The room got silent. Then Ashley's dad cleared his throat. "I was under the impression that you didn't want anything to do with this child. Have I been misinformed?"

"Yes, sir. I don't know who told you that," I looked at my dad, "but it's not the truth."

The man seemed pleased. "If that's settled then I will be on my way out of here. I have other business to tend to. Come on Ashley."

They started to walk away, but I grabbed Ash by the arm. "Do you mind leavin' with me. I need to talk to you."

Her dad smiled, but had already gotten on his cell phone and was talking about an appointment.

I started heading toward my car when my dad came out. "Shayne, can you come in here for a second?"

I walked toward the bay door and put my hands in my pockets. "Have at it, Dad. I know you're disappointed."

"I need you back to work. How long do you need to move in your new place?"

He pretended like he hadn't kicked me out of his house and fired me just days before.

I shrugged. "A few days, I guess. Ashley's goin' to need help too."

There was no point in arguing. I needed my job and I liked it.

"Just come back next Monday ready to work. Make sure you tell your mother your new address so she can change the files in the office."

Of course, he was all professional. God forbid he act like we were father and son. "Will do. See you then."

I climbed in the car and saw Ash staring at me. "Shayne, this has gone too far."

We started driving before I could talk to her. "Look, I've had a shitty couple of days. Let's just find a place that we can share for now and we'll figure things out later."

"You're willin' to put your life on hold to take care of me?"

"It's temporary, Ash. As soon as the baby is born you can decide where you want to live. I don't even care if you don't talk to me everyday. Let's just keep everyone happy until the truth can come out."

"I'd do anything to get away from that man. He's so suffocating."

After agreeing, we set out and found the perfect place. It was about twenty minutes in between each of our parent's houses, which was far enough away that they wouldn't be stopping in and spying on us every day. Ash even stopped at a couple places and filled out applications for part-time work. We talked about being cordial roommates, who chipped in and stayed out of each other's way. When it was necessary, we'd put on a good show for everyone that mattered.

After the background check was done and I gave my first months rent, we were able to move in three days later. All of the furniture from my old place was in storage and Ash only brought her bedroom set. The only room that wasn't furnished was the baby's room and we had plenty of time for that.

Staying busy kept my mind off of Lacey, but I still worried that she wasn't right with things, so one night I called her.

"Hello."

"It's Shayne. How are you?"

All I could hope was that she didn't hang up.

"I'm okay. How are you?"

"I moved into my new place. It's in that community Canterbury. My dad's lettin' me come back to work next week."

"That's great Shayne. I'm glad things are getting better for you."

"What about you, Lace? I'm callin' because I'm worried about you."

"I appreciate that you care, but I'm fine. I've been home at my parents since Monday and school keeps me busy during the week. I'm sure you remember that."

"Have you spoke to Joey?"

"No." She got quiet. "Shayne, I can't talk to you like that yet."

"I know. I'm sorry."

"It's nice to hear your voice and I'm really glad that you got your own place."

"Lace, can I call you again? I promise I won't pry. I just miss bein' able to talk."

"Sure."

"Talk to you soon, then."

"Okay. Bye Shayne."

After hanging up, I was able to smile. We talked about nothing serious, but hearing her sweet voice made me feel like one day we'd be able to get passed everything else and be friends again. Lacey was someone I would always care about, no matter who she was dating. If I couldn't have her in my bed, I at least needed her in my life.

Lacey

I'd done so well focusing on everything but the two men in my life. Joey hadn't tried to call or message me, but one call from Shayne was all it took for my mind to start wondering if he'd already moved on.

It drove me so crazy that, by the time Friday came along, I found myself driving to Sky's in hopes of seeing him, even if only for a moment. I wanted to catch him with another woman, so I could be sure that I'd made the right decision.

I didn't need to look far to find him, since he was underneath of his car working on it when I pulled up. I tried to hurry up and knock on Sky's door, but he was rolled out from under it, chasing me up the sidewalk. "Lacey, hold up a minute."

I turned and put on a serious face. "What?"

The moment I looked into those light hazel-brown eyes, I felt like I was going to melt. I noticed his perfect jawline and the way his stubble had grown in around his chin. He licked his lips before words came out and I licked mine as a direct reaction.

He noticed and a smile formed in the corner of his mouth. Instead of talking, he reached up and ran the back of his hand over my cheek. I closed my eyes, remembering the way his hands felt as they explored my naked flesh.

He nestled his face close to my ear and the air as he spoke tickled me. "Did you come here to see your friend, or me?"

I shoved him away. "Don't flatter yourself, Joey. I came here to see Sky. It's the weekend. This is where I come. Nothing has changed."

He pressed me against the building and grabbed ahold of my crotch. "Everything's changed. Stop pretendin' you don't want more."

I attempted to fight him and he held me steady, rubbing me between the legs. "I don't."

His lips were on mine and I couldn't help myself. The only reaction that came out of me was reciprocation. For days I'd tried to get him out of my head and now I understood why it was so hard. I yearned for his touch, no matter how bad or wrong it was for me.

Joey pulled away, once he knew I'd stopped fighting him. He brushed over my lips with his thumbs and kissed me softly once more. At the same time, Sky opened her door and saw us in the embrace. Her eyes opened wide.

Joey wasted no time, letting her know how things were going to go down. "She's comin' home with me. Make sure you tell Ford we don't need any drama. Once my door's locked, ain't nobody stoppin' us."

My heart was beating so fast and I felt like I was going to pass out as he grabbed my hand and led me inside his place. He kicked the door shut and pulled us against it. I still had said nothing to him, knowing that at any moment I was going to start crying uncontrollably due to being so overwhelmed.

Joey pulled away and looked right into my eyes. I felt like he was burning through me. He tugged on my shirt until I lifted up my arms, letting him pull it over my head. I ran my hands up his, feeling his hard, warm chest against the palms of my fingers. With little effort he lifted it off, then brought our lips back together.

He pulled away and sat me down on the couch, while he remained standing. "You think you know me, but you're wrong. I've never lied to you about my intentions, but only withheld things about myself that you would prefer to not know."

He paced around while still talking. "Since you don't believe me, I think I should show you the difference between you and the other women I've fucked."

The way he was talking sort of scared me. "Is this where you tie me up and beat me so that you can cum all over my face and make me leave?"

He cocked his eyebrow then began to laugh. "Um, no. Is that what you like?"

I giggled. "Of course not."

Joey got down on his knees and looked at me. "I don't want to do this, but you've given me no other choice."

"Do what?" I was definitely worried.

Joey took my bra and ripped open the hook in the front clasp. He yanked it off of me, causing me to lose my

172

balance and fall back against the couch cushion. "When I fuck other women, I don't care about taking my time. They come for one reason and I give it to them." He grabbed my jeans and started pulling them off of me, without waiting for me to lift my ass. My body was yanked halfway off of the couch and he still kept pulling. "They never fight me." I stood up and stepped out of my jeans, watching him pull down my underwear, without any regard for the details of my naked body in front of his eyes.

Joey stood up, threw me over his shoulder and took me into the guest bedroom, where he tossed me down on the bed. From there, he removed his pants, opened the bedside table and pulled out a condom. When he climbed on the bed, he didn't kiss me. Instead, he flipped me over and got behind, so he was facing my ass that was up in the air. I could feel his hand massaging it, right before he smacked it hard. The sting was replaced by his rubbing and as soon as it felt better he smacked me again. Before I could respond, or scream, he shoved himself inside of me. I wasn't wet and the friction felt like he was ripping me raw. As much as I hated what he was doing, I couldn't help but start to get turned on that we were having sex again. My body began reacting to his movements and soon I could feel the wetness of my arousal. Joey felt it too. He grabbed my shoulders and pounded into me harder. He yanked my hair back and forced a kiss on my lips. Then he bit down and sucked on my bottom lip until it hurt. When he pulled away, I cried out. It felt so good and so painful all at the same time. I wanted what was happening, but this was not the same guy that I'd been with one week ago.

Joey flipped me over and grabbed both of my hands, lifting them over my head so I couldn't touch him. He held them with one hand and rubbed my clit with the other, while he entered me again. He wouldn't look at me, but stayed focused on my pussy and what he was doing. We slammed into each other, every time causing me to hit the headboard. Loud bangs became more frequent as the bed kept hitting the wall. Joey continued going, without emotion. He fucked me like a machine would that couldn't experience feelings.

I let him go for a few seconds before I began to cry. Joey pulled out of me and stood up. He looked mad. "The next time you want to compare yourself to someone else, maybe you should come to me first. You and I both know that I didn't fuck you like I do them that night. It was more than that and you need to start believing it if you ever want to find out what's been happenin' between us, Lacey."

I was speechless. It wasn't like he'd assaulted me. I'd never told him to stop, because a apart of me didn't want him to.

What I wanted was to feel close to him. This side he was showing me was obviously his way of dealing with me rejecting him.

After he'd left me alone in the guest room, I waited a few minutes before I could go out to face him. He was standing in the kitchen, naked, smoking a cigarette, with the door cracked open.

I approached him with nothing on my body and wrapped my arms around him.

In seconds I felt his arms around my back. "I'm sorry. I didn't mean to be an asshole. I'm just so fuckin' pissed you'd walk away after that night. Was I just imaginin' that there's somethin' between us?"

It was undeniable. "No. I feel it too."

He kissed the top of my head. "Lacey, I'm no good at bein' a boyfriend and I know you need time, but I can't let you walk away from this."

He pulled away and looked right into my eyes. Our lips met and he held our mouths together. "Take me back to your bed, Joey."

I didn't have to ask twice. He tossed out the smoke, grabbed my hand and led me into his bedroom. After pulling down the covers, and letting me climb in bed, he ran back out into the bathroom and brushed his teeth. The smell of smoke didn't bother me, but I appreciated that he wanted it to be perfect.

When he came back into the room, he walked slowly. I couldn't help notice that he was already hard. I licked my lips as he climbed in the bed and scooted up next to me. Our hands connected and our bond was immediate. Joey kissed me tenderly, reminding me of the man that he'd been that first night. "Are you mad at me?"

I moved my shoulder and felt awkward. "You scared me."

He ran his fingers over my nipple while he spoke. "I'd never hurt you, or any woman, for that matter. If you weren't so stubborn, I wouldn't of had to show you the difference. You could have taken my word for it. Lacey, I'm not a whore. I just like sex. It can be casual and consensual between two people that have no interest in each other. You're different and you need to accept that or this can't happen."

"Okay," I whispered.

He stared at me. "After all of that hard to get shit, you're just goin' to agree?"

I nodded. "I think the guest room fucking helped."

"You liked it a little. Admit it." He laughed.

Joey rolled me on top of him. I sat up and placed my hands on his collarbone. We were already dry humping without doing it on purpose. I couldn't be naked on top of him and not move around. "My ass is on fire now. Next time, warn me. I felt like you were going all Nightmare on Elm Street."

"I guess you don't want to use my handcuffs and whips? Maybe I could break out my gag ball."

I smacked his chest. "You're a freak. Do you have a secret red room?"

"A what?"

I laughed, imagining him reading a dirty book about secret sex rooms. If it wasn't edible, Joey wasn't interested. "I did think about you."

"Oh yeah," he grabbed my hips and started moving me himself. "Were we naked?"

I nodded. "Of course."

"I thought about you, too." Joey lifted me up until my pussy was right at his face. I looked down and watched him kissing me there. He flicked my clit with his tongue and pulled away. "Mmm, I thought about this every night. You taste like honeysuckle and I love that shit."

The tingles overwhelmed me and I let my head fall back as his mouth sucked on my pussy. He licked me like his favorite flavor of ice-cream, like I could melt at any second, while holding onto my ass, so I couldn't back away.

I reached up and grabbed one of my nipples, positioning it so that my tongue could brush against the hardened tip. Joey moaned against my sex as he watched. I did it again, this time watching him watch me.

I could feel him sucking in my labia and nibbling on my lips and he tugged on them. His thumb came up and rubbed on my clit until I moved his hand away and began to do it to myself. Watching his mouth, so close to my fingers, lapping up the most tender part of my body was irrationally the best feeling that I'd ever experienced.

Shutters of incredible pleasure engulfed me, sending me to new heights once more.

My ass sprung up as the intensity became too much to handle. I gripped Joey's hair and cried out his name as my wet juices filled his mouth.

He moaned against my saturated pussy, keeping his face close as he gently kissed the tickle away.

As he moved back up my body, a trail of my ecstasy was left from him dragging his lips and chin over my tender skin. Our eyes met and his eager grin showed me that we were far from over. "Suck it off my chin, Lace. Taste yourself and tell me how I make you feel when I'm sucking on that little clit."

Jolts of excitement made my nipples tingle as I closed my eyes and tasted my own release on Joey's skin. He moaned and ran his hands over my back as I followed his directions. "Tasting myself makes me horny. It makes me want you to do it again." My honesty shocked me.

Joey smiled and looked right at me. "I'm not done with that pussy tonight. When we're done, you'll be squirting that hot cum, feeling what it's like to lose total control of yourself. I love watching you do it," He ran his fingers over my clit. "but I know you can do better."

My back arched with every movement he made over my tiny bud. I wanted to cum again, but knew it was time to give back to this man, who'd just given me such pleasure. I scooted away from Joey, shoving him down on his back. He smiled and held his arms out for me to come to him, but I shook my head. Both of my hands grabbed ahold of his knees as they started their slow process up to his thighs. I licked my lips, thinking about his rock-hard cock being in my mouth. Joey didn't have to question my intentions, as I gave him no time to. My lips were around his girth, taking his smooth skin an inch at a time as deep as I could go. He played with my hair while watching my every move. I could tell he liked it, but wasn't satisfied with being average. I didn't just want to blow him, I wanted to blow him away.

With no regard for modesty, or self consciousness, I removed my lips from his dick and licked the tip. He groaned, watching me do it again. When I knew I had his undivided attention, I spit on it, while taking my fingers and lubricating his whole shaft. My tongue began at the base of his testicles and slid up the back of his shaft, applying necessary pressure to his main vein.

Joey grabbed my head, forcing me to repeat what I'd just done. I looked up at him, keeping my eyes steady as I licked around his balls again. As if that wasn't enough to drive him utterly crazy, I sucked the smooth mounds into my mouth and tugged. His body jerked during the time that I released them from my lips. This time, when I lapped up his cock, I took his tip in my mouth and moved rapidly, with no real pattern. My hand rubbed his balls while the other jerked him off. I sucked him so hard that my jaws began to hurt, albeit I refused to let up.

I'd been cheated on and knew that, had I satisfied my partner, he never would have strayed. Pleasing Joey became my top priority and I wasn't giving this man a chance to question my abilities.

I pulled away from his cock, while still massaging his shaft. His thighs needed attention, so I licked them inside,

179

where the patch of hair began to thicken. His soft balls brushed across my nose as I got closer and I wanted them again. I licked them from behind, coming so close to touching his taint with my tongue. I recognized the taste of his sweat, but even the salty hint couldn't stop me. I was dripping again, reaching down and touching myself, while sucking him off.

Joey was getting close. He was breathing heavily and grabbing me wherever he could reach. The base of his stiff shaft was easy to pump, while my lips provided a place for his release. I could feel it there, ready to pour into my welcoming mouth. As it came out, the heat and flavor trickled down my throat. I kept my mouth there, making sure he was done, before I licked his tip. Tonguing his hole as if I wanted more.

Joey wiped his face and looked down at me. I could sense that he was satiated and impressed, but needed to hear it for myself. I licked his tip again, staying there next to his spent, limp shaft. "Mmm, how did it feel?"

"You know the answer already."

"Give and you shall receive." I ran my hands up his thighs, making him moan again.

He cleared his throat and grabbed my hair, forcing me to climb up to be even with him. "There's not enough hours in the day for me to be able to do the things I want to do to you."

I brought my lips to his ear and whispered, "I have nowhere else to be."

This time I wasn't going to run away. I couldn't.

No man had ever made me feel so insatiable and I believed that I was different than the others. With the amount of pleasure that he'd offered me, I wondered if I could overlook any of his flaws and accept the things he gave me instead. Did I really need that forever after, anyway?

Chapter 16

Shayne

Ashley had her first doctor's appointment and asked if I wanted to go. I didn't, at first, feeling like it was creepy for me, who'd never actually been intimate with her, to be in the room when she got naked, and felt up by a doctor.

After much consideration, and knowing she was going at it alone, I decided it was necessary to be the support she needed.

We'd been getting along fine, maybe because we'd known each other for so long. Aside from her being vindictive, Ashley had always been a nice person. Her love for Ford sent her over the edge and I couldn't entirely blame her. When his sister died, tragically, he shut down. We all knew he'd never recover and be the guy he was before that day. Ashley happened to be the odd person out.

For a while, I hated her. She expected me to be okay with her using Ford and never speaking up about the real biological father. Some truths were out, while I struggled with the other one that would eventually rock my family.

To us, we were just roommates with a common interest, but to others, we were two people starting a family. It was absurd and frustrating, but certainly distracted the other fucked up aspects of my life.

My father allowed me to come back to work. He avoided me unless it was crucial to communicate. Our relationship would never be close and I didn't really care. The man was harsh and his morals were shit.

All I could hope was that the fate of my niece or nephew wouldn't have anything to do with him.

Ashley was nervous about her first appointment, especially when we got back in the room. She wasn't required to undress, which was good for me, considering I didn't want anything to do with that. I guess it was out of nervousness, but Ash looked over and asked me a question that I surely didn't expect. "Shayne, you miss Lacey don't you?"

I was sitting in the chair across from the exam table and looked down at the floor. "Yeah, but that ship has sailed."

"I can't believe she's seein' Joey, of all people."

I thought about her upsetting call and how I hadn't heard a thing from her since. Suddenly, I became worried and decided to walk outside to check on her. It was a good thing that I had her new number, otherwise I would have been freaking out.

It rang six times before the voicemail picked up. Instead of leaving a message, I dialed it again and this time I was more shocked than anything else.

"Hello?" A male voice answered the phone.

"I must have the wrong number."

"Are you looking for Lace?" I hated that someone else called her that. It had always been my nickname for her when she visited the beach.

"Yeah. Is she around?"

"Is this Shayne?"

Right away I got defensive, but my fear was being verified. "Joey?"

I heard an air filled laugh on the other end of the phone. "Yeah, it's me."

Maybe I should have kept my mouth shut, except I hated that he was answering her phone. "You need to leave her alone, dude."

"Come again?"

"Lacey. You need to walk away. Look, I don't blame you for wantin' a piece, but she's not a fuckin' toy. She wants somethin' real, man."

"It ain't your business, Shayne."

I clenched my fist, wanting to reach through the phone and beat the shit out of him. "She is still my business. You really think she would have run to you, if I hadn't pushed her away? Lacey's smart. She'll wise up and see how you really are and if I find out it's because you hurt her, you'll have Hell to pay."

Joey started laughing. "Now you're threatenin' me? I can promise you that Lacey's in good hands. She said that nobody's ever made her cum like I do."

"Fuck you!"

"Oh she is, over and over again."

"You're messin' with the wrong guy, Joey."

"Shayne, don't call Lacey anymore and watch what you promise. There ain't no way you'll win this battle."

I went to say something else, but he'd already hung up. Feeling more pissed, I went back into the doctor's office and found that he was there, already talking to Ashley. Her belly was exposed and he had some device pressed against it. I could hear the rapid beating and recognized it from television shows. There was a little child growing and even if it wasn't mine, it was still a part of me. My mind started to ease as I listened and saw Ashley smiling from ear to ear.

The doctor put the device down and folded his hands. "Do twins run in either of your family's?"

The knot was back and consuming me with shock and awe. "My siblin's are twins."

"I'm hearing multiple heartbeats. Just to be sure, I'm going to order a sonogram."

Neither Ashley or myself could stop looking like we were going to be sick. I grabbed her hand and threw her a smile as he was writing the referral for the test. "It's goin' to be fine, Ash."

I knew it wasn't. One baby was hard enough, but two? My brother was in for a world of change and I had no clue how I was going to break it to him.

Ashley cried the whole way to the diagnostic center. I tried to reassure her, but simply couldn't find the right thing to say. Neither of us was ready for one kid, two was going to be impossible to prepare for. Giving up the next couple of years for my brother seemed to be turning out as a huge mistake. Nothing good was going to come out of this mess.

185

An hour later, after I watched a long dick looking thing go underneath the sheet, we were looking at two blobs on the little monitor. The tech confirmed that there were in fact two babies growing in Ashley's stomach. Had it not been for me seeing them myself, and realizing that they were little humans, living breathing, and family, I may not have been able to stand up. Instead of freaking out, I stared at the screen mindlessly watching them.

That moment brought so much into perspective for me.

My mind went to Lacey and what I could have had with her. I imagined her getting the sonogram while I held her hand, knowing they were my children. Realizing that she wasn't mine set a new plan into affect. I wanted this life with Lacey and I was going to do whatever it took to get her back.

I had something that Joey didn't.

I still had her heart.

Lacey

Joey had taken me to new heights, surprising me each time the two of us came together. He touched me like I was fragile and precious, not like he'd shown me how he touched other women. While in the shower, I closed my eyes and thought of the countless times he'd given me pleasure already. My skin vibrated as I brushed the washcloth over my tender pussy. It had been throbbing since our last encounter, hours ago. Joey was like a sex machine, and he never gave up until I was ready to pass out.

I let the rag drop and touched my bare fingers to my clit, moving them around in a circular motion. I lathered up my tits with my free hand and watched myself pinching my left nipple. I leaned back against the wall and moved my hand faster, pressing hard as my fingers teased my eager clit. Soon, my legs were buckling and I was silently crying out in bliss.

I stepped out after finally rinsing off, gently drying my still trembling body. Joey was on the couch, in only a pair of boxers. He smiled when I walked in, wrapped in only a towel. "I think we should do somethin' today."

I climbed on top of him, looking him right in those light hazel-brown eyes. "We are doing something."

He patted on my legs after accepting a short kiss. "I meant go out. Let me take you out to dinner, on a real date."

I was shocked, after hearing so many horror stories about Joey not doing anything but screwing random women. "You really want to take me out?"

He rubbed my arms and smiled. "Yes. Why are you sayin' it like that?"

I shrugged and smiled awkwardly. I don't know. Everyone says you don't ever do that. I just can't understand why you feel like doing it with me. You've already gotten me in bed, several times. Aren't I breaking every one of your rules?"

He tugged down the towel and massaged my tits while he looked at them. "Rules are made to be broken, especially when they're with someone like you, Lacey. You made me fuckin' crazy when you wouldn't talk to me. I've never had to chase pussy before. Not ever."

Our lips met and I teased him with my tongue. "So, was I worth the chase?"

He cocked his eyebrow, while pinching my nipple and biting down on his lip. "I can't get enough of you. Does that answer your question?"

I should have been satisfied, but for some reason, I wasn't. Joey was amazing and also mysterious. There was so much I didn't know about him. "It answers that one, but you still haven't said what you want from me. Is this just sex? Are we friends with casual benefits? Forgive me for being blunt, I just need to know what I'm getting myself into. After Shayne, I can't be in the dark about anything."

Joey pulled me close, cuddling with me on the couch. He grabbed the remote that he still kept behind his head instead of an end table, and turned the volume down. "I reckon you deserve answers then. Lacey, I'm not real sure what this is between us. I'm not the kind of guy that goes lookin' for women. I have understandin's and nobody complains. You're not like them. I get that you want some kind of label, because that's all you've ever known. I'm just not sure I can make promises without breakin' them. Do you understand?"

I really didn't. "You say I'm different, but not different enough to just want to see me?"

"Don't put words in my mouth. I never said that. I've never had to answer to a woman. My life's been too busy to settle down. Things have changed and perhaps bein' with you could turn into somethin' more. It feels right, but I don't know how long it will last, so I don't want to lie about it. It's all new. I might just wake up one day and decide I need to be single. Do you understand?"

I was annoyed, but for some reason, I did understand. "I appreciate that you're being honest about it. Most guys would tell me what I wanted to hear to shut me up."

He brushed the hair away from my face. "I'm not most guys."

"No, you're not." I smiled and tried to think about being happy where we were at. It had only been a few times that we'd been together. Obviously, it was too soon for anyone to put labels on it, but I felt weary, like everything could change in an instant. The more I fell for Joey, the scarier it was going to be to allow myself feelings that would in turn break my heart again.

After we laid there talking for a while, I reached over and grabbed my phone. I needed to put some clothes on, or at least hang up the towel and walk around naked. It was damp and getting on the sofa fabric. Joey watched me as I looked at it. "I can't believe that I haven't gotten any phone calls today. I figured Sky would be blowing it up."

Joey laughed. "It didn't ring while you were in the shower." I turned to look at him and he was staring at the television when he spoke. Deciding that it was a good time to change, I hurried into the bedroom to do so.

Like every time I'd gotten a shower here, Joey had set out a t-shirt of his for me to put on. The shirt he'd picked out had a lapel on it that would have scratched my chest, so I went into his dresser to find another one.

I did find a plain one, but that wasn't all that was in his drawer. Over a dozen photos of naked girls, laying sprawled out on beds were in a pile. I glanced at them quickly and then put them back where they were. When Joey came in and saw the shirt, I could tell he knew that I knew. He sat down on the bed and patted the spot beside him. I was reluctant, but made my way there. Our eyes locked and he shot me a smile. "Ask away."

How was I supposed to approach this without seeming jealous or disturbed when frankly, I was both. "There's like a dozen different women in those pictures, Joey."

He pointed to the dresser. "Go get them." I couldn't help but notice that he seemed unaffected, like it wasn't a big deal at all.

I walked over and grabbed the pictures, then placed them in the palm of his waiting hand. "I wasn't snooping. I just wanted a more comfortable shirt, I swear."

He took the pictures and spread them out on his bed. Then he pointed to one. "Her name is Courtney. I met her in culinary school, first. We were teamed up to work on a project. Her boyfriend was also in the program and she loved him enough to sabotage our team, for his to do better."

I wasn't following. "I don't understand how this naked picture has to do with culinary school."

He smiled. "It's simple. One night we had a few drinks. Getting her to come back to my room was easier than I expected. Once I got her naked, I took the picture. The next morning she woke up and begged me not to tell anyone. I waited a week before I showed her the picture and told her if she ever crossed me again, I had leverage against her."

"You're ruthless."

"I was determined to make my dream come true. No little two-timing bitch was going to fuck it up."

I pointed to the others. "What about these?"

He pointed to two others. "For two months I worked in Baltimore. The first week there I met these two crazy chicks that just wanted to have fun. Tawny and Sheena were their names. Those two I took for fun. Then I decided that I wanted a collection, so every woman that I hooked up with I took a picture. You may think I'm an asshole. Some people write in journals. I kept photos to remember them by."

I grabbed all of the photos and put them back in his drawer, still not sure how I felt about them.

"They're yours to keep. Thank you for being honest."

"You think I take them out and look at them?"

"I don't want to know."

"Your picture ain't goin' in that drawer, Lace. Don't even worry about it."

"I wasn't." I felt hurt. Like I wasn't good enough to be something he reminisced about. "Am I not good enough to be in your collection?"

He grabbed my hands and pulled me between his legs. "You're different. I want you here, because I like being with you. Your picture belongs on nightstands and wallets, not hidden in drawers."

I wrapped my arms around him and kissed him on the lips. "I really shouldn't like you this much."

He laughed and kissed me again. "I warned you."

"You did."

"I'm not the guy that everyone says I am, Lacey. I get that I did things that some people would frown upon, but I knew what I wanted and I went for it. Every woman that I've been with has understood that I couldn't give them anything other than a good time."

"Stop explaining. I don't even care." To an extent, I didn't care. Joey made all of my problems disappear. With every kiss and every touch I was consumed by pleasure, leaving me needing more.

He said I was different. Whether that was a crock of shit, or really the truth, it was enough to make me come back. It was time for me to live in the day, instead of reaching for forever when it was too hard to grasp.

"I don't want you to leave."

I climbed on top of him, pinning him to the bed while holding on to his hands. Joey didn't fight me. "If you want me to stay, then you need to lose the shorts. I want you naked."

He flipped us around and ran his hands up my t-shirt. "That goes for you, too. Take off this shirt and show me that pussy."

He sat up and I lifted the shirt to my abdomen, revealing my naked sex. Joey licked his lips and ran his hand over my smooth naked pussy. "I'm going to lick this pussy until you explode."

I gasped and watched him scooting down.

It was going to be another long night.

Chapter 17

Shayne

Twins.

She was having fucking twins and I'd told my whole family they were mine.

I didn't sleep much that next night, or the one after it. It didn't help that I could hear Ashley crying her eyes out constantly. What kind of support would I be to her if I walked away now?

I woke the next morning with a pounding headache. I'd reach my limit of stress and I was about to explode. My emotions were through the roof and I hated myself for being such an idiot.

In the back of my mind, I continued to remind myself that I was doing this for my brother; that his future was worth protecting.

Still, hearing those heartbeats did something to me. They reiterated that these were two innocent children. I had to protect them.

Ash was going through her own set of emotions. She was crying constantly and comforting her was uncomfortable, since we weren't really that close. It was necessary for us to make peace and move forward, if not for ourselves and the fact that we were living together, but for the sake of the unborn children that I'd committed to help raise, temporary or not.

I found Ashley in a ball on the couch. She had some movie playing, but her head was down against her knees. When I sat down beside her, she looked up with eyes full of tears. She sniffled through her words. "I'm fine."

I put my arm around her. "You're not fine, Ash. I get it. I know you're scared."

"It's not just that. After hearing them, those heartbeats inside of me, it hit me. They're little lives growing inside of me and I've been so awful. I don't deserve to be a mother, Ford was right. How am I going to give them a good life?"

"Don't say that." I kept comforting her, rubbing her back for support. "Ash, you may not have expected to get pregnant that night, and yes it changed your life, but that doesn't mean you can't be a better person. Sure, you went a little crazy when it came to gettin' Ford back, but you were desperate."

"Don't be nice to me about Joey, Shayne. I know you helped him get back with Lacey."

"I'm not denyin' it. They belong together, as weird as it sounds. I'm not meanin' to be a prick and hurt your feelin's, but it's true. Ford loves Sky and she loves him back. Think about how broken he's been since Harley died. Can you imagine how hard it was for him to feel again? She brought him back to life, and whether you want to believe it or not, it's the truth."

She got quiet and put her face down against her knees again. I pulled my hand away from her back and just sat there. She spoke without looking at me. "It hurts so much. I can't stop lovin' him. We were supposed to grow old together."

I sighed and thought back when we were younger and had our whole lives ahead of us, not that we still didn't, but the game plans had changed before our eyes. "You're not alone, Ash. I'm not Ford and I know we're not a couple, but I'm not goin' to walk away."

She finally sat back up and leaned her head against me. "Do you hate me?"

I brushed her hair away from my face, since it was itching. "No. I may not agree with things you've done, though."

"I'm so scared."

"Ash, regardless whether me or my brother claim these children as ours, it won't matter. They're a part of my family and my parents will love them. We all will. That's what family does. We have each other's backs. That's also why Ford's so pissed at me. He thinks I had your back and not his. It doesn't matter if everything worked out. He'll never trust me again."

"Don't remind me of the reasons we shouldn't be friends. You must resent me, at least."

"I get it. Right now, I'd love to beat the shit out of Joey, so I get it. I can see how jealousy makes people say and do crazy things." I felt stupid talking to Ash about Lacey. Since she was Sky's friend, she couldn't let herself be amicable towards her. Lacey was just as much the enemy as Sky.

I don't think Ash would have been rude if Lacey came over, but she certainly wouldn't want to become her personal friend. Her heart ached for my cousin and I wondered if she'd ever be able to get past it.

Since I'd never been in love before, not the kind where I felt like I couldn't live without that person, I couldn't fully understand why she was holding on. All I could hope was that one-day I'd feel that way about someone. I thought, in time, I could feel that way for Lacey and be the man that she wanted me to be. The truth was, I didn't know if I could. Still, getting her away from Joey was my main goal. I didn't care how or when, but I knew I wanted it to happen. He didn't deserve her affections and neither did I.

Lacey

Running into Joey was becoming inevitable. If I wanted to see my best friend, which I did, I knew there was a good chance he'd pop in, taunting me with his seductive voice and innuendos. Maybe I was glutton for punishment. Perhaps I was the one leading him on, giving him false hope that he could have me whenever he wanted. It wasn't like I was fighting him anymore. No. The moment Joey came on to me, in any way, I was his puppet.

Every Friday night I found myself in this same predicament. I'd no sooner pull into the driveway and he was hunting me down, offering me another night of memories that I wouldn't soon forget. I couldn't say no, because as much as I wanted to hate it, our intimacy just kept getting better, to the point of exceeding any sort of expectation I could ever possibly have. Joey knew it too. His cocky demeanor drove me insane, so much that I began to get off on it. Tonight was no different. I made it to Sky's door before I heard his opening. He lit up a cigarette and finally looked up at me. "How was school this week?" I pulled my hand away from Sky and Ford's door. "Boring as usual. Why do you care?" A half smile formed in the corner of his mouth. "I was just wonderin' how many times you thought about me fuckin' you." His words turned a switch on inside of my body. No matter how dirty this man spoke to me, it fueled my fire for him. "I am there to learn, not

198

to relive some mediocre sex."He laughed and took another drag. "Woman, you can say whatever you want, but I know what you're really thinkin'."

"You don't know me. You just think you do."

Joey leaned back against the gray siding. His eyes looked me up and down. "You're sexy as Hell when you're lyin'. Lacey, I bet you sat in those classrooms drawin' little hearts on your folders while thinkin' about me lappin' up that pretty pussy of yours."

"Shut up! I don't do that." He was pissing me off insinuating that I spent every second of my days thinking of him. Sure, there were many moments spent replaying our hot sex together, but that was a secret he would never know.I opened the door and started to walk into Sky's apartment. "So, when should I expect you?"I peeked back out of the door. "Why don't you stand here and wait." I shut the door quickly, laughing and wondering how long he would stand there waiting for something that wasn't going to happen.

One thing about spending my free time with the happiest couple in the world, was my inability to accept that I was always the third wheel. Each time they kissed or made out, I imagined kissing Joey. His evil bantering had gotten me so worked up that it was impossible to not imagine being with him. Add that to the fact that he was so good with those big, wandering hands. With one touch, he had my panties wet and my willpower gone.While sitting on the couch, hearing them whispering sweet nothings, I pictured it being me and Joey. Then my mind reverted back to being in his arms and in his bed. His perfect lips knew just how to caress my skin. His focused eyes guided him to his awaiting prize and when he undressed me and discovered my wet surprise, he dove right in, devouring my pussy and lapping up my juices. His lips would sparkle from my wetness. I craved this man and everything that he was able to make me feel.Realizing that Sky had been calling my name, I looked over to see her smiling at me. "Where were you just now, Lace? I said your name three times."

I could feel my cheeks turning red. "You probably don't want to know." It was embarrassing that he was getting to me so much.

Ford shook his head. "He's under her skin. I'm sure that's been his game this whole time."

"He's not," I lied.

"You little tramp. He is so. Just look at you over there, thinking about how you're going to sneak off again and accidentally end up in his bed." Sky knew I was full of shit.I could keep denying it, or just cop to what they already knew.

"Fine. He's A-MAZING in bed. Like I can't even put it into words."

Ford threw up his hands. "Spare us the details. There are some things that I never want to know about my cousin."

"What should I do? Everyone keeps telling me he's bad news, but all he brings me is pleasure. When we're alone he's different. It's like no other woman exists. I know that's not the truth, but is it so wrong for me to just want to have some fun, to forget all of my problems and be carried away by him and his sexiness?"

Sky reached over and grabbed my hand. "It's not wrong. We just don't want you getting hurt."

"I told you before that Joey doesn't do girlfriends," Ford reiterated.

I stood up and straightened out my clothes that had bunched from sitting. "Maybe I don't care anymore. Love is over-rated. No offense, but I'm sick of putting my heart on the line. I want passion and adventure and I know just where to go to get it."After grabbing my thing's, I walked towards the door and looked over at my shocked friends. " I'll see you in the morning."

Sky whispered something in Ford's ear and he shook his head and smiled. "It's her choice."

I didn't wait for my bestie to try and talk me out of it. She didn't understand what it was like seeing her so happy when my heart was crumbling. I wanted a distraction, no matter how temporary it was. Maybe if I didn't expect anything, I couldn't get hurt. Once I was standing in front of Joey's door, I felt all of my courage leave my body. My idea to go and offer myself wasn't as exciting as it had been in my head. Just as I turned around, ready to walk back into Sky's and hear them make fun of me, the door opened. Joey cleared his throat and waited for me to turn around. I was too embarrassed to speak."Did you need somethin'?

"Uhh, they're out of milk. Can I borrow a cup?"I felt like a moron. He held the door while I walked in, smelling the scent of his soap from a shower. I tried not to be obvious, knowing he was focused on my every move.When we got into the kitchen, he pulled out a glass and opened the fridge. I watched him pour the milk into the glass and hand it to me. Our hands touched and in an instant I felt the connection. He peered into my eyes, keeping the distance between us to a minimum. "I just thought about ya, while I was in the shower."

I should have been repulsed, maybe offended even, but instead I was turned on. "Glad I could help. "I licked my lips and grabbed the milk.

"Are you really, Lace? Are you glad that I busted a load while thinkin' about your fine ass bendin' over for me?"I felt the fire igniting between my legs and knew if I turned around to look at him, we'd end up in his bed.

"It's flattering."

I made it to the doorway that separated the kitchen from the living room. "Put the milk down, Lacey. I saw Ford carryin' in a gallon this mornin'."

My mouth dropped. I was flabbergasted, at a loss for words. He knew I was lying the whole time. I dropped my shoulders and turned slowly. Joey surprised me by grabbing the glass and pulling me into his arms. "At some point you're going to have to start admittin' that you want me."

I bit down on my lip and whispered, "never", while glaring into those light hazel-brown eyes.

Joey leaned in, lightly touching his lips to mine. "Why is it so hard to admit that you like me touching you?" The back of his skin traced over my arm. "Fightin' me only makes me want you more, but you know my rules. If you want this, you have to ask."

His skin was braising mine and I shivered as his hand lightly coursed over my lips. "You know why I'm here."

"I do, but you're goin' to need to follow my rules. I can't have you screamin' for me to stop halfway through. I mean, I've got needs, too."

"I won't. You know that." He was crazy if he thought I was going to beg him. I wasn't desperate.

He pulled away and dumped out the glass of milk. I stood there, waiting for him to come back, except he didn't. He rinsed and dried the glass, then put it away in the cabinet above.

When Joey walked by me, heading into the living room, I felt my adrenaline kicking in. I didn't have to beg this man, because he enjoyed me just as much as I enjoyed him. That had never been a secret. So I did what every girl in my situation would have done.

I took off all of my clothes and sat them on the kitchen chair. After a few deep breaths, I walked into the living room, past Joey who was sitting on the couch, and into his bedroom.

After nearly ten seconds, he came in and jumped on his bed, pulling me on top of him. "You never play fair, Lace."

We kissed, so deeply that the hair on the back of my neck stood up and I could feel myself getting wet. He hadn't even touched anywhere sensitive. When his hands did start to explore my naked skin, my nipples hardened and I sat straight up so he could see the way my body responded to him. He smiled and suckled on my nipple, while looking into my eyes. I grabbed his chin and led it back up to my mouth, where our tongues played and teased. Our kisses became vigorous, sometimes clanking our teeth together during the intense moments. I tugged on his t-shirt and ripped it off of his head, just wanting to be able to feel his fiery skin against my palms. Joey's nipples were hard and I pinched them at the same time, sending him squirming. I shoved him back on the bed and tantalized one of them with my tongue. Each time I got close enough to suck it into my mouth, I pulled away. He bit down on his lip as I repeated the same movements with the opposite side. Joey played with my hair, using his hand to direct my head from one nipple to the other, while one of my hands trekked below, to the elastic of his shorts. I could feel his erection pressing on my ass as I sat on top of him, so I knew it was in there waiting for attention. In a quick movement, I grabbed ahold of him, pushing my body down between his legs. He adjusted, getting comfortable for me to get to work. "I love this cock." It wasn't a lie. I loved what this man could do with it. It pleased me like no other before it.

My lips surrounded his thick shaft, gliding down it with the help of my own saliva. I sucked him off hard, jerking him with the same tempo. He bucked and groaned each time my head bobbed, which only made me want to do it harder and faster.

Swiftly, he grabbed a chunk of my hair and pulled me off of him. I licked my lips and tried to go for it, but he wouldn't allow me to. "Hold on there, sweetness. I can't spoil myself that fast. We've got all night to enjoy each other, don't we?"

I nodded. "You want me to stay all night?"

He pulled me up to his face and kissed me softly. "You got a problem with that?"

I leaned in and kissed his collarbone, dragging my lips back up his neck. "None at all."

Joey's strong arms flipped us around until he was the one on top of me. He pinned my arms above my head and held them with one of his, while the other traced down, tickling circles around each of my nipples. The sensations took my breath away.

Once he had my nipples hardened and reacting the way he wanted, his fingers followed down to my eager pussy. I felt them rubbing over my labia, soaking up the wetness that was already there. He pulled them up to his lips and sucked them into his mouth. Watching him, tasting me like that, was so erotic. I closed my eyes to try to control the butterflies that were overwhelming me. Every inch of my body was tingling and I wanted this man, so badly that I was ready to beg. "Please, Joey. I want you so bad."

He pulled his fingers out of his mouth with a shit-faced grin. "Say it again."

"You heard me." I looked right at him. "I want you so fucking bad."

"Oh yeah," he groaned, flipping me over and then sitting on the back of my legs. I was confused, but he grabbed my hands and kept them together, over my head. Joey dug his fingers into my pussy, then trailed my juices from there to my asshole. I felt him there, spreading the lubrication over my most sensitive of areas. "Wait, don't do that."

"Shh, trust me, Lace. I won't hurt ya. I need to do this. Your ass is too fuckin' sexy to ignore. Don't you know that every man wants what they shouldn't have?" I felt pressure first and then a pinch as slowly his finger entered into my ass. I could feel every millimeter going inside and violating me. At first it felt as if it were tearing me. I scrunched up my face and tried not to focus on the immediate pain, but as he pushed inside further, I began to relax. Joey wasn't hurting me, he was trying to take me to new heights.

As I finally stopped fighting him, he removed his hand that was holding mine up. Shortly afterwards, that hand was massaging my pussy, rubbing my creamy lubrication all over my outer lips. Then he located my clitoris, pinching it between his two fingers, while pumping his other fingers in and back out of my asshole. I could feel my inner walls tightening and throbbing, and as my body reacted, so did Joey and the speed of his pleasing me. He pinched my clit, then rubbed it fast, so fast that I screamed out, allowing him to still pump his finger into my anal cavity. "Let go, Lacey. Cum like you've never done it before. I want to see it gush out of that pretty pussy. Do it now!" His fingers rubbed even harder over my clit, so intensely that I could barely breathe. I arched my body and shoved my face directly into a pillow as I bellowed out nonsense and felt a warm rush pouring out of me, like I'd never experienced before.

Finally, when I relaxed, Joey removed both of his hands and climbed off the bed, leaving me there naked and vulnerable. He wiped off his hands and stood at the edge of the bed, watching me turn to face him. When our eyes met, he leaned down close to me. "I knew I could make you squirt."

I felt embarrassed. "I didn't."

He laughed and pointed to a wet spot on the bed. "You did and it was sexy as hell. Now flip your ass over and spread your legs, it's my turn now."

I was shaking, but did as he said. I'd just had a finger literally up my ass and if that could give me pleasure, I trusted Joey had even more tricks up his sleeve that I was ready to discover.

208

Chapter 18

Shayne

The phone conversation with Joey was still bothering me, so I waited until that following Monday to call Lacey, because I knew she be back home for school.

It rang a few times before she answered. "Hello."

"Hey. It's Shayne. How are you?"

"I'm good." I could hear that she was happy and knew it was because of him.

"That's good." It pained me to say. "Listen, I know you have school this mornin', but I was wonderin' if we could meet tonight. There's somethin' I need to talk about and I think you're the only person I can trust with it. I know it's askin' a lot, but..."

"Can you come here? My parents won't be home. They have some thing at the restaurant and are going to stay there until it's cleaned up. We'll have privacy to talk."

"Yeah. Do you want me to grab some dinner? I can get you that sandwich you like from that new place in Easton."

She giggled. "That would be cool. Shayne, you're not coming over to try something stupid, are you? I...I can't do that with you and you know why."

"It's not like that. I really need a friend, Lace. Things are all fucked up."

"I'll see you tonight. Any time after four is great."

"Alright. See you then. Thanks for this."

"Shayne, it's fine. I want to be friends with you. We were friends before all of this happened. We need to get back to that."

"I'll see you tonight, Lace."

"Bye."

After we'd hung up, I was too excited to see Lacey. Work went by slow and I couldn't stop thinking about being close to her again. I knew we weren't a couple, but in the back of my mind I couldn't help hoping that I could make her want me again.

Traffic was horrible after work and I didn't get to her house until after six, after picking up her favorite food. She greeted me with a smile, but offered no hug. I don't know why I was hoping for one. It wasn't like she'd missed me, while being shacked up with Joey for the last few weeks.

We sat at the table facing each other during our meal, saying pretty much nothing the entire time. Being in a room with her was a bit uncomfortable. I didn't know how to begin a conversation, or what would be offensive to her.

After we ate and cleaned up, I grabbed her hand and held it as she looked back at me. "I miss you so much, Lacey."

She pulled her hand away, but didn't move. "Shayne, please don't make this awkward."

"I'm not. Sorry. I just wanted you to know that."

"Is that your whole reason for coming? Did you think I'd let you back in so easily?" She stood with her hands on her hips expecting some kind of explanation. "Of course not. I came here because I need advice. My life is so fucked up right now. I don't know what I'm doing anymore."

Lacey leaned against the counter and looked concerned. "Why. What's wrong now? I thought you had things figured out?"

I covered my face with my hands, unable to look her in the eye. "Ashley's havin' twins. We found out a couple days ago. I tried to call you then, but Joey said you were in the shower."

"You tried to call me? When? I didn't have any missed calls."

"Saturday, maybe it was Friday. I don't remember. He said to stop callin' you and that I needed to leave you alone."

"What?" She looked pissed and I couldn't help but feel glad about it.

"I thought he'd tell you, Lace. I'm not tryin' to cause problems." Really, I would have loved to be the reason that she hated him.

She picked up her phone and started dialing and I grabbed it out of her hand. "What are you doin'?"

"I want to know why he lied to me and why your number was erased from my call log. Look at it." She held up the phone. "There's not one single call from you."

"He's probably jealous of what we have. Think about it. You still love me and it probably bothers him."

211

She raised her eyebrow and gave me a look like I shouldn't have dared to say something so boisterous. "Don't say that, Shayne."

"It's true though, isn't it? You still love me."

She wouldn't look at me. Instead she started washing the dishes.

I leaned over the counter and got her attention. "Your love is what makes me want to keep goin'. Do you know what it's like livin' with Ashley? She's pregnant with twins. I'm a damn mess. Do you know how hard it is knowin' that you're fuckin' someone else? It's killin' me, Lace. I keep thinkin' that if I do all of these nice things, you'll come back and give me another chance."

"It doesn't work that way, Shayne. We can't be like that again."

"I don't care about Joey, or anyone else." I walked over and touched the back of her shoulders. Since she refused to face me, it was easy to keep my arms there without seeing her disappointed face. "Tell me you don't miss me. Tell me you never think about all of the good times we had together. I'm not talkin' about sex, Lace. We were closer than that and it took you leavin' me for me to realize it."

She turned around, finally, looking me right in the eyes with tears coming out of hers. "I do miss you. I waited so long to be your girlfriend and when I finally was, it felt better than I thought it would. I could see us having a real future together. I wanted it." She looked sad again and wiped off her

212

tears. "But this relationship changed so fast. Trust is everything to me, Shayne. Without that, we've got nothing to go on. You act like this is so easy for me. It's not. I've been miserable and I know you hate Joey, but he's kept me sane. He doesn't make promises that he can't keep."

"He lies too. Look at the phone call. Are you just goin' to ignore the fact that he threatened me and neglected to tell you I called?"

"No. I will deal with him later."

She started to walk out of the kitchen and I followed her. "Lacey, don't walk away. We need to talk about this. I can't let you go."

I grabbed her by the arm and spun her around, causing her to smack into my chest. We looked at each other and I could feel a connection. She could feel it too, because she had suddenly stopped fighting me. So I leaned down and kissed her, passionately, like my life depended on it. Lacey pulled away when I tried to put my tongue in her mouth. Her hand came across my face, swiftly shocking me by the force of the slap. "Don't you ever do that to me again."

I pulled her close to me once more, this time pleading with my words. "Please don't be mad. Lacey look at me. Look up at me and tell me that you don't miss me." Then I decided to change my plan. Pleading wasn't working. I needed another way. "If we're really done, not because you don't love me, but because you can't trust me, then be with me. Sleep with me one last time, Lace. Let me make love to you and get closure. I can't hurt like this anymore. Please. It's killin' me feelin' like this. I know you owe me nothin', but maybe it will help both of us, in some way. Don't you want to be able to let go?" My eyes were burning. I was so damn desperate that I was almost in tears.

Lacey didn't answer. She couldn't because she was too busy bawling. She knew right from wrong and my plea had only confused her feeling more. Knowing that she was a one man kind of guy, I'd put her in the position to do something that she was very much against.

I pulled her into a hug and kissed the top of her head as she cried, feeling bad about making her react this way.

When she finally calmed down enough, I let go of Lacey, took a deep breath, and looked down at her. She reached her arm up and touched my cheek with the palm of her hand. Just feeling her touch me gave me hope, because I knew she still cared. That was when I felt the first tear fall down my face. I hadn't cried in years, even when Harley passed away. Sure, I'd been upset and even had tears in my eyes, but this was different. Lacey watched me for a moment and then laid her head against my chest again. "I'll do it Shayne. I'll be with you one last time, so that we can both walk away with closure. This isn't fair to either of us, lingering on. I want to be friends, but I can't with these feelings. I can't move on until we both know it's over. If we do this, Shayne, it's to say goodbye, and nothing else. Promise me?"

She'd given me the green light and I knew I had one last chance to win her back. "Yes, I promise."

Lacey

We'd made it up to my room before either of us
touched one another. My shirt came off first, perhaps to give
him the motivation to move forward with our stupid plan.

Shayne's kisses were aggressive, like he'd waited
forever to be able to do it. I didn't stop him though, after
longing for what felt like forever. This wasn't ideally what
closure looked like, but I was willing to do whatever it took to
get him out of my system.

With each brush of our lips, every touch from his
hands, and the way he looked at me, I thought about Joey. This
wasn't something that I was going to be proud of doing. I kept
telling myself that I missed Shayne, that I wanted this and it
was necessary, when all along it was apparent that it was
wrong.

Our charge for closure would leave us more broken,
that was a given.

Just as I was about to pull away, I realized something.
Shayne was here with me, giving me every ounce of what he
had to offer, and it wasn't enough. It didn't give me butterflies,
or send me to new heights with every touch.

In fact, as much as he tried, I wasn't turned on. My
mind wanted Shayne, because I felt like he'd broken my heart,
but my body wanted Joey; the man who had claimed to not lie
to me and done it anyway. I should have walked away from
both of them. That's what I was going to have to do.

Shayne broke my train of thought when he scooted down between my legs he tugged off my clothes and I lifted my legs, allowing him an easier pull. He ran his hand up and down my pussy, looking at it like it was a delicious pie.

Still no butterflies.

Shayne didn't ever initiate this with me. He was all about himself, always. Right away I could tell he was silently begging, pleading for me to want him back. His lips pressed over my smooth skin, while his tongue began to lick over my clit. Of course it felt good, but I still wasn't feeling that burst of pleasure that Joey often gave me.

I hated comparing them, albeit I couldn't stop. With every brush of his tongue, every motion of his hands, I imagined being with Joey.

I grabbed Shayne's hair and tried to get into what he was doing. It felt great and in time I would cry out in bliss, except it wouldn't take me to new places, and knowing that crushed my optimism.

This was the man that I wanted a forever with and I couldn't focus on the fact that he was lying in my bed, attempting to make sweet love to me.

It was possible that unconsciously, I'd shut down my ability to feel what was happening, due to the fear of falling apart when it was over. I certainly didn't want to think of this being our last time together.

My sudden realization woke me up a bit. Shayne licked harder, pressing his tightened tongue firmly against my bud. My body began to respond and I refused to fight it. I wanted to feel butterflies and scream out his name. My toes curled and I pulled on his hair harder as I felt that magical feeling overcoming me.

Shayne kissed my thighs, each side the same, before kissing his way to my bellybutton. He drove his tongue in it, like he was tongue-fucking me. Thankfully, I was feeling so good, that it didn't gross me out like it normally did. He got off on it, so I let him be. I put my elbow behind my head so I could watch him loving on me. His hands came up and cupped my breasts, just as his mouth sucked up one of my nipples.

I was wet and ready, thankfully.

Shayne stood up and started removing his clothes. When his boxer briefs came down, he stood at full attention. His length, beat out his girth, and I did get chills imagining him being inside of me. I loved Shayne, but for the life of me, this wasn't the amazing goodbye that I'd thought it was going to be. It was mediocre, leaving me desperately needing more. Shayne's focus had changed already and he wanted to be between my legs. In fact, he grabbed them and pulled them to the edge of the bed. Just as he was about to enter me, I pulled away. "What the Hell? Did you change your mind?"

I pointed at his naked shaft. "That gets covered, or this isn't happening!"

He smiled and tried to come at me on the bed. "Baby, we've done it a million times with no rubber."

I kicked him off me again. "That was before I knew the truth. It was before I knew you slept with those two sluts at Parker's college."

He froze and I wondered if he'd lose his erection at that slap of truth.

He didn't.

Shayne shook his head, but said nothing as he grabbed his pants and pulled out his wallet. Little things like that had never bothered me before, albeit I'd never considered that he kept them in there to hook up with random strangers.

I watched him bite open the condom and felt the burning start in my eyes. I'd changed my mind, but didn't have the heart to tell him to stop. Shayne leaned down and kissed my lips, but I kept my eyes shut, avoiding letting him see the tears forming. I couldn't bring myself to hurt him.

He entered me slowly, continuing to kiss me, until I responded. While focusing on his body and the way I'd memorized his physique, things became easier. We grinded together and I wrapped my legs around him. Shayne drove into me, then pulled all the way out. I gasped each time, enjoying the pleasure, finally, as he invaded my sensitive opening again and again.

I threw my head back as his tempo increased. My nails dug into Shayne's back and I finally opened my eyes. He leaned in and kissed me tenderly, giving me a reminder of the man I loved. He was still in there, masked by another part of him that couldn't be faithful. I wanted this nurturing man back; the one that called me and shot me a random text for no reason.

Sweat ran down his back as our pace continued. We switched positions and I sat up, riding him, causing a special friction that only this position allowed. Shayne grabbed my ass and dug into my skin. His head arched back and he shut is eyes tightly. I could feel him shooting hot cum into the rubber that separated us.

As he finally finished and regained composure, he pulled me on top of his hot chest. "This can't be over, babe. I can't let you go."

The tears came back instantly. I lifted off of him and sat on the edge of my bed. "Shayne, I'm so sorry. I thought this would help, but it made it worse."

He grabbed my shoulders and pulled me into his arms. "What are you talkin' about?"

I looked at him, with warm tears running down my flushed cheeks. "We're done. Shayne."

They were the only words I could get out before the sobbing began. The look on his face was agonizing. He'd given me his all, but it wasn't enough for me to reconsider. It was a terrible shame, but the truth. We were done.

"Lace, please."

"I hope we can be friends."

Friends? I threw him that horrible line that everyone used and walked out of my own bedroom. All I wanted to do was disappear. It wasn't just the pain that I was under. I'd hurt another person, leaving him torn and confused. I knew I couldn't do this again.

Both of these men needed to leave me alone. I was done with this drama, the worrying and the pain.

I was done with it all.

Chapter 19
Shayne

I didn't spend the night at Lacey's, after she reiterated that it was really over. My last attempt at winning her back had failed. I don't know if it was the sex, but shortly after, while we were still lying there naked, she let me know the cold truth.

She was done with me and there wasn't anything else I could do about it.

To drown my sorrows, I headed for the nearest bar. After more drinks than I could count, everything went fuzzy. When I say fuzzy, I mean that I woke up the next morning in a strange place, next to a very naked stranger.

Her arm was wrapped around me and since I was freaking out already, I didn't want to alarm the girl. Slowly, I eased my way off of the bed, without waking her. Once I found the bathroom, I closed the door and found a pink towel hanging that I wrapped around my waist. In the mirror my reflection shocked the Hell out of me. I had circles under my eyes, which only happened when I hadn't slept the night before. While splashing water on my face, a petite brunette, with large brown eyes opened the door. "Hey. I was wondering where you went off to."

"I, um." I looked down at the pink towel. "Have you seen my clothes?"

"They're in the living room. You started taking them off before we got in the front door, not that I'm complaining. For someone that drank as much as you, it didn't affect how you moved in the bedroom." She looked behind her and smiled. "You better get dressed, loverboy. My sister is here visiting and she's a bit of a prude. If she wakes up and sees a guy wrapped up in the towels she bought me last Christmas, she will freak the fuck out."

I looked down at the pink towel and raise an eyebrow. "Help me get all my clothes and you can have the towel. No offense, but I need to get the fuck out of here. I'm late for work and my dad's goin' to kick my ass."

"He called earlier. I shot him a text back that you were too sick, throwing up with the runs. He said to stay home and keep that shit away from his workplace."

Surprisingly, I smiled, impressed that this stranger had not only offered me a good time, but covered for me when I wasn't able to do it for myself. "Thanks."

She smiled and ran her hand over my chest. "There's a pack of toothbrushes in the cabinet. My sister is famous for forgetting hers. Anyway, help yourself. I'll be right back with your stuff."

I found a pack of six pink toothbrushes and cringed at the idea of having to use it. Knowing that my breath had to have been horrible, I filled one with toothpaste and started brushing. When the door opened, I thought it was just going to be the same girl bringing me my clothes. Instead, a very shocked familiar face stared back at me. "Shayne?" She laughed. "You've got to be kidding me."

"Megan?" The same girl that I met at my friend Boner's place was standing in front of me. She didn't look happy to see me and I knew why, but I had to ask. "This is your sister's place?"

She nodded, looked down at the towel, and then covered her face. "Oh my god! RACHEL! You slept with HIM?"

The girl, that I now knew was Rachel, ran up to the bathroom and looked from me to her sister. "You know each other?"

"We've met, under different circumstances," She answered.

The two sisters then looked to me for further explanation. I threw my hands in the air. "Small world?"

Megan pointed at me. "This guy you spent the night with is a total man whore. This is the guy that Lacey Travis was dating."

"Lacey? From high school? I haven't seen her in years." Rachel argued.

"Remember, I told you I ran into her mother and she told me all about her cheating boyfriend? This is the guy. I can't believe you brought him home with you. Did you pick him up at a bar? Oh my God, do you not have any morals at all? Sometimes I wonder if I was the one who got all the good genes."

Realizing that I was the reason the two of them were arguing, I figured it would be smart to take myself out of the equation. "Look, I'm just goin' to go. Sorry if I caused either of you problems. It wasn't my intention."

"Not so fast!" Megan grabbed the towel, it loosened and fell to the floor. All I could do was stand there watching her face turn beet red. She threw her hands over her face. "Cover yourself!"

I reached down and picked up the towel, before grabbing my clothes and walking into the bedroom.

Rachel followed me inside. "I am so sorry about my sister. She's worse than my mother sometimes."

I pulled my pants up. "It's all good. I really need to go anyway."

"So, we should do this again." She sat down on the bed with confidence.

I leaned over and kissed her head. Since I didn't remember it, at all, I had no idea what we'd actually done. "Yeah, sure."

"I put my number in your phone."

That was sort of stalkerish. "Ok great."

I left the bedroom and found Megan in the living room. She had a cup of coffee and was sitting in a chair. "You really are a whore."

"Megan, it's not what it looks like."

"Yeah right. Do I look stupid to you? One day your hitting on me and the next you're in bed with my sister, who I know you don't know. That's pathetic."

She was right. I was pathetic.

"I'm out of here."

"Good riddance."

There was one problem. I didn't know where I was, or where my car was.

I had to go back inside and ask for help and I really didn't want to.

After exhausting my options, I knocked and waited. Megan answered the door. "What do you want now? There's nobody else in this house that wants to sleep with you."

"Look, I don't know why you think I'm so terrible. She took me home last night."

"You're pathetic." She shook her head and grabbed her purse before pushing me back out the door. "Let's go."

"Wait, how do you know where my car is?"

"My sister hangs out at one bar. Obviously, you would know that if you knew anything about her." We climbed into a car I recognized from the beach.

Once we got on the road and left the unfamiliar neighborhood, I started to feel like I knew where I was. "You never mentioned a sister."

"Please don't talk to me. I'm so mad at you that I could pull out into oncoming traffic in hopes of you losing a couple limbs."

I grabbed my dick as if to protect it. "You weren't this feisty when we hung out last."

"You weren't fucking my sister when we hung out last. Ugh! You're dick is going to fall off, you know."

"I use protection."

"Men like you are the reason that women become lesbians."

"You are vicious when you're mad." I was watching out the window to make sure a dump truck wasn't coming in my direction. "Look, Megan. I'm really sorry. I had too much to drink last night. I swear, I didn't plan on going home with anyone. I was just as surprised as you were."

"Please shut up. I'm taking you to your car and we never have to see each other again."

It bothered me that such a nice girl thought I was scum. "Can we start over?"

Megan pulled up next to my car and put her vehicle into park. "I wouldn't want to be your friend if you were the last men on the planet. You're the whole reason that I'm still a virgin."

The V word made me insanely curious. "Did you just admit that you're...?"

"Yes, I'm a virgin."

"But, we made out. You let me touch you."

"Jesus, Shayne. I'm not that naïve. I can enjoy myself without being deflowered. Can you get out of my car now?"

I opened the door and looked back at her. She was sexy when she was mad, but I was too messed up in my own way to play head games with another woman. I'd pictured my morning playing out differently. All of my hopes of being with Lacey were gone. An empty hole was in my heart and I only had myself to blame.

"Sorry if I ruined your day, Megan. I'll try not to run into you ever again."

"One can only hope." She turned away before she even got done speaking.

I waved, knowing damn well she didn't notice. It irked me that someone could hate me so much. Was I really the monster she saw me as? Surely I had to have some good qualities.

By the time I made it back to my apartment, I was beat. Ashley made me some tea and hung out with me while I told her everything that had happened the night before. She said I was a fool to think Lacey would have taken me back. In fact, she told me that no woman would fall for that idea after goodbye sex, no matter how good it was. Maybe she was right. Maybe Lacey and I were really over. After all, I'd already gone and slept with someone else the same night we were together. My repetitive mistakes kept landing me further from what I thought I wanted. I needed to focus on something other than satisfying my sexual need for a while.

After running into Megan again, in such an awful way, I started to think maybe it was meant to happen. No matter which direction I chose, I kept screwing up. Megan reminded me that I was in charge of my actions and it was my job to change, for real this time.

Lacey

School was the last thing on my mind and maybe I should have called Sky to let her know that I wouldn't be there, because when she showed up at my house, she was freaking out.

"Lacey, I've tried to call you all morning. How come you weren't in class today? It's the one class we said we'd never miss since we were both in it."

"I had a bad night."

'What do you mean? Were you sick?"

"No, worse. I kind of told Shayne that he could come over."

"You what? Please tell me that you didn't do something stupid?" I appreciated that she was concerned, but didn't want to hear her tell me that she told me so. Not again.

"So what if I did? It's not like I can take it back now."

"What did you do? Did you sleep with him? I thought you liked Joey."

"I do like Joey, but this was about me and Shayne. I needed to know for sure that I was making the right decision. I had to know that it was okay to walk away from him and move on."

"So where is he now?" She sat down on the couch across from me and folded her hands. "Did he stay the night?"

I shook my head and began to cry uncontrollably. "No. He's gone. I told him we were done, right after. He left so hurt

230

and angry with me. Then I asked him if we could be friends. Who does that?"

"Lacey, Shayne cheated and lied to you. You're acting like this is all your fault."

I looked up at her, unable to accept that this had nothing to do with my actions. "Joey lied too, you know. Shayne called and Joey erased the number. He told Shayne to leave me alone. He had no right to do that, but he did. Why do I always get with guys that can't be honest with me? I'm like a jerk magnet."

I felt the couch move while my hands covered my face. My sobs were still uncontrolled, but Sky's hand tried it's best to comfort me. "You are not a jerk magnet."

"Why can't I find someone that wants just me? Every guy that I care about sleeps around. Maybe I just suck in bed. Maybe I can't give them enough to keep them happy."

"Stop saying that. Do you hear yourself? I think you need to stop looking so hard for love. It doesn't have anything to do with you as a person."

I nodded. "You're right. I need to not see either of them. I should focus on school and my future and ignore guys for a while."

We hugged and she held me tightly. "It's going to be okay, Lace. You have me and I'll keep you straight."

I felt confident that she meant what she was saying. I was going to get through it and stop hoping to change two men that didn't want to be changed.

231

The first thing I needed to do was tell Joey. He deserved to know why I couldn't see him anymore. He needed to know that no matter how perfect the sex was, it was never going to be enough for us to ever be more. Joey was a means to an end. The old Lacey was gone and the new one wasn't falling for any man's ploys to get her into bed. She would be in control and protect her heart from being broken again.

Chapter 20

Shayne

I told myself that I was going to walk away from Lacey; that I was going to let her go this time without a fight. Unfortunately, it was easier said than done. I waited a day before I started calling her. Of course, she never answered, so I bombarded her voicemail with messages, practically pleading with her to call me back.

I went to work, came home, and thought about the things Megan had said to me. She had me hating myself, more than usual. Even Ashley, who seemed to be my only confidant, couldn't get me out of my funk.

She made me dinner and had it waiting for me when I got home from work. After showering, I found her sitting in the kitchen with a table full of food. "Hey. I thought you might want to eat, seein' as you probably haven't all day."

I sat down at the other end and ran my hands through my hair. "Yeah, thanks. I guess I didn't even think about it."

"You can't keep beatin' yourself up over it, Shayne. You tried. You went above and beyond to make things right. Maybe you should move on."

I raised my brow and looked at her. "Please don't give me advice, Ash. You of all people don't have room to talk. Look what you did to try and get Ford back. We both know how that ended up."

"It's because of what I did that I know I'm right. Look, I don't expect you to trust me, or be my friend, but I'm tryin' to help. We live together and now I'm havin' twins. The only person that's been a constant so far is you, Shayne. I just want to make things a little better for you. Maybe if I can help you, I'll be able to forgive myself for the things I did."

When her over emotional hormones kicked in and she started crying, it made me feel terrible. I wasn't the only person going through Hell. We were both suffering. As much as I wanted to hate Ash, I knew she was the only woman I could be close to without wanting something more. I stood up, walked over to her side of the table, and hugged her. "Don't cry, Ash." I ran my hand through her dark hair. "We're goin' to get through this, together. We're a team in this. Maybe it's best if I focus on the babies. We've got a long road ahead, and our families are counting on us to make the right decisions. I say we take this pity party and use it to our advantage."

"How do you think that's goin' to happen?" She looked up with tears in her eyes, like I was being a fool.

"No more drama. We concentrate on bein' good parents. We read books and shit; whatever we have to do to prepare. No more bullshit with ex's or one-night stands. I'm done with it all."

We stared at each other and she patted my hand. "Okay. We'll do it together, for the babies."

"For the babies," I repeated.

I stood up and walked over to my seat, admiring the casserole sitting in the middle of the table. "So, what did you make?"

"It's Mexican. I got it off one of those shows. I'm just warnin' you, it might taste like ass. I've never been good at cooking."

I put a piece on my plate and took a bite. "It's pretty good for bein' ass." I winked and saw her smiling at me.

Our troubles were far from gone. My heart ached for Lacey, but I knew I was doing what she wanted. Even though we were done, I wanted her to be able to see that I'd changed. Hell or high water, I was going to be a better man and prove everyone wrong about me.

Lacey

Shayne and Joey had both been calling me and I knew I owed at least one of them an explanation as to why I'd been avoiding them. Telling Joey that our tryst was over by phone wasn't feasible. He'd want a real explanation; one he could believe.

By that weekend, my anxiety was sky high. I'd gotten myself so worked up about everything that I hadn't considered not being able to go through with it.

Joey was at his door when I pulled up, shirtless, holding it open without saying anything.

I made it inside and watched him shut the door behind us. He came up to me and put his hands on my shoulders. "Why haven't you been takin' my calls? I finally get your number and you won't answer it when I call you." He leaned in and kissed me softly on my lips, almost making me forget what I'd come there to do.

I pulled away, but he still had a hold of me. "We need to talk about something."

He pulled me in for another kiss and I didn't know how to stop him, so I just blurted out something that would get his attention. "I slept with Shayne."

He pulled away and stared into my eyes. I felt horrible and my stomach began to knot up. He scrunch up his face. "What do you mean? I know you slept with him,…"

"This week. He came to my house and we slept together."

I was afraid of how he'd react, but Joey kept his cool. He sat down on the couch and took a sip of his beer, then leaned back and looked at me. "Why are you tellin' me this?"

I sat down next to him. "I'm tired of all the lies. I can't take it anymore."

Joey reached for my hand and touched the top of it. "I don't lie to you, Lace."

"Yes, you do. You erased my phone when Shayne called, didn't you?"

He smiled. "Yeah, you got me there. That's different though, and you know it. Shit, Lace, I even told you about other women in my life. I've never told any other person that."

"I can't see you anymore." I looked away, afraid to see the way he was going to judge me.

"What are you goin' to go back to Shayne now? You think he's good for you? Can he give you what I can? Does he make you feel the way that I do?"

"No!" I was so frustrated. "He doesn't, okay? This isn't about Shayne."

"You came here to tell me that you were together and now you can't see me anymore. What else would it be about?" Joey stood up and paced around the living room. I watched him shake his head and clench his jaw, while I thought about how to best explain.

"Being with Shayne made me realize that I'm on a collision course. I can't keep doing it to myself. It's ripping me apart from the inside. When I'm with you, I forget who I am. You make me feel alive and like nobody ever has before, but it's a temporary high. The moment I walk out your door, I think about you being with other women. I think about the pictures and what else you could be hiding from me. I think about all of the people that have warned me about how you are. It's just too much."

"Lacey, you're so wrong. I'm not hidin' nothin' else from you. Sure, I lied about Shayne, but that's only because I wanted you for myself. You think I wanted to share you? You're the only woman that I've ever had to fight to be with. Once I had you, I knew one thing." He walked over and got on his knees in front of me. I was already crying. "I knew I didn't want to let you go."

I tried to look away. "I wish you really meant that, Joey, because being with you is wonderful. You and I both know, it was just about the sex. It's not like you even do relationships, so don't give me that shit that I'm different. Look, I've thought a lot about this and it's best if we just stop."

"I think you're scared that you might have feelin's for me."

He shocked me and I remembered back when I thought he was a cocky bastard. "I'm stopping this before that can happen."

For a moment I saw this spark in his eyes, almost like he was going to fight for me to stay. "I guess you need to do what you think is right, Lacey." I stood up and tried to hug him, but he backed away from me. "You should probably go. I mean, I don't want you to have to be around when I'm callin' someone else to come entertain me, because that would just be rude."

By the time I made it to his door, I was already bawling. Sky was a knock away, but I chose to leave the property. I couldn't handle seeing Joey with another woman. Realizing that only let me know what I was walking away from. Sure, he wasn't willing to be in a committed relationship, but that didn't mean that I wasn't falling for him. I needed to get as far away from him as possible.

Joey had made it clear that he was going to move on and that all I was to him was a fuck. No matter what kind of bullshit that he fed me to make it happen, I was just a conquest. Being able to watch me walk out the door with no remorse was enough proof for me.

I drove fast, speeding home, where I knew I could be alone to suffer in peace. I didn't want to talk to anyone, not my parents or my friends. I needed to be in seclusion, where I didn't have to talk about being hurt and alone. I wanted to cry without explaining why.

Once I was in my room, I buried my face on my bed. My sobs were loud, but like every night, my parents weren't home. They wouldn't understand that my heart was broken.

They'd tell me everything would be okay, when I wasn't sure it ever would be.

I'd tried to be with Shayne, to be able to say goodbye and not feel awful about walking away from him. I wanted to forget about the way I'd loved him for so long. I needed to escape his hold on me.

Joey was the key. He helped me see that another man could give me more. He'd showed me that I was desirable and made all of the pain go away. Saying goodbye to him was what was killing me. I felt more empty than before, and extremely alone.

I felt like saying goodbye to Joey was harder than breaking up with Shayne. For the life of me, I couldn't understand how sex with the man had left me with feelings that I couldn't explain. My heart ached for him to reach out to me. I wanted my phone to ring; for him to beg me to come back to his place so we could talk about being together.

But it never did.

After that night, I promised that I'd stay away from Sky's until I knew I was able to see Joey without hurting. It was the hardest thing that I'd had to do, pretending that I could be strong on the outside when my insides felt like they'd been stabbed a zillion times.

After four whole weeks, Joey hadn't called. Shayne still left messages, but I erased them before listening. All of my progress would have been for nothing if I allowed myself to feel bad about ignoring him.

I saw Sky at school, but she knew better than to talk about either of the guys. Instead, she talked about Ford and how well he was doing working for her father. As happy as I was for her, I still envied her life. Ford was the perfect guy. He was so in love with Sky that he never even looked at other women. Several times I asked what she did to keep him so happy, thinking maybe there was some secret, but she said I was crazy. She told me that I needed to keep doing what I was doing and happiness would find me.

There was only one problem with her theory. I wasn't going to find love someday, because I already was in love, with a man that never offered me anything but a good time. The longer I was away from Joey, the more I knew that my feelings for him had grown into something more. The worst part about it, was knowing that he'd never feel the same way about me.

Chapter 21
Shayne

After a while it's normal to get sick of moping around. For weeks I'd dwelled on all of my failures instead of taking into account everything I was doing for my family. They may not have known it, but I was protecting them, being responsible, and making sure that we had a part in the newest members of our family's lives.

It had taken my dad a month before he would finally talk to me about anything non work related. Even though his grudge was still apparent, I found compromise when he broke down and invited me and Ashley to come to dinner.

My sister was the only person who appeared to be genuinely excited, but it was a step in the right direction. Ashley seemed more nervous than me. They knew we weren't a real couple, so it wasn't like they were expecting us to hold hands or be affectionate.

We were just two people that shared one night together. Out of that night we made a baby and chose to raise it as two loving parents.

On the outside it sounded almost perfect. For me, never willing to be tied down, it made sense. Nobody expected me to be this knight in shining armor.

We were invited over on a Saturday and Ashley must have changed her clothes ten times. She was nervous and I tried my best to reassure her. "Will you calm down? You barely look pregnant. Everything you've put on looks cute."

"Cute? I don't want to look cute. I need to look mature, like a mother."

I rolled my eyes and covered my face to prevent her from seeing me frustrated. "Ash, please put something comfortable on. You don't have to impress any of them. It's not like they've never met you before."

She sat down next to me and put her head on my shoulder. "I know. I'm trying to be at my best knowing that this lie could blow up at any time. Since your family already hates me, I'd like to have some sort of dignity once the truth is out."

I patted her leg. "Everyone will love the twins. Ain't that what matters the most?"

She smiled. Since we'd been living together, Ashley had changed. She cared about what other's thought and had been so focused on learning everything she could about being a mother. Her stepmother was close to our age, which did nothing for Ashley's need for a mother figure. She tried though, always doing what she thought was going to get her in good graces with Ashley.

Her real mother left town a few years back. She married some other government official and barely spoke to her daughter. I always thought Ashley would end up being selfish like her, but this pregnancy had changed her.

"I'm just goin' to wear this. We can go whenever you're ready." She smiled, but I could tell she was anxious.

"I've been ready for nearly an hour," I teased.

She gave me a dirty look as we headed out the door.

The car ride was quiet. She fidgeted with her hands, picking at her fingernails and biting them at times. I looked through the mirror toward the backseat and clenched my jaws. "Guess I'm goin' to have to get a new ride soon. This car isn't made to hold car seats, especially two of em'."

She looked back and laughed. "I never noticed. Wow, guess you never get action in that thing."

"This car was for pickin' up women. The action started when we got back to a bed."

Ashley laughed more. "You're never goin' to change are you, Shayne?"

"Be nice. Honestly, it gets lonely. I sit around and watch my friends and family settling down and a part of me wants that."

"You had it with Lacey. That girl chased you for years, didn't she? I remember seein' her around."

"Yeah, her family had a place at the beach near mine. I've known her for years, since we were teenagers."

"What will it take for someone like you to settle down?"

I looked over at her and then back to the road. "Please tell me that you're askin' in general. You know you and I won't work, right?"

Ash nudged my arm. "Eww. No! I'm not askin' for me. I was just bein' a friend, you douche. Two guys in the same family are too much for me."

"Hey, you got what you wanted. Didn't you always say you wanted to be a part of our family? The two kids in your stomach made that happen."

"That wasn't what I meant." I offended her and I felt bad. She'd been the only solid friend in my life lately.

"Sorry. I didn't mean to piss you off."

"It's fine." She paused and looked out the window. "Shayne, can I tell you somethin'?"

"Sure."

"You're my only friend. I can't talk to anyone else. You know my secrets. Somehow, you always do. I know for a while you hated me, but I appreciate everything you're doing. I don't know where I'd be without you."

Ashley reached over and grabbed my hand. I squeezed it. "We're cool. I know I said I hated you, but I was only sayin' it because I was so pissed."

"I know I shouldn't have lied to Ford. At least he's happy now. Your sister said he's doin' real good at his job."

"He talks to the family more. It's good that he's back to bein' normal. I mean, we all thought he'd marry you."

"When Harley died everything changed. A part of Ford died with her. Now his mother's back after all those years. He's got a lot on his plate. I never would have said this months ago, but I'm glad he has Sky. She seems like she's just as crazy about him."

"She's a great girl. She's good for him. They both want the same things." The car got quiet. I'd hit a nerve, but Ashley needed to talk about it, just like I needed to talk about Lacey. "How about Lace and Joey. Did you ever see her runnin' to someone like him?"

Ashley laughed. "Now that's hysterical. He makes you look like an angel."

"I know, right. What was she thinkin'?"

"I've known Joey since we were little kids. He's always had a way with the girls, even his brother. I guess it's in the blood or somethin'. I can happily say that I've never been with either of them. Jamey's goin' to be just like Joey."

"We had words, you know. I called Lacey a while back and he answered. He told me she was different to him and I needed to back off."

She looked right at me with a shocked face. "Really? Do you think she put him up to it?"

"She didn't even know about it."

"Wow. Do you think he's changed?"

"Hell no! He just wants to bang her. I guess he thought that if she got back with me he wouldn't get to bang anymore." I tightened my grip on the steering wheel. Thinking of Joey and Lacey made me insanely jealous. I'd never suffered from that kind of feeling before, especially not about a girl.

"You need to forget about her. I'm not sayin' that to be mean. She gets to you like Ford got to me. Once I realized that and finally gave up, I started to feel better. Plus, I had these little ones to worry about." Ford could have had a good life with Ashley. She was gorgeous. The girl had a great body and she was easy to hang out with. Sure, she had a wild side, but I found it spunky and attractive. Had she not been with either of them, I would have definitely wanted to hit it. That wasn't me though. We were friends and that was it.

We pulled up at my parents and I turned the car off. Ashley looked at me like she was going to throw up. I grabbed her hand again. "It's goin' to be fine, Ash. Were two friends that are expectin'. That's the truth. The paternity is irrelevant, right now."

"It's still lyin'."

"Don't get all honest on me, Ash. We can do this."

She squeezed my hand. "Okay. Let's do it."

Lacey

"Stop moping and get your butt over here. Ford got some movies and we're planning on vegging out all weekend." Sky had been begging me to come over for the past week.

I still didn't want to run into Joey. Seeing him would bring the pain back. His last words to me were all I could think about, no matter how much time had gone by. "You know why I don't want to come."

"I didn't tell you?"

"Tell me what?" She had me scared. "He's got a new girlfriend?"

"No. Well, I suppose he could. He left for Italy a few days ago."

"Vacation?"

"No." She got quiet for a moment. "Lace, Joey moved there. He got an opportunity to be the chef for some consulate. We didn't find out until the day before he left. His brother's staying in his place until the lease is over with."

I could feel my lips trembling as she spoke. Not only was Joey gone, but he was on the other side of the world. "He's not coming back?"

"Ford said it's a dream opportunity. His mother was really upset. She was finally getting used to him living on his own and then he did this."

"Sky, are you lying to me? Did you know about this and just not tell me?"

"No, I swear. He came to us the night before. He was short about it and didn't give us any details. To be honest, we hadn't seen him much lately anyway. Ever since the two of you called it quits, he kept his distance."

"I bet he had plenty of women to take my place."

The line got quiet again and I wondered if we'd been disconnected. "Lace, I've never seen a single woman visit Joey. He'd go to work, then come home. Are you sure that he didn't want something more with you?"

"No. He made it quite clear."

"I think he lied. We're talking about a guy that did everything for his mother. What else could make him want to leave everything behind? Something had to happen."

I thought about Joey being so far away. My heart was breaking all over again and I couldn't even picture never being able to see him. I'd been foolish to not come around. "If that's the truth, then I made him leave."

"You did tell him you slept with Shayne. Maybe that's what set him over the edge." She told me like it was and I valued that in our friendship, but at the very moment I wanted to slap my best friend. I was in agony and needed to find answers, not be lectured.

"How do I reach him?"

"I have no clue. I guess his mother has a way."

"I've got to go, Sky. I will call you later if I'm going to stop by."

"Lacey, what are you going to do?"

249

I was sobbing and hoped that she could understand me through my tears. "I need to know the truth. Everyone told me he'd never want a relationship. What if he did? What if he was being honest to me? Oh my God, I could have ruined everything."

"Lacey, calm down. We'll get his number. Everything will be okay."

"No, that's not good enough. I've got to find him. I need him to know that my feelings were real. All that fighting, it was only because I was crazy for him. It was the chase that made me want him, but nothing could ever compare to what happened when we were alone. I can't explain it. No man will ever make me feel like that, except Joey. He needs to know, Sky."

"I can call the diner for you and get his contact information."

"No. I need to do it myself. This is all my fault and it's my job to fix it."

I hung up the phone, knowing exactly what my plan was going to be. I didn't care what it took, I needed the truth no matter what I had to do to get it. If there was a chance that Joey was in love with me, I had to know.

Chapter 22

Shayne

The house smelled wonderful when we walked inside. Peyton was the first person to greet us and I felt like I was going to vomit when I saw who her guest was. Jamey sat in a lounge chair in the living room. He nodded when our eyes met and for a split second I thought it was Joey. Ashley must have sensed my anxiety, because she grabbed my hand, getting my attention to go to her, instead of him.

My sister came over and hugged me. I whispered in her ear, "What is he doin' here, Pey?"

"Seriously?, We've been seein' each other for a month. God, you are so out of the loop. Dad is fine with it for once, so back off."

I grabbed my sister by the arm when she started to walk away. "He's nothin' but a player."

She jerked herself out of my hold. "Screw you, Shayne. Just because you screw up your relationships, doesn't mean people can't change. Jamey's living at his brother's place now. He's got a good job and I really like him."

"Don't say I didn't warn ya, Pey. He's bad news."

"For once can you stop bein' a big brother. I'm not gettin' married, Shayne. We're dating, that's all."

Jamey was standing next to my dad, talking about something. I wanted to walk up and throw him against the wall. My animosity grew when I saw my dad patting him on the back when he said something funny. Ashley wrapped her arm around me. "We were just talkin' about that family and here's one of them. What the Hell is goin' on?" She whispered.

"I don't know. I sure as hell am not alright with my sister bangin' this guy. Jesus, what else?"

"Calm down. They're just kids. It isn't like it will last. I'm more curious as to why Joey would let Jamey move in with him. I thought he moved to get away."

"Well, I don't want my sister over there. Next she'll be bringin' his brother over here and I will have a serious problem with that."

My dad came over with a smile on his face. He hugged Ashley, like she'd never betrayed anyone in our family. "How are you feelin', hun?"

Ashley shrugged. "I've been better. I get sick a lot, but Shayne takes care of me."

"Twins, huh? They run in the family, so one of my kids was bound to have a set. It's a shame ya'll weren't married. Raisin' one baby is hard, but two at once is extremely difficult."

I put my arm around Ashley, not even realizing what it was insinuating. "We'll do just fine, dad."

He looked from me to Ashley and took a deep breath. "I hope so, son. So, you remember Jamey, don't ya?" My dad pulled Jamey over toward where we were standing.

"Yeah, of course. He's Ford's cousin." Jamey smiled, but I refused to smile back. He stuck out his hand for me to shake and I squeezed it extra hard.

"Good to see you again, man." Jamey was just as fake as his brother. I wanted to take him out back and beat him to a pulp.

Seconds later, my mother was calling us all into the dining room. Ashley stayed close to me, avoiding the elephant in the room, while I was preoccupied with how I was going to break this kid's neck. Dinner was the easiest part of the night.

Afterwards, I walked outside for some air. Jamey came out and lit up a smoke. He offered me one, but I passed. "I thought you were back with your ex, Lacey."

"Who told you that?"

"I just figured, after what she did to Joey."

Had it not been for my curiosity, I would have already punched the kid. That's how much I disliked him. "What are you talkin' about? What did she do?"

He took another drag before speaking. "Apparently, Joey had it bad for her. Next thing we know, he's takin' a job in Italy and leavin' the country. If you ask me, it had somethin' to do with her. I ain't never seen him so bent up."

"Wait. Are you tellin' me that he wasn't just sleepin' with Lacey? They were more?"

He put his hands up. "I don't know how she saw it, but I've never seen my brother like that, neither has our mom. She's torn up about him leavin'. I don't know if she's ever cried the way she has lately. When he asked me to stay at his place until the lease ended, I moved in the next day. It's all fucked up."

Joey had left his family and friends behind because he was broken up about Lacey. It made no sense, unless he'd fallen in love with her; the kind of love that makes you do crazy things. I got that knot in my stomach again, knowing that I was the cause of all of this. Lacey slept with me and it ended her relationship with Joey. "How can I get in touch with your brother?"

He shook his head. "I don't know, but my mother does. I reckon you can call her at the diner. She's there until eleven."

I put my hand on his shoulder. "Thanks. Oh, one more thing. If you hurt my sister, in any way, I will kick your ass. Got it?"

He chuckled. "Yeah. We're cool, man."

"We better be."

I walked back inside and found Ashley helping with the dishes. "Hey, we were getting ready to have dessert."

"Do you mind if we take it to go? I just remembered that there's somewhere I've got to be."

After saying thank you for the meal, we headed out. I waited until we were in the car until I let Ashley know what was really going on. She seemed shocked, not just because Peyton was seeing Jamey, but the stuff with Lacey too. "So what are you goin' to do?"

"I'm drivin' to the diner and findin' out how we can get in touch with Joey. I need to make this right, Ash. All I ever wanted was for Lacey to be happy. For this dude to leave the country, he's got to have it bad for her. If there's a chance that he's in love with her, she should know. I can't keep ruining people's lives. As much as it sucks for me, they deserve a chance."

"What's gotten into you, Shayne. You hate Joey."

"You're right. I don't like him. But, I care about Lacey. If her sleeping with me did all of this, I need to make things right, or at least try."

"It's not like he's goin' to want to talk to you, Shayne. If he left because you banged his girl, I hardly think he'd listen to anything you have to say."

"I have to try."

I knew I was being irrational. Most guys would be happy that their ex's love interests moved that far away from them. Joey was no longer able to stand between my trying to win Lacey back. As much as I wanted that opportunity, I knew it was too late for me. Joey had helped Lacey move on. A part of me wished that she didn't care about him, but I knew that wasn't the case. Lacey had this thing about being honest. Joey asked me to stay away from her because he wanted to be with her. He didn't lie to Lacey just to screw her like I'd originally thought. She'd dumped him for the wrong reasons and I knew that if she found out the truth, she'd never forgive me or herself.

We pulled up at the diner about forty minutes later. After walking in and getting a table, I waited for Joey's mother to come and wait on us. She was standing up at the bar, hugging a blonde that was crying. At first I didn't recognize who it was, until she turned around. Lacey stood there, with Joey's mom. She was sobbing and had makeup running down her face.

I couldn't help myself. I got up and walked over to them. "Lace, are you alright?"

Lacey

Of all the people that I wanted to see, I had run into Shayne and Ashley. I'd driven all this way in tears. Joey was gone and I had to talk to him. I was desperate.

Miss Viv. walked away so we could talk.

"What are you doing here, Shayne?"

"You first. What's goin' on?"

I started crying so hard I didn't know if he could understand what I was saying. "Joey's gone and it's all my fault. I ruined everything. I didn't know, Shayne. I swear, I didn't know."

"You didn't know what?"

"Everyone thinks he left because of me. I walked out on him and told him we couldn't be together. I didn't know his feelings were real. Now he's gone."

Shayne pulled me into his arms and I refused to pull away. I needed the comfort out of some desperate attempt to have someone understand me. "Please don't cry, Lace. It's goin' to be okay."

I shook my head. "No, it's not. I love him. I'm sorry. I know it isn't something you want to hear from me, but it's true. I fought it, I really did. I just can't anymore. I can't imagine never seeing him again."

"Shh, we'll get in touch with him. I'll talk to him. It's goin' to be fine."

I shook my head again and finally pulled away. "I'm not calling him, Shayne. I'm going to Italy. I've got to see him. He needs to hear it in person."

"Don't be silly. You can't fly halfway across the world. Just call him."

He wasn't getting it and neither had Joey's mom. Nobody could understand that my irrational, desperate thinking wasn't going to go away until I was on a plane, going after the man that I needed to be with. Nothing else mattered. I didn't care about finishing school, telling my parents, hanging out with my friends. All I cared about was finding Joey, before it was too late, before he'd moved on and found someone to replace me.

"His mom is giving me the address. Sky's been trying to book my flight for the past hour. I'm going and you're not going to stop me."

"It's too dangerous. Bad things happen to women traveling alone." Shayne wouldn't shut up.

Another voice shocked me. "Go with her, Shayne. Make sure she gets there in one piece." Ashley stood a couple feet from me. She had her hand on her stomach and I thought about the twins she was carrying. So much had happened between me and Shayne and he was still trying to protect me. It didn't make sense, but my options had run out.

"I will be fine. Once I get to the airport, I'll take a cab to his apartment. His mom says it's a good neighborhood and I should be fine, even if I have to wait. She said there's a coffee shop right across from his place."

Shayne reached out and took my hand. "I'm sorry for my part in all of this, Lacey. If I would have just let you go, none of this would have happened. I just wanted you to be happy. It sucks that it can't be with me, but I get it. Just know that I'll always care bout you."

Hearing him say it, made me finally feel at peace. Shayne was letting me go and a huge weight lifted off of me. "You were my first love, Shayne."

He kissed my hand. "I know. Maybe if I wasn't such a prick, things could have ended up differently."

"Maybe."

"Call me when you get back, Lace. I'd like to know you're alright."

"I will."

Shayne and Ashley sat back down at their table while I waited for Joey's mom. The woman was so desperate to get her son back that she didn't even argue with me about my decision. The guilt was horrible when I thought about being the reason that she was so sad. My plan had to work. Even if he didn't love me, maybe he'd still consider coming back for his family. Either way, I couldn't live another day without knowing the truth.

I walked out to my car with Joey's information and saw Shayne heading towards me. I turned around and tried to be humble, instead of breaking down again. "I'm fine, I promise."

"Do you know your flight information?"

"I know I'm flying out of Dulles. The earliest was a redeye to Rome. Sky hasn't called me back with the exact details."

"How are you gettin' there?"

I appreciated him caring, but I was fully capable of getting to an airport alone. "I'm driving. I've been there before to drop my dad off when he went on a hunting excursion. It's no big deal."

"I don't want you parking in the middle of the night, all alone. I'm drivin' you. How about I take Ashley home and meet you at your parents. It's on the way to the airport anyway. We can get back on route fifty and take it all the way to ninety-five."

I thought about driving alone in my condition. "I can't ask you to drive me to go see the other guy. It's not right."

"I'm offerin'. That's different. Besides, I insist."

"Fine, I'll text you my flight info. I need to be there two hours in advance, just in case."

Shayne agreed to wait for my text and headed over to his own vehicle. Once I hit the main highway, I cried the whole way back to my parents. I'd been miserable since I walked out of his door that night, but this was torture. All I wanted to do was feel his arms wrapping around me. I wanted to hear him telling me that I was different. This time, I wanted to believe him. He needed to know that I'd been fighting my feelings for him since that first night.

My text from Sky made me cringe when I saw how much a plane ticket was going to cost me. Twelve hundred dollars later, I was booked on a nonstop flight. With less than four hours until take off, I called Shayne to let him know.

This was really happening. I was doing something crazy and I wasn't coming back until Joey knew that I wanted him.

Chapter 23

Shayne

I dropped Ashley off and headed toward Lacey even before she'd text me the information. After stopping by to grab some antacids for my upset stomach, I arrived shortly after. She carried one bag out to the car and I put it in the back for her. Once we were both inside the vehicle, I felt like I was going to suffocate.

Lacey remained quiet for a while, staring out the window as I drove. We stopped at a Dunkin Donuts before the Chesapeake Bay Bridge to keep us both awake. Dulles wasn't that far, but traffic was usually horrendous no matter what time of the day or night it was.

"What if this is a mistake?"

Her question was filled with angst. "If he's anything like me, he's crazy about you, Lace. Is that what you're worried about? Do you really think he'll reject you?"

She shrugged. "Maybe. What if he's hooked up with someone else? I'm sure there's lots of beautiful women in Rome."

"There's beautiful women everywhere, but that doesn't mean he wants them anymore. His brother says he's crazy about you. He said that he's never seen him act the way he did about you."

"What if he hates me? God, we should just turn around. This is a terrible idea."

I reached over and grabbed her hand. She was shaking, like she did when she was scared or upset. "Calm down. Look, maybe I'm the wrong person to explain this to you, but you need to listen anyway. Guys like gettin' laid. We like the way it feels to be intimate with a woman, even if there's no emotional connection involved. It's just about the pleasure and nothing else. When a man starts to have feelin's for someone, their needs change. I'm not goin' to lie and say that Joey wouldn't sleep with someone else, but if he was, he was doin' it because bein' alone is killin' him inside. The idea of you bein' with someone else is keepin' him from sleepin' and even eatin'. He would do it to relieve the stress he's under, not to fall in love with someone else."

Lacey adjusted in her seat, like I'd made her feel uncomfortable, or I had the plague. "You're speaking from personal experience aren't you?"

I nodded, but kept my eyes on the road. "Yeah, maybe."

"Why are you doing this then, Shayne? Why drive me to go be with someone else?"

I glanced at her before looking back at the road. "Because I'm sick of bein' selfish and gettin' nothin' but grief. I'm not right for you and I know it. Yeah, it fuckin' hurts. I feel like shit every day thinkin' about not bein' able to be with you, but I know it's the way its got to be. I had my chance and we both know how that went. Plus, I'm no fool. That last time we were together, you were different. I could tell I wasn't the one

263

you wanted to be with that night. I was just too selfish to admit it. These past couple months have sucked for me, except they've let me know just how fucked up my life was. I need to change, Lace, because I want to be happy. Besides, I've got too much on my plate right now with the twins comin'. Once that happens, the whole family is goin' to shun me. I'll be needin' your friendship then, so I figure by helping you, maybe you can find it in your heart to finally forgive me."

She reached for my hand and squeezed it. "I do, Shayne. I'll always be there for you."

"That means you have to answer my calls, you know."

She laughed. "Yeah, I'll work on that."

We talked about other things, not related to either of our problems for the rest of the drive. After nearly two hours, we arrived at the airport. Lacey got out and came around to my side of the vehicle. Her arms wrapped around my back. "Thank you, Shayne."

I kissed the top of her head and felt like I was saying goodbye forever. It felt like if I let go of her, she was never going to come back. It was difficult to look her in the eyes. "Anytime, Lace. If he hurts you, call me and I'll be on the next flight."

She began to laugh, but I could tell she was starting to cry. "I might hold you to it. Maybe you need to remind me that this isn't the stupidest thing I've ever done in my life."

I leaned my forehead against hers. "It's not stupid. It's incredible."

She looked right at me and I watched her trembling lips trying to say words. All I heard were sobs.

We stood there, for what felt like forever, in the drop-off lane at the airport. I didn't want to let her go, but she couldn't stand there forever. We kissed, one last time, full on the lips. I ran my hand up and held the back of her head, then finally let go. I wiped the tears from her cheeks. "Have a safe trip."

"I'll call you when I get there, I promise."

Then she walked inside.

I sat back in my car and watched her until she disappeared between the crowds of people. My heart was empty, but I felt happy.

Once I got onto the freeway, I could feel the stinging. I'd been fighting with my emotions for a while and this time, I'd given up. Tears fell down my face and I eventually had to pull over to get a handle on myself. Life was all about decisions, and even though I knew I'd made the right one, I was still the one who ended up alone.

I called Ash once I knew I was good enough to talk again.

"Shayne, are you okay?"

"Yeah. I'm on my way back."

"Do you want me to wait up?"

"Do you mind talkin' to me while I drive? I could use the company."

"That bad, huh? I'm sorry, Shayne."

"It's not your fault. I made my own choices. It's just hard sayin' goodbye. As much as I hated it, I can see how he'd change for her."

"Like Ford did with Sky."

"Yeah. Do you think there's someone out there like that for you and me?"

"I hope so. You'll find love first. I mean, I'll be too busy raisin' these twins. My life is pretty much set in stone now. One day you'll be free of it all and just be an uncle."

"Ash, there are men out there that would love to be with you. We just need to be patient."

We talked for the rest of my ride, making it go by a lot faster. When I walked in the door, I found Ash asleep with the phone still next to her ear. I picked her up and carried her to her room, tucking her into bed.

I may not have gotten the girl I wanted, but I gained a friend that I could talk about anything with. My family didn't have to approve, in fact, I liked that they didn't, because my business was my own to keep.

One day I would change their minds about me. I didn't know how yet, but I wouldn't stop working on it until I got it right.

Lacey

Sitting alone in an airport, with a very long flight in front of me, wasn't exactly easy. I bit all of my fingernails and contemplated calling Shayne a dozen times to come and pick me up. The plane arrived early and boarding started shortly after. Since it was a late night flight, it wasn't full. I had the whole row to myself. Realizing that I hadn't packed magazines or anything to bide my time, I decided to try and go to sleep.

That didn't go very well. The turbulence was horrific and a few times I thought the plane was going down. As much as the stewardess kept reassuring me, I wasn't good with it until we touched ground. Even then, my stomach was in knots and I puked in the bathroom several times before I could get myself together enough to hail a taxi.

Of course, I didn't speak Italian, so I had to hand the driver the written address and hope that he didn't take me to some hostel and kill me.

We pulled up a narrow cobblestone road as the sun was setting. My driver barely spoke English, but he managed to point to the building before handing me back the address. I stood in front of an old metal door with shaky hands, praying that this wasn't a huge mistake.

Before I could put my fist up to the door, I heard someone coming up behind me. There was giggling and a deep, familiar voice. I turned to see my biggest fear. Joey was standing there, with another woman. I froze and so did he.

The woman, with her strong accent spoke first. She said something in Italian and when I shook my head, she changed to English. "You need help?"

Joey turned to look at her. "Gia, she's here to see me. Why don't you go out without me tonight?"

The woman looked from me to Joey. "You sure?"

"Yeah." She kissed him on each cheek before walking back down the road.

Joey turned to me with confusion in his eyes. "Lace, what the hell are you doin' here?"

I covered my face. "I'm so sorry. I thought...Oh God, I feel like such a fool."

Joey pushed me gently to the side and unlocked his door. He grabbed my bag and pulled me inside. After climbing a set of stairs, we went through another door and entered into the main apartment.

I was crying so heavy that I couldn't even see the place with a clear set of eyes. Joey pulled me along and sat me down on a couch, where he kneeled down in front of me. "I can't believe you're here. How did you...What are you doin'?"

I shook my head, unable to tell him the truth. I couldn't admit that I'd come all this way to profess my love, to a man that clearly didn't leave Maryland because of me.

He grabbed my hands and put them up to his lips. "How did you find me? Did my mother put you up to this?"

I sniffled and finally opened my eyes. It was blurry, but I could see that he was concerned. "Why didn't you tell me you were leaving?"

He leaned back and put his head down. "I didn't need to explain my reasons to anyone, Lacey, especially you. You made it clear that we couldn't be together."

"No! You don't understand."

He stood up and started pacing. "Lacey, tell me why you're here. You see, I'm tryin' real hard to move on. I moved here to get away."

"Get away from what? Are you in trouble?" I couldn't understand what he was running from. Clearly since he'd already been hooking up with new people, me being the reason was out. There had to be something else.

He scrunched up his face. "No! I didn't do anything wrong. Stop actin' like you don't know."

I stood up and followed where he was walking. He came to the refrigerator and leaned against it. My hands touched his back and he didn't move. "I really don't know."

He faced me and looked right into my eyes. His were sad and red. I lifted my hand and touched his face. "Don't, Lace."

"Why? Why can't I touch you? Do you hate me that much? Did you leave because you hated me?"

Joey turned his head and rubbed his lips across my hand. "I can't hate you."

"I don't understand." He didn't hate me or want me. I was nothing to him, just like all the other women in his life. I backed away from him, moving my hand away and crossing my arms over my chest.

I walked backward and he came forward, chasing me. He pulled my arms open and held them at my sides while peering into my eyes again. "What don't you understand? I told you how I felt. I told you that you were different. I knew I shouldn't have let myself feel that way. My mother always told us not to give a woman our heart. She said they'd just break it, but you were different. I couldn't help myself. I had to know what it felt like to open myself to you." He scratched his head and spun around like a mad man. "Then you go and sleep with Shayne, like I meant nothin' to you. Do you have any idea what that felt like to finally fall for someone and have that happen? I had to leave, Lacey. I couldn't see you again, even if it was by chance. It hurts too much knowin' you don't want me that way." Joey walked into the bathroom and slammed the door behind him. "You need to go."

I ran toward the door and placed my palms against it. "Joey, don't shut me out. There's something you need to know. I can't tell you through the door."

A few seconds passed and he opened it. His eyes were watery and I could tell he was emotional. This was a side of him that I'd never seen and I was scared of how he was acting. "Are you here because someone's hurt? Is it my mom? Tell me, Lacey." He was panicking.

"I came because I love you," I sobbed. "I came as soon as I found out you were gone. I know it was stupid, but I couldn't tell you over the phone. I needed to see you. Now, after seeing you with that other woman, I know I wasted my time."

Joey grabbed me and pulled me into his arms. His lips were on mine. Warm passion ran through my veins as our tongues met and danced together. His hands started on my waist, but made a beeline up my shirt and under my bra. I felt his palms running over my nipples, which became hard instantly.

Joey pulled away from our kissing and pressed his head against mine. His eyes were closed, so I closed mine. "I thought if I took this job I could forget about you and the way you made me feel, but I was wrong. I can't get you out of my head."

My heart ached thinking of him using other women as a means to forget me. "So you picked up other women?"

Joey laughed and held me closer, like he was teasing me for being jealous again. "That woman is my bosses wife. I don't have a lot of stuff here yet, so I borrow theirs from time to time. She came to get their blender because they're expectin' company tomorrow night."

"So, you weren't hooking up?"

"Woman, you make me crazy!" He put both of his hands through his hair. "Why would I want to be with any other women, when all I want is you? Don't you get it? I'm crazy for you, Lacey. I drink beer to forget you and pass out dreamin' about you. You think I wanted to let myself feel this way? Damn it, I've gone my whole life without carin' and the first time I open my heart, it gets torn to shit."

I began to cry again, realizing how bad I'd hurt Joey. If he'd opened up to me about his feelings, I would have never walked away. "I'm so sorry," I grabbed his hands and looked right at him. "But I'm not leaving this time. I came all this way, not just to bring you home, but because hearing that you left crushed me. I don't care about the past, or the head games that both of us were playing. This thing between us is real."

Joey stood there looking at me for the longest time. He said nothing, like he was thinking about what to say but couldn't find the words.

Finally, I couldn't stand it. "Say something."

He picked me up, carrying me through the house and into his bedroom. From there, he set me down on the bed and pulled off his shirt. "You flew here to be with me, Lacey. I need you naked, so we can fuck, because I'm tired of picturin' it in my head. I need to have the real thing."

Chapter 24

Shayne

I woke up that next morning feeling like someone that I cared about had died. Maybe it was because I hadn't heard from Lacey and needed to know she'd arrived and everything was okay. If that prick Joey messed things up after she'd gone all that way, I was going to hop on the next flight and kill him myself.

As amazing as it was, Ashley was already awake. I knew because I could smell coffee brewing, even though she didn't drink it. I found her in the kitchen, eating a giant bowl of hot farina. "Hey."

She took a big bite before replying. "Hey, yourself. Are you tired?"

"I don't know what I am. Everything's so fucked up." I grabbed a cup and filled it with hot coffee. "I mean, I know I'm doing the right thing, but I feel like shit. What if she was the one and I let her go?"

"Well, when I lost Ford, this last time, when I knew it was forever, I felt like I couldn't breathe. You know what I was willin' to risk to get him back and that wasn't even the worst of my plans. For God sakes, I was willin' to live with that lie as long as I could trap him into bein' with me. It's only been months, so I get that nobody can forgive me, but what I did was out of bein' so damn desperate. My point is, if you love Lacey, it's goin' to be hard to get over her."

"That's the thing. I feel like shit, but even with the guilt, I still think I could go out and hook up with someone else. I hate to admit it, but I've never had that feelin' like they were the only person for me."

"Do you look at other women and think about Lacey?"

I shook my head. "No, not really."

"There's your answer, Shayne. You see, when I looked at other men, I only thought about Ford. None of them even compared to him, in any way."

I took my coffee and drank the rest of it. "Maybe you're right. It doesn't mean that I don't care about her, though. What if somethin' bad happened to her?"

"What if somethin' good happened and she's just busy. I hate to say it like that, but she did fly halfway across the world to be with Joey. We both know that she wouldn't have done that if she only planned on talkin' to him."

Ash was right. I was a fool to think that she'd even remember to take a second to call me. Lacey was probably naked and in his arms. I cringed thinking about it, but appreciated that she could be happy. After all, wasn't that what I wanted for her all along?

I patted Ashley on the leg. "How about we go out for brunch and go out lookin' for baby stuff. Those little ones you're carryin' are goin' to need a kick-ass nursery, right?"

Ash turned to look at me with a big smile on her face. "Really? Shayne you don't have to spend your money on me. My dad set up an account for me to get on my feet. I don't know the bank information, but I'm sure I can get it before we go out today."

I thought about her father and how he would always try to control his daughter, by offering to support her. I hated it. She needed to free herself of his hold and raise her children by herself.

We both needed to move on and start worrying about things pertaining to our futures, instead of dwelling on things that we couldn't change. Lacey and I were over. I knew it needed to sink in and I realized that it was what was right. A part of me would always care about her, but for now, she couldn't be my responsibility.

I still had to worry about my family, my living arrangements, and my future. It wasn't like I could play house with Ash for the rest of our lives. There was going to come a time when each of us needed to start dating and living separately. We couldn't pretend forever.

Lacey

Our naked bodies moved with the motions of each of our thrusts. Joey caressed my skin as if it were our first time. We'd been making love since I got there, only stopping for short breaks to recover.

I couldn't tire of this man because he took me to places that I never knew existed, each time we came together. I couldn't be sure if it was the same for him, but he seemed to be enjoying me equally.

I reached over and pinched his nipples between my nails, getting that rise out of him that I expected. He wrinkled up his face and let out a groan, before picking up his stride, pumping into me like a jack-hammer. Our bodies slapped together and both pain and pleasure sent me over the edge. I dug my nails into his wide shoulders and felt myself going into a blissful frenzy.

Joey looked pleased, watching me lose control from his doings. Still, he wasn't just satisfied with letting me relax. His thumb reached down and began vigorously rubbing my already sensitive bud. "I thought about this pussy every damn night. Show me again, Lace. Show me how it puckers up for me."

His eyes were focused on my pussy, watching for it to react to his words. I could feel it pulsating, delivering the action he wanted to see. A gush of wetness rushed out of me, coating his erect cock. He smiled again and licked his lips, while my body shuddered. I reached for him to hold me, but instead, he entered me completely and got back into the same groove as before.

I closed my eyes, turning my head to the side, trying to relax enough to breathe normally. Out the window, I could see the sun coming up. Realizing that we'd been up all night, made me suddenly exhausted. I yawned and looked back at Joey, who was intently focused on blowing his newest load.

I studied his face, so focused on the matter at hand. He was motivated by desire, but not just that anymore. Joey had fallen in love. He'd opened his heart up for the first time, allowing himself to feel what it was like to share a mutual affection with another person.

That person was me and it gave me chills to think about it. As his thrusts continued, I watched him, envisioning our first moments together, before he'd let me in. It didn't matter that it had been about the sex, or trying to forget my problems. We were here, together, because I couldn't stand imagining my life without this man.

This time, when my body began to shake, it was because I was crying.

I was crying for this beautiful man that I'd almost let slip out of my life. Tears ran down my cheeks realizing how close I'd been to losing him and how happy I was to be here, in his arms where I needed to be.

Joey grabbed my shoulders and jarred his body forcefully against mine one final time. His eyes closed and his head fell back as he shot his hot cum into me for the fifth time in one night.

He collapsed on top of me, finally giving in to the reality that we hadn't yet slept. I held him tightly, ignoring the sweat that covered our bodies. As I started to sob, he lifted his head and looked at me, curiously. "What's wrong, Lace?"

"I almost lost you," I cried out. "I'm just so happy to be here with you, Joey. I'm sorry for staying away and fighting what was really happening between us. I should have trusted you, listened to you more."

He wiped my tears away with both of his thumbs. "Stop cryin'. It' ain't your fault. I could have been clearer, but I wasn't sure how to be. It ain't like I've been in this situation before."

I nodded. "I know."

His lips pressed against mine and he held them there. When he pulled away, we were looking right into each other's eyes. "I thought you were usin' me to forget Shayne. I didn't want to admit my feelin's to someone that didn't want me back. Leavin' was easier."

"No," I shook my head. "It wasn't easier. I thought you didn't want to see me anymore. I stayed away because I was afraid that it was easy for you to forget me. It hurt me so much. I thought that sleeping with Shayne sent you over the edge and you decided that you didn't want me anymore, in any way."

He rubbed my cheek and smiled. "It was the opposite. When you told me that you slept with him, I felt like I couldn't breathe. My damn stomach hurt so much and I wanted to hurt him so bad. That was so hard for me, Lace, hearin' you say that you gave yourself to another man; a man you loved."

He was right. I had loved Shayne, in a way that was so different than the way I loved Joey. "I know you won't understand this, but I slept with him because I wanted the closure. I did it because I knew that there was something happening with us. Sleeping with Shayne had nothing to do with love. It was about saying goodbye to something that I'd held onto for too long."

He shook his head and looked confused. "Are goodbye fucks somethin' that normal couples do?"

I shrugged. "It was a mistake."

Joey rolled off of me, grabbed a towel and stuck it between my legs, before pulling me close to him again. "You're here now."

I reached up and touched his lips with my fingertips. He kissed them, while keeping his eyes focused on me. "I'm so sorry I hurt you. If I would have known how you really felt, I never would have touched him again. I swear I wouldn't."

"Lacey, Shayne still wants you, that's no secret. If you gave him another chance..."

I pressed my fingers over his lips. "Shh, it's never going to happen."

We got more comfortable, laying on our sides and facing each other. Joey played with my fingers, lacing them together and tickling my palm. "I'm goin' to fuck up at some point, because I've got no idea how to be in a relationship."

"You're doing great." I could feel myself dosing off. The sun was in full view out the window and I knew I couldn't fight it much longer.

He brought my hand to his lips and held it there. I closed my eyes, letting myself fall into somber.

"I'm so in love with you," were the last words I heard him saying.

Chapter 25

Shayne

I decided to take Ash to the beach, where there were many outlets to shop. We arrived and had lunch before we got started. Ash's appetite had not only increased, but she ate anything in sight. We shared an appetizer and talked about our shopping list when out of the corner of my eye, I recognized two girls sitting together.

Megan and her sister sat there, peering over at me. I waved out of courtesy and got a dirty look from Megan and a smile from Rachel. Ash turned around to see what I was looking at and both girls looked away quickly. "Friends of yours?"

I chuckled and took a sip of my soda. "I don't know if you would call it that. I hooked up with one and tried with the other, not knowing they were sisters. The one was a bitch, but her sister seems like a good time. It happened that night Lacey said we were over. I was drunk and don't remember shit about it."

Ash shook her head and laughed at me. "Do you even know how many women you've slept with?"

I shrugged. "Yeah. I might not know all their names, but I think I remember all of them."

She talked with a mouth full of food, showing me how comfortable we were together. "I guess I'm a big cock block. If you want a night to yourself, I can go stay at my parent's house."

I chuckled. "You're fine, Ash. It ain't like I hook up with someone different every night. Besides, I'm tryin' to be better."

"You don't have to change your life because of all this. You deserve to be happy too."

As much as I appreciated her giving me my space, the truth was that Ashley's predicament kept me busy. It was finally feeling like it was going to be alright. I'd be a good uncle and no matter what, I'd always be there for them. "I'm where I need to be, right now, Ash."

Our meals came and we started eating and getting back to small talk when Rachel walked up to our table. "Hey, Shayne."

I looked up at her standing there. "Hey. You visitin' your sister?"

She looked back at her sister putting on a coat. "Yeah. So how have you been? Is this your girlfriend?"

"No." Ash began to laugh. She sat back and rubbed her stomach, displaying a small baby bump.

Rachel's eyes got huge. "Oh my God. Are you two having a kid?"

Ashley said "no', while I said "yes." We both looked at each other.

I looked back at Rachel. "Yeah, it's a long story. This is my roommate Ashley. Ashley this is Rachel."

They smiled and greeted each other. I could tell Rachel was confused and honestly, so was I. I couldn't believe that I'd just come out and said that I was the father, to someone that obviously wanted to hook up again. What was wrong with me?

"You should give me a call sometime. We'll hang out again."

Megan walked up to her sister and grabbed her arm. "How many times have I told you to stay away from this guy?"

"Hi, Megan," I said as I motioned a wave.

She curled her upper lip. "Hello and goodbye, Shayne."

It drove me nuts that she hated me so much. Without thinking, I stood up and grabbed her arm. "Can I talk to you alone for a second?"

Rachel looked as shocked as I felt. Megan pulled her arm away from me. "No! There's nothing you can say to me that I would find amusing."

I looked at Rachel and then back to her sister. "I need to tell you somethin'. Please."

She rolled her eyes and we walked outside, while Rachel lingered somewhere behind us. Once she headed toward the car, Megan turned around to face me. "What do you want, Shayne?"

"Why do you hate me?"

"Really? You wanted to get me alone to ask me that? Dude, you slept with my sister. You sleep with everyone. It's disgusting!"

"I'm not that bad." It wasn't like I really slept with everyone. I had limits.

"Look, I don't know why you want to talk to me, and I don't even care. Please leave me alone, Shayne. I don't want to be your friend and I want you to stay away from my sister. She doesn't need any diseases."

I crossed my arms over my chest and stared right at her. "That's cold. I don't have diseases. I just thought maybe we could start over. I'm not the bad guy you think I am."

She pointed back toward the restaurant. "You're here with a pregnant chick, that you claim is carrying your child, yet you're out here, trying to hit on me."

"I'm not hittin' on you."

She crossed her arms like mine. "Whatever. Can I go now?"

"Ash is a friend. We live together. I'm not the father, but the real one doesn't want to claim responsibility, so I promised to take care of her. In fact, we're here shopping for the nursery."

She seemed shocked. "What's in it for you?"

I threw my hands in the air. "Nothin'. I'm tryin' to be a good friend to her. She needs help. You still think I'm the devil?"

Megan looked down at the ground. "Are you telling me the truth? You're really going to take responsibility for a baby that isn't yours?"

"Twins. She's havin' twins."

That shocked her even more.

"Megan, I'm not trying to sleep with you. If I just wanted to get laid, your sister is practically spreadin' her legs waitin'. I don't want that. I'm sorry I hooked up with her. Lacey had kicked me out of her life and I was all fucked up about it. Your sister found me at the bar and took me home. I woke up, not knowing what happened or where I was. I swear. I know you probably don't believe me, but that night we stayed up talkin' meant a lot to me. You're a nice girl and I just want a chance to be your friend."

She shook her head and looked away. "This is weird, Shayne. Don't you have friends at home? Why me?"

"You're different. I want a friend who is neutral. I'm related to most of mine and I live with Ashley."

"So you two must have benefits living in that situation."

"I've never touched her. You can go right inside and ask her that. She dated my cousin for years and I'd feel wrong about bein' with her that way. She's a real cool girl, who has gone through Hell. She lost her best friend and the love of her life, then ended up pregnant after a one-night-stand."

"That sucks."

"Yeah. We're both pretty fucked up."

Megan took a step toward me. "I don't like you, Shayne, but I'm wondering if maybe you aren't as bad as I assumed. I suppose that if you're serious about needing a friend, you could call me from time to time. If you keep your distance, I will consider answering. I will never forget seeing you with my sister, nor will there ever be a chance of us getting together."

I put my hands up like I was surrendering. "That's cool. I'll prove to you that I'm not the guy you think I am." Sure, in the back of my mind I was picturing kissing her and getting her into bed. I was a man and I had needs. First I needed to convince her that I wasn't the devil. She was a nice girl and I was willing to take my time to get to know her. "So, I guess you'll be hearin' from me."

"Whatever. Look, I'm not telling my sister about this. She thinks you're awesome and it sort of repulses me, since she knows nothing about you."

This girl fought for her innocence. She was a challenge and it made me want to know her more. I wanted to know why she'd never given herself to someone. "I can't change the past."

"Have fun shopping, Shayne. If I don't ever talk to you again, good luck with the twins."

I watched her get into her car before heading back into the restaurant. Ashley was picking at my plate when I sat down. I lightly smacked her hand away. "Lay off my fries."

She laughed. "They were gettin' cold."

"I'm starvin'."

"How did that go? She seemed like she wanted to rip off your balls."

"I think she still does." I popped a couple fries in my mouth before continuing. "I met Megan a while back and we stayed up all night just talkin'. She's a virgin and really serious about her values. She hates me for sleepin' with her sister. I was tryin' to make peace."

"She thinks we're together doesn't she?"

I shrugged. "It don't matter. I'm pretty sure she'll never talk to me again."

"You like her don't you? The one you didn't sleep with?"

"Yeah, she's different."

Ashley smiled, but kept her opinions to herself. I knew it was a slim chance I'd ever talk to the girl again, so it wasn't worth talking about it. "Can I get dessert?"

I laughed and handed her the menu folder. "Since you're eatin' for three, I guess it's fine," I teased.

"I'm always hungry. It sucks. My ass is going to be huge and I'll never find a man. I'll have to marry some old geezer from town without teeth."

"Shut up. You're beautiful. It don't even matter how fat your ass gets."

I meant it as a compliment, but for some reason, Ashley's face turned red. "Don't talk like that. We have to live together. We need to be ugly to each other to keep the peace. I

287

like livin' with you and knowin' you don't expect me to sleep with you. It's comfortin."

"All I said was that you were good lookin'. It's nothin' I haven't told you before. Woman, your hormones make you whack sometimes." I laughed it off, but wondered why she'd gotten so scared. Was I making her feel uncomfortable at home too?

I watched her eat an entire brownie sundae before we headed out to shop. After visiting the baby store, she'd picked out the cribs and the bedding. By the time we'd left she had a whole list of things she wanted. It made me feel good to be able to be involved. The twins were going to be spoiled and contrary to what everyone said, I could see Ashley changing before my eyes.

She was going to be a good mother and I'd make sure of it, whether or not they were really my kids.

Lacey

I still couldn't get over the fact that I was in Italy. Joey's arms held me so tightly for hours. It was as if he thought if he let go, I was going to disappear. I too, was caught up in being with him again. The familiar scent of his skin reminded me of how much I'd missed it. His hands fit perfectly over each of my ass cheeks and his naked body was hot enough to have to open the windows in the winter.

We were consumed in each other, forgetting about anything else important that could have needed attention.

We'd finally confessed our feelings. Joey said he loved me, and no matter what anyone could have told me in the past, I believed him. His eyes didn't lie and I knew that I had, in fact, been the main reason he had to leave town.

An ache filled my heart when I thought of the exact moment that I found out he had gone. So many things raced through my mind, but nothing was more clear than my urgency to find him and bring him back to me.

We finally woke up and according to the clock it was afternoon. Not only had I not told my parents that I'd left the country, but I also hadn't called Shayne to tell him I'd arrived safely. None of it mattered, when I considered having to leave this bed, and Joey's arms.

He kissed me tenderly on my cheek. "How long can you stay?"

I sat up on my elbow and looked over at him. He was relaxed and content.

"I didn't think that far ahead."

"Well, now that you're here, how long can you stay with me?"

"Not long. My parents will flip when they find out that I ditched school to leave the country." I feared the conversation when they did find out.

"Lace, what if you stayed here with me? We could travel on my off days and not worry about anyone tryin' to come between us."

I shook my head, shocked that he would ask me to move across the globe for him. "I came here to get you to come home." Sudden confusion was written across his face. "Everyone misses you. We can be together now."

He shook his head and scooted his body away from mine. "It's not that simple. This job wasn't just about me runnin' away. Sure, if I would have known that you'd be with me, I wouldn't have accepted the offer, but the truth is, I applied for this position last year. When a spot opened, I knew it was an opportunity of a lifetime. Walkin' away from this could end my career. Do you know how many chefs get this kind of break?"

Tears filled my eyes again when I realized that he wasn't coming home with me. Not even my love could change his mind. Joey's future was important. He'd worked so hard to get where he was. "I don't understand. You said you wanted to be with me." I had to still try.

"I do."

"I can't live here, Joey. I can't leave my whole life and drop out of school."

He stood there, looking down at me on the bed. Since he was in his boxers, I concentrated on his face, instead of his fabulous body. As much as I wanted more sex with him, the most recent confession was about to give me a nervous breakdown.

I began to sob, thinking about walking away from this man that I felt like I didn't want to be without. He'd entered my heart even when I didn't want him anywhere near it. Now, I couldn't bear to let him go.

"I can't leave, Lacey. I'm sorry. I know you must hate me, but this is what I've wanted my whole life. I'm not askin' you to live here forever. It's just for six months to a year." He reached for my hands and kneeled in front of me. "Just consider it. Things would be so much easier if you were here with me. I'm so fuckin' lonely and the thought of you goin' home will drive me nuts."

I cried harder. "It's not that simple. I have to finish school. My parents don't even know I'm here. They won't understand, because I never told them about you. I'm so sorry."

Joey looked down at the sheets. "I understand. It sucks, but I understand."

291

I pulled his hands toward me, getting his attention. "If I could, I'd stay here with you, in this bed for as long as possible. You and I both know we have obligations. We can't drop our lives and not regret it at some point."

"I know. What do we do now? Do we spend the next couple days fallin' deeper for each other and then act like everythin's okay when you have to go home?"

Joey was upset. The pain was written across his face. My heart ached for him and the thought of leaving. After all of the miscommunications between us, we were finally on the same page. Walking away from him would be horribly difficult. "We can have a long-distance relationship."

He shook his head and paced around the room. "I don't even know what that is, Lace. You're askin' me to pour my heart out to you every night, when I can't be with you physically? What kind of relationship is that?"

"People do it all the time, "I argued.

He ran his hands through his dark hair, frustrated. "It's stupid. It's worse than not bein' together at all. I don't want to worry about you bein' so far away. I don't want to hear your voice on the phone and miss you like crazy." He threw his arms up. "I don't want to feel like this!"

I tried to regain composure over myself, instead of being a babbling baby, but he was breaking my heart. This wasn't how I'd played things out in my head. I wanted to be with Joey, but it wasn't going to happen unless we were living on the same continent. It seemed as if we were doomed before ever having a chance at a real relationship.

I sobbed, so hard that he sat down on the edge of the bed and started rubbing my legs. "Don't cry, baby. Please don't cry."

"I can't help it. I want this with you. No other man has ever made me feel the way that you do. You're acting like you'd rather walk away from this, than try to make things work. My heart is breaking. I came all this way for you, because I loved you so much that I was willing to cross the ocean to bring you home to me. Now, you tell me that can't happen. How am I supposed to feel? How am I supposed to look you in the eyes when I know that we have to say goodbye to each other? I'm sorry, Joey. I'm not like you. I can't do it without hurting."

The room was quiet aside from my weeping. I wanted him to reach out and tell me things would be okay, but Joey didn't move. He laid down beside me and covered his face with his hands. Not that I was watching him anyway. My eyes were too filled with tears to be able to pay any attention to him.

We both lay there, side by side, with nothing left to say to each other. I'd come and experienced just a taste of what it would be like to have his heart and have given him mine, but that was all it could be. Before things got worse for both of us, I was going to have to get up and leave. I couldn't be that close to him and not want more. I think he knew it too, since he was keeping his distance.

Without waiting for him to question me, I headed into the bathroom to shower. When I was done, I'd say my goodbyes and walk out of his life.

Maybe I shouldn't have gotten involved so soon after Shayne. Maybe I should have let him be and not chased him down. I felt worse than when we were apart before and this time, it would be because it was what he wanted.

Chapter 26

Shayne

I didn't wait very long to call Megan. I didn't just like her because she reminded me of Lacey. I liked her because she hated me and the challenge kept me invested.

It was a little after nine in the evening and I knew she'd still be awake. Who went to bed that early at our age? Finally after it rang four times, she answered.

"Hello?"

"Megan, it's me, Shayne."

"Yeah, I saw your name. Are you going to make me regret telling you to call me? I mean, I thought you'd at least have the decency to wait a few days."

"No. I just wanted to say that it was great to see you earlier today, that's all." I waited for her to respond and wondered if she'd hung up.

"I don't know about nice, but it was something."

"I'll cut to the chase, Megan. You're interesting and I like talkin' to you. I want to take you out to dinner, as friends of course."

"Didn't I just say that we could be long-distance friends? I never agreed to a date."

"Not a date. Just two people having conversation over dinner." I waited for her to reply and the silence meant she was thinking it over.

"I will meet you at a restaurant, a well lit one, with plenty of people in it."

"Jesus, I don't murder people."

"Shayne, let's be clear about one thing. You will never get me into your bed, backseat, or anywhere else for that matter. I have no interest in sleeping with you, not now and not ever. I only agreed to be your friend, because I felt sorry for you."

"I will text you the details of where to meet. I know how you feel about me, Megan. You've made it very clear."

"Goodnight Shayne."

"Goodnight."

Ashley smiled at me from the other side of the couch. She had her whole hand in a bag of popcorn and threw a piece at me. "She's goin' to cut off your dick if you try to get it near her, you know that right?"

I shrugged. "I plan on bein' nice and havin' a plutonic meal with her. Hopefully she can't reach it from under the table."

Ash laughed. "Are you sayin' it's small?"

I threw the popcorn back at her. "Don't even play. You know I will whip that shit out right now and show you."

She covered her face. "Eww. Take that somewhere else."

Before I could say anything, She shot up straight and grabbed her stomach. I was immediately at her side. "What's wrong?"

She grabbed my hand and put it on her belly. "Feel."

I could barely feel little taps against my hand. Then they finally stopped. We looked at each other, but I didn't remove my hand. "How long have you been feelin' that?"

"A few days, I guess. I thought I had gas or somethin'. One of those books said it was called flutterin'. I laid in bed last night feelin' them. That's when I knew what I had to do."

I looked at her with worry in my eyes. "What do you have to do?"

"I need to devote my whole life to these two. It's time I stopped worryin' about myself and started living for them." She smiled and looked down at her belly.

I kissed her cheek, catching her off guard. "You're goin' to do great, Ash."

"I hope so."

We stayed up watching a movie. Ashley was probably thinking about the twins, while I was focused on how I was going to get back into Megan's good graces. This was definitely going to be my hardest challenge. Since I'd slept with her sister, she wasn't going to let me touch her, at all.

When I got into my room, I lay there staring at the ceiling, thinkin' about Lacey. I don't understand why my mind kept going back to her, because she was obviously happy in Joey's bed. Just picturing them together made me cringe. I hated that he'd won her heart and promised myself that I would kick his ass one day, if he hurt her.

By midnight, I'd already looked up a few places to eat and shot Megan a text message. It was late and I was sure she was asleep, but I needed the distraction. Getting her to like me was going to be it.

Anything was better than sitting around thinking about the girl that I let get away.

Lacey

I don't know how long I'd been crying. Joey continued to hold me and I did manage to sleep in between the sobbing. It wasn't like he was being mean to me. The man didn't know how to be a boyfriend. He'd slept with women with no strings since puberty. How could I be angry when he honestly was confused himself?

My heart still ached though.

Our time together was limited and I hated thinking about it.

By the next morning we'd settled nothing and Joey had to get up and head to work for six hours. He showered and dressed before sitting down next to me on the couch. "I'll be back in time to take you out for dinner. Promise me, you'll still be here."

I nodded. "Yeah."

His kiss was long and soft. I took in his scent and immediately thought about having to say goodbye to him for real. I held back the burning in my eyes, so he didn't see me getting upset again. I needed to be strong. This was a mutual decision. We couldn't be together until we were both done what we needed to do.

I didn't have a problem with waiting for Joey, but knowing his track record, and the fact that he said he couldn't do long-distance, I feared that he'd pick up other women and share his bed with them.

Once he left, I lost it again. After some time, I curiously walked around his apartment and stared out the window. Finally, I got a coffee from across the street and sat outside, listening to the people speaking such a beautiful foreign language.

The stone streets and kind folk were welcoming, but one thing that I couldn't help notice was the slew of beautiful women everywhere I looked. My stomach was in knots as I watched them smiling and passing by me.

This was where Joey lived, surrounded by these exotic women. By the time he came back to the states he would have bed some of them. It was only a matter of time before he got lonely one night and wanted company. Sure, it would mean nothing to him, but everything to me when, or if I ever found out.

It was making me sick thinking about it. The last thing I wanted to do was share this wonderful man with other women. This was the reason that I'd broken things off with Shayne and now I was going to be in the same situation with Joey.

With two hours left before he got off of work, I found a pen and paper and started writing him a note.

As painfully heart-wrenching as it was, I needed to walk away. There was no way in Hell that I could look him in the eyes and be able to say goodbye to him. I was too in love with him to be able to do that.

My thoughts were jumbled and I didn't know where or what to say, until the pen hit the paper.

Joey:

Being with you has been some of the happiest, most exciting times of my life. I'll never forget how you helped through my tough break-up with Shayne. Thank you for letting me know a side of you that no other woman has known. I will never forget that you gave me your heart.

To say that I love you back would be an understatement. When you pop in my mind, my stomach does butterflies and I feel like a giddy teenager, awaiting my first kiss. Our connection has always been mutual, even when I was fighting you off. I think that's why I fell so hard for you, because I could feel that it was going to be amazing.

You didn't disappoint. Everything you said was true. You were the best that I've had and probably the best I will ever have, but all good things must come to an end.

As much as I don't want to do it, I have to walk away now, before I fall apart before your eyes. Being with you, here, in this beautiful place, hearing you say those three words back to me, is something I will never forget. Words could never describe how much love I feel for you.

The thing is, I can't hold on to hope when it comes to us. You said it yourself, that you don't know how to have a long-distance relationship. I get it, I really do, but it doesn't make it hurt any less.

I'm leaving today, before you get home, because I can't say goodbye to you without hurting. I can't look you in the eyes and tell you that we're over. It's not what I want, but what has to happen. Let's face it, you're gorgeous and women notice that. I can't be halfway across the planet from you and not wonder when or if you're hooking up with someone else. Maybe Shayne is to blame for my trust issues, but I have them now and I can't help myself.

I hope one day, when you come home, you'll forgive me and we can be friends. That's lame and cliché, but it is the truth.

I love you, Joey, with everything in me, I swear I do, but I can't hold onto hope when I know I will only be disappointed. I can't ask you to change for me, or be faithful when we're so far apart.

Thank you, for everything you've given me. I will treasure our time together for the rest of my life.

Love, Lacey

By the time I made it down to the street, I couldn't speak to tell the taxi driver where I needed to go. I had to write it down and hope that he could read English. Thankfully, we arrived at the airport a while later. I struggled with my decision when I got my return flight and then sat around waiting for it come. The whole time, I stared at the doors, hoping he would come rushing through and tell me he was coming home. It was selfish for me to even daydream about. Expecting a man to give up on something he'd worked his whole life to become was ridiculous. I couldn't take that from him, no matter how much I wanted it. He needed to see it through, so that he could be happy in his future. The last thing I wanted was to be the person that held him back.

Not only did I cry the whole way home, but also when I pulled out my cellphone and wondered who to call. It was nearly seven in the evening and I was a train-wreck. For no reasoning other than being a mess, I called Shayne.

I needed to be able to get home without someone asking me a million questions. I was broken and knew he wouldn't want details. All I could hope was that he still cared enough to come and get me.

Chapter 27
Shayne

My plans to win Megan over were going great. Instead of waiting for an opportunity to come, I made one, the next day. I'd arranged to meet her in the evening, right after work. She argued with me at first, but I think she knew I wasn't going to let up on her until she agreed.

I located her car in the parking lot and took the spot next to it. She was playing on her phone and looked over when I pulled in. I knew she wasn't amused by me, not that I blamed her. The animosity between us was no secret. She didn't care for me much and I was on some mission to change her mind.

I ran over to her door and opened it, like a gentleman would do.

"Good evening, Megan."

She stepped out and gave me a weird look. "Hey. Keep in mind this isn't a date, Shayne. Opening the door for me isn't necessary. You don't have to pretend to be someone that you're not."

I wasn't alright with her assuming that I was the world's biggest douche. Sure, she had good reasons for not liking me, but she refused to give me the benefit of the doubt, about anything.

"When we met, was I an asshole? Did I or did I not stay up with you all night and never ask for anything else?"

Megan waited until we were inside and seated to answer me. "When we met, I already knew things about you. You weren't an asshole, but it's probably how you work. I can see how you would meet a girl and charm her into thinking you were nice. Then, when they finally let you in their pants, you showed your true colors."

"How I work? Damn, woman. Should I give you the knife to cut off my genitals now, or can we have dinner first?" I had to laugh at the way she thought she knew everything about me. "Can you clarify that for me?"

"How you swoon women into sleeping with you. It's ridiculous. I don't get it at all. How could someone give themselves to a complete stranger?"

The waiter brought us our drinks and I pondered on how to respond. This girl was determined to bring me down and I wasn't going to be taken easily. I was going to get in this girl's pants, whether she believed it or not. "There is no swoonin'. Did you ever think that maybe they want to know what it's like to be with me, to fuck me? Have you considered that they enjoy it as much as I do? Besides, let's face it, all you know is what you've heard. Maybe I'm not as bad as you think I am."

"I have a good idea of exactly how you are."

I pointed to her. "I'm goin' to prove you wrong."

"Fat chance."

"Can we please enjoy our meal? I didn't ask you to dinner to rehash your hate for me. I'm tryin' to make peace

305

here. I'm tryin' to show you that I'm not the asshole you think I am."

She went to open her mouth when my phone started ringing. I grabbed it, preparing to ignore the call, until I saw who it was.

"Lacey?"

She was crying hysterically. "Shayne, can you come and get me?"

"Where are you? What's goin' on? What did he do to you?" I was freaking out and I think Megan was embarrassed at how loud I had become.

"I'm at the airport. My flight just got in." She sobbed harder and I knew that it wasn't worth asking her for details when she was in this sort of condition. Something bad had to have happened for her to come home so upset.

"I'm leaving now. It's goin' to take me a few hours. Can you hang tight until then?"

"Yeah."

"See you soon, Lace. I don't know what's goin' on, but it will be okay. I'll make sure of it."

I hung up the phone and looked at Megan, who obviously wanted an explanation. "Megan, I know I basically forced you to come here, but Lacey's in trouble and I have to help her. You should stay and enjoy your meal. I'll call you tomorrow." I pulled out my wallet and tossed money on the table before starting to walk away. My mind was on Lacey and hearing her so upset had me worried.

306

Megan grabbed my arm. "Wait! Do you want some company?"

"She's at Dulles. It's a far ass drive."

"I don't have plans. Besides, she may need to talk to a woman about whatever's going on. I can take my car so we all fit. Unless, you want to be alone?"

I didn't have time to consider if this was some kind of female test. There was always one happening and I was forever failing them. Still, I knew that whatever was going with Lacey wasn't going to end in the two of us sleeping together, plus the ride was long and boring alone. "Yeah, it would be cool if you came. I'd like the company."

We grabbed our things and headed toward the airport. Joey messed with the wrong girl this time. He was going to pay for hurting her, even if I had to fly to Italy to do it.

Megan and I talked about a lot of things before we reached the airport. Traffic was moderate and it took us an extra half hour. After over three hours of being stuck in the same vehicle, I felt like we'd made progress. Megan was starting to ask me personal questions. She wanted to know me, which was the first step.

As we approached the terminal for arrivals, I saw Lacey sitting on the curb. She had her hands up to her face and was clearly emotional. I threw Megan's car into park and went running over to her.

After scooping her up in my arms, I held her tight and let her cry. "Shh, it's goin' to be alright, baby. You're safe now."

307

Seeing her so upset made my blood boil. More than ever, I needed to settle a score with Joey. If Lacey wouldn't tell me what was going on, I'd call him and find out. He wasn't getting away with breaking her heart. She didn't deserve it yet again, from another man she loved.

Lacey

I'd spent four hours stuck in an airport, after an even longer flight. I was exhausted and lost. My heart, soul and everything that kept me together had shattered into pieces. I'd walked away from Joey, without giving him a chance to fight me. I knew myself better than that and it was clear that I couldn't allow myself to trust him, not when he was so far away.

Shayne ran toward me, before I even noticed a car sitting there waiting. He threw his arms around me and for the first time since I watched Joey walk out of that bedroom, I felt safe. I wasn't using him, asking him to come and pick me up. I may not have trusted Shayne with my heart, but I trusted him with my life and I knew he cared enough to help.

I didn't expect him to have been on a date and for him to have brought her along. I watched a familiar girl get out of the front passenger seat and climb in the driver's side. She said nothing and neither did Shayne about her being there. Honestly, I didn't care. I just wanted to go home and lock myself inside where nobody could get to me. We both got into the backseat and pulled away from the parking spot.

Shayne continued asking me what was wrong as we drove away from the busy airport. I stared out the window, until I couldn't take him asking anymore. "I left him there."

"You what? What do you mean?"

"He was so happy to see me," I cried while I tried to explain. "We were so happy, all consumed in each other. I thought he was coming home with me, so that we could be together. It's what we both wanted. We were finally on the same page." I cried even more. "So I thought."

"I'm not followin' you, Lace."

I knew I wasn't making sense, but it was difficult to explain when I didn't want to talk about it in the first place. "Joey wanted me to stay there with him. He said he couldn't leave until his job was complete and that his future was at stake."

"Babe, you need to get to the part where he broke your heart."

I faked a smile. "He didn't. I left him." I shook my head and covered my face again. "After much consideration, I decided to come home, where my life is. It wasn't like I could just move there and be with him. My parents would disown me."

"He'll be back, right? He isn't stayin' there forever?"

I thought about why Shayne would ask that. A part of me wondered if he wished that Joey never came back. It was no secret that he hated me being with the guy. "He'll be there six months to a year. I don't know all the details, because I got too upset when he started to tell me." I was fighting back the tears again, while thinking about him being that far away. He'd have gotten my letter by now and I knew it would hurt him. In my experiences, when a man gives his heart to a woman and she breaks it, he's kind of broken from opening up ever again. It hurt me knowing that I was hurting him. "Look, I left Joey because it's impossible for me to trust a man who is living half way around the world. I can't even trust a guy that lives thirty minutes away."

Shayne disregarded my comment and chose to ignore the fact that he was the reason for my distrust. "So, he just let you go? He just let you walk away and hop back on a plane, all hurt and messed up like you are?"

I shook my head. "Not exactly. I waited for him to go to work and then I left him a note. He's probably just finding out."

"Jesus Christ. Are you fuckin' with me right now?"

"No. I'm not kidding. We outweighed our options and it was clear that it wasn't going to work out, so I took it upon myself to find a resolution. Joey needs to focus on his career, because it's all he's ever wanted. I can't ask him to give that up for me. I also know that I wouldn't be able to handle him living so far away. Since he's never been one to settle down, a long-distance relationship is out of the question. I made things easier for him. He didn't have to watch me walk away. He didn't have to hear me telling him that we weren't going to work out. It's for the best."

Shayne and I were both in the backseat and he was giving me the most concerned look that I'd ever seen him give. "Lacey, don't you see what you've done? You raced on a plane to get to him and then you just come home, giving up. I'm not

311

buyin' it. I'm not buyin' how you're okay with this decision. It's not for the best. It's fuckin' bullshit. Look at you." He motioned toward me. "You look like Hell and I've never seen you so upset, not even when we broke up. Don't sit there and tell me it's for the best, when clearly, it's not what you want."

I cried even more and felt him pulling me into his arms. He said something to the girl who was driving, albeit I was too caught up in my own sobbing to hear him. "It hurts so much."

I sniffled, sobbed and then bawled some more. By the time we'd made it back to my parent's house, I was done talking and just wanted to go to sleep. Shayne walked me to the door and said hello to my mom, before he started to walk away. I stopped him halfway down the sidewalk. "Shayne wait!"

He turned and faced me. "You good, Lace?"

"I'm not good, but I wanted to say thank you. Tell your friend thanks as well. I didn't mean to cock block you on a date, if that's what it was."

"It wasn't a date, not really. She offered to come. Look, no matter what I'm doin', you will always be more important. Remember that." He kissed the top of my head before walking to the car.

My parents wanted an explanation, even though I knew they assumed I'd been at Sky's the whole time. Instead of worrying them, for now, I lied and said that's where I was and I'd forgotten my cell phone charger. When my mother saw my eyes, she asked if Shayne and I had been fighting. They were so out of the loop that they thought I was still seeing him. It reminded me how against it they would be about me moving to Italy to be with a man they knew nothing of.

I found my way to my room and locked the door behind me. I didn't want to talk to anyone. All I wanted to do was cry myself to sleep.

I'd never felt so depressed and alone. My heart had been so full of love and excitement just days ago. Being in Joey's arms felt like Heaven. Now, I was left vulnerable, wishing I could turn back time.

I had a chance at happiness and I threw it away.

Was I making the biggest mistake of my life?

Chapter 28

Shayne

"Maybe I was wrong about you, Shayne." Megan's comment caught me off guard. We were pulling out of Lacey's driveway and I figured she'd had enough of me after being ignored for the whole drive.

"I'm really sorry things were so weird. I've never seen her like that."

"You really care about her, don't you?"

"I'll always care about Lacey. After she broke things off with me, I thought I wanted to do whatever it took to get her back. The thing is, we aren't good together. She wanted a forever kind of love and I don't know what that feels like yet. It wouldn't have been fair for me to lead her on. She deserves happiness."

We pulled onto the main highway and she was quiet for a few minutes before she replied. "I am guessing you hate the Joey guy?"

"Me and Joey share a cousin. It's complicated. I've got to see him on holidays and him bein' with Lace is difficult. You think my track record is ridiculous, well, you've never met Joey. The guy is a gigolo. He fucks for amusement and nothin' else. I don't get how Lacey fell for him, but she did."

"If he's such a player, why would she want him?"

"Because, apparently, he's in love with her." I shook my head and looked out the window. "It figures right? The one girl I care about and she falls for someone I loathe. I suppose I deserve the torture, in some ways."

Megan kept watching the road as she spoke. I wasn't sure if she was just conversing with me because she was curious or because it was helping with the drive. "So, she got on a plane and went to Italy, then broke up with him and came home? It makes no sense."

She had a point. Why was Lacey willing to give up so much? Had I really messed with her head that bad that she wasn't willing to wait for what she wanted. Did she really think it would be better if she walked away and tried to move on? "I'm not one to root for the other guy, but you're right. The only person that can make Lacey happy is herself. The sooner she realizes it, the sooner she can follow her heart."

I don't know if I'd made her feel uncomfortable, but for the rest of the ride Megan talked about other things. We discussed her job and the twins. I didn't get into details about who the real father was. It was irrelevant to our friendship anyway.

After the long ride, we decided to grab some fast food and call it a night. We sat in Megan's car eating. "I'm sorry our dinner got ruined. I swear I wanted something other than a drive-thru."

Megan laughed. "I think I got to know you more this way. It certainly showed me that you care deeply about your friends. Look at the way you take care of your pregnant friend. It's insane that you would put yourself out there like that. I

315

was wrong about the person you are. I mean, I'm not saying that I want to sleep with you, but I think we could be friends."

She held out her hand and I shook it. "Deal."

We both laughed. Then Megan did something that shocked me. She leaned over and kissed me on the cheek.

Instead of pushing my luck, I simply smiled and got out of the car.

On the drive back to my apartment, I tried to call Lacey, but she didn't answer. It was late and I knew she probably wanted to be alone. I just wanted her to know I was there if she needed me, as a friend of course.

When I walked in the door, I found Ashley asleep on the couch. She had a bag of chips in one hand, the remote stuck in her cleavage, and a jar of pickles in the other hand. I snapped a quick picture from my phone before cleaning up and carrying her to her bed. Halfway there, she wrapped her arms around my neck and kissed me. Her eyes were still closed and I didn't think she even knew what she was doing. She mumbled something as I put her on the bed and rolled over, as if it had never happened.

I watched her sleeping for a minute, taking in her growing belly. It wouldn't be long before the twins were here. I still had a bunch to do to prepare, as well as have a heart to heart with my brother regarding plans. I needed to know how long he expected me to play daddy. The more time I spent with Ashley, the more attached I was to the twins. They weren't even here yet and I already loved them. Feeling them moving did me in. I was starting to wonder if making this decision was going to end up ripping out my heart. It was important to talk to Parker, before I let that happen.

Lacey

I was under the assumption that when I got to my own bed, in my home, I'd feel safe enough to get some rest. Unfortunately, that wasn't the case. I spent countless hours tossing and turning, thinking about the man that I'd left behind.

Out of habit and curiosity, I checked my social media pages.

Joey had messaged me and I was petrified to open them.

I stared at the notification for a while, before I could bring myself to do it. My hands were shaking and I imagined the worst. I scrolled down to the oldest one and started from there.

Lacey, I don't know what I did to deserve this. Did you come here to rip out my heart one more time, because that's what you've done? I brought you flowers and whistled my whole way back to work, in which I got off an hour early. I was more than excited to know you were waiting for me. You can imagine the pain I felt when you weren't there and had left that note.

I don't care what I said the other night. Given the chance, I would have talked you out of your decision. I sure as Hell didn't tell you I loved you so that you could leave me.

This sucks. I'm guessing you're still on a plane heading home. In that case, just know that spending even one extra day with you was worth so much to me. No matter where you are, or who you end up with, just know that you're the first woman I ever loved. I'll never forget the way your body felt in my arms, or the way you looked when you were lying naked in my bed.

Love, Joey

My eyes were so blurry that his last sentence was difficult to read. I wanted to continue, but needed to gain some composure before I had a nervous breakdown and had to be committed. My mind was thinking irrational things and all I wanted to do was disappear so that I wouldn't have to hurt the way I was.

Once I grabbed some tissues out of the bathroom, I was able to bring up the second message.

Why can't you talk to me? I'm hurting too, you know. Don't you get it? I was just getting used to moving forward. I'd focused on my job and tried to forget about how much I missed you and then you come walking through my door. You gave me fucking hope and then you took it away. I , at least, deserve an explanation, other than this fucking note. We're not kids, Lacey. You're being ridiculous. None of this makes sense to me. Why leave if you were happy? Why rip out my heart on purpose. Did I hurt you? Did I do something that I'm unaware of?

Just talk to me.

I wanted to talk to him. I wanted to hear him telling me he loved me and that we would find a way to be together, but it wasn't going to happen that way. The inevitable had already occurred. Joey and I had missed our opportunity to work things out. Our lives were in two different places and there was no logical solution to that problem. We were doomed, probably from the beginning. I should have taken my best friend's advice and stayed away from him.

I stared at the blank screen, thinking of what I could possibly say to him.

Only two words came to mind, so I typed them and hit send.

I'M SORRY.

The next few days were a blur and I refused to look at any of my new messages, on account of them being from him. I even avoided talking to Sky and Shayne. I knew that they didn't deserve the silent treatment, but I had nothing positive to say and explaining myself would only make my wounds worse. In order for me to heal I needed to block out the world and give myself time.

There wasn't a single second that went by that I didn't think about Joey. He consumed me in one way or another and the ache for him grew. It was when I truly realized the difference between puppy and adult love. The more I thought about it, the more I understood that Shayne had always been my past. He was someone I imagined being with, but never really had completely.

Joey was the opposite. He was someone that I never imagined being with, but didn't want to ever let go of. I could close my eyes and picture us in the future. I could see us settled down together and him coming home to me every night.

For the most part, I chalked my irrational thoughts up to being desperate. A part of me refused to let go of my feelings. It was useless to think that one day I was just going to wake up and have forgotten about our connection. Each time we separated, I found myself needing him more.

One day, more than a week later, while I was in class, I got a text message from a weird number. The vibration caused me to jump out of my seat, so I checked it immediately.

I LOVE YOU- Joey

My heart skipped a beat, before my mind could let myself get upset.

We weren't together. He was free to move on and see as many women as he wanted. I'd given up on us and made that clear.

His words were like a ticking time bomb. An hour later I was in the bathroom, dousing my face with water, trying to calm down. I was fighting a losing battle with my heart and didn't know what I was going to do.

All I knew was that the path I was on was destroying my livelihood. Something had to give.

If Joey couldn't let me go, then I had to force myself to push him away.

That night, I pulled up my account and left him a message. It wasn't the best decision, but he had to stop holding on to me.

Joey,

Please stop messaging me. We're over. There's nothing you can say or do. It was fun, but I can't do it anymore.

Lacey

Hitting send was like drilling nails into my feet. I knew the repercussions of my words. I also knew that he'd come back one day and when he did, he'd want explanations. When that time came, I'd find something to say, but for now, it was all I had left in me.

Chapter 29

Shayne

When my mattress gave way, I opened my eyes to a bright room and a pregnant chick sitting on my bed. She handed me a cup of coffee. "Good morning."

I sat up and grabbed the hot cup out of her hand. "Thanks."

"Parker's on his way here."

I knew I had a shocked look on my face. "I was going to go see him."

"Shayne, let's be honest. We can't keep pretendin'. I messaged him last night and he agreed to come and talk to me. We've never done it before, so I think it's important."

"Do you want me to leave?" I wasn't sure if she wanted me to be a part of the conversation, being that they were the real parents. I was just some asshole taking care of her and holding her hand through all of this.

She reached over and touched my hand. "No. I want you to stay. He needs to hear how you've taken care of me. He needs to know what you've sacrificed. You think I don't see how miserable you are, bein' here with me and bein' seen out in public with me, now that I'm showin'?"

"Ash, I'm not embarrassed."

"Deep down you know this isn't your mess to have to fix. I know you keep doin' it anyway, but enough is enough.

You need to date and be happy again. I'm just holdin' you back from that."

Ashley couldn't have known how attached I was becoming to her and the twins. She couldn't know that I enjoyed her company and liked her being my roommate. We were awesome friends and I could tell her anything. In a way, I felt like she was pushing me out. "You're wrong, but I'd like to hear what my brother has to say. The shit is gettin' real."

I hadn't calmed down, even when she left me to get up and get dressed. I couldn't shake the feeling that I had no say in what was about to happen. My 'do the right thing' brother could have decided he wanted to step in, for some reason it bothered me. Ash and I had been living together for months. Our friendship had grown and I cared for those twins, more than he could. He didn't even want them, claiming they were the biggest mistake of his life. Watching Ashley's stomach grow and feeling them move, was like nothing I'd ever experienced before. They were little miracles and shouldn't be taken as pieces of property.

Since I didn't want Ash to notice how much it was bothering me, I kept to myself until my brother arrived. When I saw him standing on the other side of the door, I wanted to tell him to go away, but instead let him in and shook his hand. "Long time no see, bro."

"Yeah, man. How you been?" Parker walked directly into the kitchen where Ashley was sitting on a stool. He froze, seeing her baby bump for the first time. "Whoa."

324

"Nice to see you, too, Parker."

He threw up his hands. "Sorry. I wasn't expectin' you to be so big."

I could tell from the look on Ashley's face that she took it the wrong way. She looked shocked, as if he called her a fat heifer and laughed afterwards.

"She's carryin' twins, little brother. That's what happens." I did my best to take up for her, but I could see that she was still offended.

She folded her hands on the counter. "I think we should cut to the chase. We all know why you're here, Parker. I'm goin' to be honest with you. You haven't done shit for me and that night we spent together was a huge mistake. It never should have happened. Your brother has not only supported me, but stepped in and done everything to make sure your children have a home and they are provided for."

"He volunteered that shit on his own. It wasn't like I could leave school. I've got responsibilities."

My brother was naïve. He had no clue how to be a parent, because he was just a kid himself. Ash was a good five years older than him and even she had her moments. "I did it because it was the right thing to do. Look at you, you've got your head so far up your own ass that you can't see how serious this is. It's not somethin' that's goin' to go away. For the next eighteen years, these kids are goin' to need a father."

Parker sat down and placed his hands over his face, moving them up and down. He was frustrated, but I was about to kick his little ass. "What do you want from me? I didn't come here to be ambushed."

Ashley looked at me and smiled, but I knew it wasn't a happy one. "Shayne, can you give us a minute alone?"

I was a little mad with her question. If anyone needed to leave the room it was my brother. I stood up and started walking toward the balcony. "Whatever."

I stood out there, thinking about the whole situation and how my family was going to be devastated. Parker needed to tell the truth, before more time passed. My parents would forgive him. They would help him.

Then I started thinking about Ash and the twins. I thought about living in this apartment alone. I pictured my brother setting up the cribs and preparing their arrival. My hands clenched the railing thinking about it. I wasn't sure when it had happened, but at some point, I'd become attached to them. I didn't want to share and I sure as Hell didn't want them leaving.

Unfortunately, it was out of my hands. Ashley was going to make Parker come clean. It wasn't my place to ask her to continue with the lie.

After a while, she came out on the balcony. Her feet were bare and it was quite cold. "You need shoes on."

"Your brother just left."

"He didn't say goodbye."

She looked right at me, with no real apparent look on her face. "He's goin' to do the right thing, Shayne. It's for the best."

What could I say? They were his children, not mine. This had been temporary the whole time and I knew that.

It didn't hurt any less.

Lacey

I wanted to think that life would be easier as the weeks went by. I steered away from the internet and hadn't visited Sky and Ford at their apartment since I'd been home from Italy. After her begging, I'd agreed to spend the weekend with them.

I drove to the familiar location, pulled into the driveway, and stared at Joey's door. Before I could get choked up, I grabbed my things and headed for Sky's. When I heard someone calling my name, I felt dizzy, until I turned around and saw a younger version of Joey standing in front of me. Behind him was Shayne's sister Peyton.

"Hey, Lace. How have you been?"

I shrugged. "Fine. What are you doing here?"

She looked at Jamey and then back to me. "We're together. Since he's watchin' the place for his brother, I come here on the weekends, so we can be alone."

"Your dad allows that?"

She rolled her eyes. "I'm an adult. I don't care what he says."

I pointed toward Sky's door. "It was nice seeing you, but Sky and Ford are waiting for me. We're going to order dinner."

Jamey grabbed my bag so I couldn't walk away. "Wait. My brother gave me somethin' to give to you when you came to visit. I'm sorry it's taken me so long, but you haven't exactly been around. Stay here, I'll be right back."

I didn't know what to do. My legs wanted to run toward Sky's and never look back. I had no idea what he had for me, but anything that had to do with Joey was a bad idea.

Jamey came out and handed me a box. It was about the size of a shoe box. I smiled. "Thank you."

"Tell him hi for me. He hasn't called to check in for a while now." I was puzzled to think that he hadn't told his family we weren't together.

"Sure."

I walked away before they saw me starting to cry. By the time I made it inside Sky's, I'd calmed down enough where she didn't notice. I placed the box and my bag in the spare bedroom and went out to be with them.

No matter what we were doing, or talking about, all I could think of was the box, sitting in the other room, waiting for me.

I knew I shouldn't open it, because whatever was inside was going to rip me apart.

Finally, after hours of watching movies and eating Chinese food, I made my way to the guest room and sat on the bed, staring down at the box in front of me.

He'd taped the edges, so it wouldn't fly open. I used my fingernail to break it and lifted the lid off.

Inside was an envelope with a letter taped to the front. I recognized his writing, from notes he kept on the refrigerator. My name was written on the outside.

I opened the note and stared at it before I could let myself read.

Lacey:

It's been three days since I found out that you slept with Shayne again. I guess part of it was my fault, for not being clear. You see, I've developed feelings for you, that I've never had for another woman. When you're in my arms I feel complete and when you leave, I miss you.

I know I came on to you the wrong way. It was all I'd ever done, and I never expected us to be anything more than fuck buddies. The thing is, hearing that you slept with Shayne, ripped me apart. You can imagine what it's like to hear that the person you're in love with has gone back to their ex.

Yeah, I said it. I'm in love with you.

I'm not writing this letter to win you back, or make you sad. I just thought you might want to know that you were never 'just sex'. From the first moment I held you, I knew it was something entirely different.

I've been offered a position in Italy, and due to recent events, I've decided to seize the opportunity. It's the chance of a lifetime and passing it up could change my future drastically.

I want you to know that I'll think about you everyday. You opened my eyes and my heart to feelings that I never knew existed.

Thank you for being with me, even if our time was limited, I will never forget it.

Love: Joey

PS: I burned the naked photos of those women and put the charred remains in the bottom of this box in a bag. I also enclosed that t-shirt you looked so good in. Smile, Lace. You're the most beautiful woman in the world when you do.

With no regard for my emotions, I picked up the t-shirt and smelled it. His scent was still on it. After holding it against my face and sobbing uncontrollably, I removed my clothes and slipped on Joey's t-shirt. Then I crawled in the bed and pulled the covers, up before looking at the burnt pictures, enclosed in a plastic bag. I could see that they were the real pictures. Under the bag, there was one picture sitting upside down. It was printed from a computer, so I flipped it over, curiously wondering if he'd forgotten to burn one.

This picture was different. It was me, sleeping in his bed. In marker, he'd written 'Joey' where his pillow sat.

I pulled the picture up to my chest and cried at the memories of waking up in his arms. I missed him more and more each day, and even time wasn't alleviating the emptiness that was inside of me.

Sky knocked before coming into the room. She crawled in the bed next to me and hugged me close. "What's wrong?"

"Joey left this stuff for me." I handed her the letter and gave her a second to read it. With the look of shock, she sat the letter down and looked over at me. "You can't keep going on like this. You've got to call him, Lace."

"It's been too long. Joey's a grown man. He has needs. The women there are beautiful. He's probably forgotten all about me."

She smacked me hard on the arm. "Stop being a stupid bitch! He's poured his heart out to you and you keep walking away from it. Lacey, you're the one who is to blame for all of this. You're the one making your life miserable. This man, the one that wrote this note, is crazy about you."

I shook my head, still in denial that I could ever be happy. "It's just too late."

She stayed with me while I cried, but said nothing else. I got that she thought I was making a mistake. I questioned myself daily. Many times I wanted to hop on a plane and show up begging him for forgiveness.

I woke up in the morning to an empty room. Deciding that I needed to be alone, I packed up my things and left before either of them woke up. They didn't need to see me this way and I couldn't deal with them telling me I was making a mistake.

Chapter 30

Shayne

After Ashley announced that Parker was going to do the right thing, I sort of shut down. We'd spent so much time together and for some reason it was bothering me that it was going to be over. I didn't get it, since we were just friends.

I refused to talk about it anymore and kept myself busy with work and getting the things for the twins in order.

On the weekend, I headed to the beach to hang out with Megan, in public, of course. She was finally being nice again and I enjoyed getting out of the house. It was weird, how all of the sudden my mind was on Ashley and the twins so much. I saw Ash every day and it wasn't like we didn't speak to each other.

We hung out all of the time, and shared a lot of similar interests. Her dad insisted that we have lunch with him one a week and it was fine, since he never questioned the paternity.

Since I was avoiding the subject, I didn't want to ask Ashley when my brother was planning on coming forward with the truth. Each day that passed had me more confused.

Then out of nowhere, I got a text that I needed to come home. Ashley was only six months pregnant and she was being rushed to the hospital. I dropped everything I was doing and raced as fast as I could to get to her.

I did everything as planned, by calling my brother and letting him know she was having complications. With him on the way, all I could do was be supportive.

It took me a while to be able to see her. Once inside of her room, I found her in tears. I pulled up a chair and sat down beside her. "What happened?" I was too afraid to ask about the twins. If something happened to them, it would kill me.

"I was trying to get something on top of the fridge, when the chair gave out and I fell. I started bleeding and called for an ambulance." She was already crying and I feared the worst.

"It's goin' to be okay."

She shook her head and let me lean in to comfort her. "I thought I lost them, Shayne. The pains were terrible. I thought I killed my babies."

I looked at her and couldn't explain the happiness that came over me when I realized the twins were alright. "They're okay?"

She smiled through her tears. "They were able to stop the contractions. The doctor says they are okay. He says I'll probably have to stay on bed rest, and will end up delivering early, since it's multiples."

A knock at the door caught us off guard. My brother walked in like he was disgusted. Ashley became uptight. "What are you doin' here?"

I was confused. She'd told me he was going to do the right thing. It made no sense why she wouldn't have wanted me to call him.

He looked at me and then back to her. "It would have been cool if you told your roommate what I was plannin'."

"Wow, you can't even ask if their all okay? What the fuck is wrong with you?"

Ashley grabbed my hand and squeezed it. "Shayne, don't."

I pointed to Parker. "He doesn't get it. He doesn't get that this is serious."

"Yes, he does."

Parker shook his head and handed me a set of papers. I didn't understand what they were until I looked at them. "What the hell? When did you do this?"

I was looking down at papers giving up parental rights and he'd signed them. "I figured I'd give them to you now, since I was here."

I looked from Ashley and then back to Parker. "Why would you do somethin' so stupid?"

"Shayne, I ain't ready to be a parent. I can't do it and we all know it. Ashley and I made the decision, because too many people are goin' to get hurt. It ain't fair to make you lie about this anymore. Ashley's agreed to tell her dad that she doesn't know who the real father is, and that you were just being a friend to protect her secret. You're free from it all. Don't you want your life back?"

The question echoed in my ear, but I refused to answer it. Did they all really think that I just sat there, looking at the papers and then at the two of them. "Ash, is this really what you want?"

She shook her head. "I can't keep expectin' you to play house with me, Shayne. You'll never know how much your friendship means to me, but I'm not bein' fair to you. I'm goin' to break the news to my dad and move back home. He'll make sure the twins are provided for until I can figure things out for myself."

"So that's it? You're just goin' to move out?"

She nodded and it felt like she'd kicked me in my heart. I stayed there with her, until her parents showed up. My brother left shortly after our conversation and there was no changing his mind. He wanted nothing to do with those kids and it made me sick. They were our blood and he was pretending they didn't exist.

I went home that night and sat down in the twin's room. We'd started painting it different colors and one of the cribs had been put together. I opened the closet and looked through the neutral colored outfits and blankets. Ashley had decided that she wanted to be surprised about the sex and I couldn't wait to find out what she was having. Whether it was nieces or nephews, I knew that I was going to love them.

Of course, her decision was impacting everything. I couldn't tell them I was their uncle. I couldn't ever let them know that we shared the same blood.

I sat in that nursery and sulked, thinking about having to give up two unborn children that I'd already fallen in love with.

Normally, if I was upset, I would have turned to Ashley for conversation or advice. Admittedly, she had become one of my closest friends and helped me through a lot since we'd been living together. Thinking about her not being around got me more upset.

Then I remembered something she'd said to me about love. She told me that she knew it was real when she couldn't imagine not being with them. I thought about the twins and Ashley and what I'd signed up for. I questioned myself over and over.

When I was more confused than sure, I called Lacey. I needed advice and someone to tell me that I wasn't just being irrational. My head was in a disarray and I couldn't focus on anything except finding a way to keep her from moving out.

"Hello?"

"Hey, Lace, it's me. I'm sorry to call so late, but I'm in a bad way and I need your advice."

"Are you okay?"

"No. I'm not."

I proceeded to explain everything that had happened and the feelings that I was experiencing. Even after a few snickering comments, it was obvious to Lacey as well. "Shayne, I think you're falling in love with them."

Hearing the words were freaking me out. "Yeah right. She's just a friend. I've known her for years. This was a favor for my brother."

"Are you arguing with me, or yourself?"

"How could I let this happen?"

Lacey laughed at me. "You don't let it happen, you fool. Love catches you by surprise when you least expect it. You've been living together for months. It's only natural that you would develop feelings for her and the twins. You're invested in them now."

"What do I do now? She's movin' out. Her mind is made up." I was fighting my feelings over what was taking place.

"Shayne, I never thought I'd be saying this, but one of us has to find happiness. You go after her. Did you ever consider that she's leaving because she has feelings for you and feels guilty about it? You took her in and protected her, when nobody else would. She'd be a fool to not want you."

"I talk to her about other girls. She knows I've been seeing someone."

"Exactly. She thinks she's in the way."

"She's not. She's never been in the way."

"I can't tell you what to do, Shayne, but I think you need to talk to each other, before it's too late."

"You're right. What about you, Lace? How are you doin'?"

She got quiet. "I miss him more and more each day. I thought I'd feel better as time passed, but the void in my heart is still there, reminding me every second of what I've given up. What if he was the one? What if he was my one chance at happiness and I pushed him away?"

"That's not true and you know it. Look at us. We suck at romance."

"True. At least you have a chance."

"Ford's goin' to kick my ass again, but I think I want to date Ashley. I need to know if I'm being desperate or this is for real."

"I better get going. I've got class in the morning."

'Thanks for the advice, Lacey. I'm glad we're friends."

"I'm glad too, Shayne."

We hung up and I knew what had to be done. In the morning, as soon as visiting hours started, I was going back to that hospital and I wasn't leaving until I knew where I stood.

Lacey

I'd slept in his shirt every single night, because it made me feel close to him. I missed him so much. My depression had never been so bad and my whole body ached every day.

Sky did her best to comfort me, but I was empty inside.

On a Friday, I drove to her place, planning on spending the night. Like always, Joey's car and motorcycle was in the driveway. My heart skipped a beat when I glanced at them. After getting out, I noticed a bunch of other cars were parked along the road.

Once inside of Sky and Ford's place, I noticed that they were getting ready, like they had plans to go out. I'd only packed comfortable clothes and had nothing to wear to go out anywhere, not that I was in the mood.

Sky came out in a skirt and blouse. She was hooking an earring in her ear. "Hey, you need to change."

"Why?"

"We're going to a party."

"I'm not in the mood. I'll just stay here until you get home."

Sky pulled me by the arm. "I knew you'd fight me. Come on. You can wear something of mine."

I pulled away. "Seriously, I didn't come for this shit. I don't want to go."

She put her hands on her hips and gave me a dirty look. "You're going. Don't make me kick your ass."

She practically undressed me and threw something tight over my head, pulling it down to my thighs. The black dress was way too hot for a normal party. "Where the hell are you taking me?"

She smiled. "It doesn't matter." She drug me into the bathroom, doing my hair and makeup. I felt like a cross between a princess and a hooker when she was done. "Look at you!"

I smiled and pretended to be excited. The three of us gathered together and headed outside, where I thought we'd be getting into a car. They looked at each other. "Shit, I forgot something. Can you help me for a minute?" Sky asked Ford.

"Can I get the keys? It's freezing out here."

I felt something being placed over my shoulders. It was black and leather and I turned to see who was offering me a coat.

My eyes had to be mistaken.

He couldn't be there, looking back at me, like he was. "Joey?"

He placed his warm hands on my cheeks. "Just so we're clear, I don't deal well with breakup letters."

I was still in shock and my breathing was out of control. "When did you get back?"

"This mornin'."

"Are you visiting?"

342

He shook his head and rubbed my cheeks with his thumbs. We stood there, staring into each other's eyes. "I came all this way to chase this girl. You see, I don't chase women, but this one slipped away from me. She thought she was doin' the right thing, I suppose. She didn't get that I would have done anything to keep her with me. She didn't understand that my future was nothin' without her in it."

"She sounds like an asshole," I whispered.

"Well, maybe I wasn't clear enough about my intentions."

"Maybe you should tell her now." I didn't know why I was referring to myself like he was talking to someone else, but he was going along with it too.

"That's what I'm standin' here tryin' to do." He leaned in, kissing me softly on the lips. My knees got weak and my arms wrapped around him, like they belonged there. "You hurt me, Lacey."

"I'm so sorry. I didn't want to stand in the way of your career."

"You wouldn't talk to me. You completely shut me out, like I meant nothin' to you."

"It hurt too much. I've been miserable without you."

"You have a terrible way of showin' it."

"So what happens now?"

"You see, you didn't count on me comin' back so soon did you? You thought I'd move on and pretend this never happened?" He motioned between us.

I shrugged. "Something like that."

Joey grabbed my arms and his face showed pain. "I don't give up that easily, woman. I told you before, I always get what I want. If you'd stayed long enough, you would have realized that I wasn't goin' to let you walk out of my life. I'd fight for this, because it's all I want. I'm a grown man, who knows what he wants in life, but I don't want any of it, if I can't share it with you. I'm sorry it took me so long to get back. I had to tie up loose ends and make sure I had a job to come back to."

"You're not going back to Italy?" I couldn't believe this was really happening.

"Lacey, I came home to be with you. I chose you over everything else. It's time to change and leave my old life behind me. I want more. I want you."

I was crying so hard and couldn't bring myself to speak. It was too surreal to me, that he was here, holding me and confessing his love for me.

"I love you," he whispered against my lips.

Our kiss started slow and then became so much more. Months worth of pain were being sucked away from my heart and it was filling with something new, something full and hopeful.

I clung to him and felt him doing the same. It was freezing, but I was burning up. We broke our embrace and looked at each other again. "I don't know what to say."

"Say you love me back. Tell me that comin' home wasn't a mistake. Say somethin'."

"I love you back."

There was a house full of people waiting for us, but we stayed outside holding each other. It was like one of those sappy movie endings that never happen in real life, except it was really happening. Joey was back. He'd come back for me and risked it all for a second chance.

I wasn't going to hurt him this time. I knew better.

This time I'd never let him go.

We started walking toward the party. "I thought you liked Italy."

He shrugged. "I can't get a decent cup of coffee and croissants are over rated. Who wants to eat pasta with a spoon, when they could be comin' home to you every night? I missed you, woman."

That's when I knew he was all mine.

Chapter 31

Shayne

Ashley was released the next morning, but since she was on bed rest, her parents insisted that she stay with them. I hated the idea, but knew she needed to be cared for when I was at work. We sent messages and I visited her every night, but it was never the time to talk about things.

The longer I waited, the more I doubted myself. She was having twins and I couldn't put myself out there and then change my mind months later. It wouldn't have been fair to her or the children.

By the weekend, I'd set myself crazy. I broke my plans to hang out with Megan and decided to invite Ash to come and spend the weekend at the apartment with me. I promised to pamper her and make sure she stayed in a laying position.

Her parents were reluctant, but Ash insisted she could ride in a car and make it there without stressing herself.

We got there with no problem and I helped her into her bed, when she complained about not being mobile.

I brought the fifty inch flat screen into her room the night before and had a huge spread ready for when she got settled. For hours we sat in her bed, watching movies and stuffing our faces. It felt right, being there with her like that.

By the end of the night, we were snuggled up together, but not in a romantic way. We'd talked about names of the twins and even liked some of the same ones. She had her head against my chest and my arm was around her shoulder. I kept wondering how we'd got to this point in our relationship and not noticed it happening. We were definitely closer and now that I was paying attention, the signs were all there.

When the twins started moving around, she had to adjust to get comfortable. I put my head against her stomach, over the fabric of her clothing. She watched me waiting for them to kick me. I took my hand, lifted my head and laid it back down against her naked stomach. Ashley seemed shocked.

I could feel them moving around in there, and without thinking about what was happening, I kissed her belly.

When I looked up, she had a frozen look about her. "What?"

"What is this Shayne?"

"You tell me." We just sat there looking at each other, hoping that the other person would speak first.

She laughed at me. "You're bein' weird. Did you think I fell in love with you for takin' care of me? Is that what this is?"

I looked down and then back up to her. "Isn't that what's happenin'?"

Her eyes were huge looking back at me. She shook her head and started backing away from me. "Don't play games with me, Shayne. I'm not one of those girls."

"No. You're not." I ran my hand over her face and she closed her eyes. I could tell from the way she was reacting that

I wasn't imagining it. Whatever was happening between us was mutual. I got closer to those puffy lips, never taking my eyes away from hers. Our lips met and I closed my eyes, hoping I wasn't going to get slapped. She tasted like popcorn and salt and as our tongues met for the first time, I felt something changing. It wasn't the fact that kissing her was getting me turned on, or the reality of what was happening. I was surprised at how right it felt to kiss her.

After all this time spent living together something had happened between us that neither of us expected.

I pulled away and we shared a moment of silence as we looked to each other for answers. "Shayne. Don't do this."

I kissed her again, before I replied. "Do what?"

"Don't get my hopes up just to end up hurtin' me. I've already been through too much to have my heart broken again."

I leaned my head against hers and thought hard about being faithful to someone. This wasn't just a person that I'd known for years. This was someone who knew all of my secrets. I trusted her completely and she not only tolerated me, but had developed feelings for me when I was at my worst. "Ash, I know you're not goin' to believe me, but I think I'm in love with you."

When she said nothing I pulled away so I could see her reaction. Her eyes were full of tears and I wiped them before they could run down her cheeks. "Please don't say things like that to me."

I wondered if she was begging me to stop because her feelings weren't the same. I had to know. For weeks I'd been tearing myself apart over it. "Do you love me?" She stopped pleading and looked away. I grabbed her chin and forced her to look at me. "Yes or no, Ash. Am I imaginin' that there's somethin' happenin' between us?"

She shook her head and whispered, "no."

"What happens now?"

Ash shrugged again and I intertwined our fingers. "Shayne, I can't be with you. I know too much about you. You're not the kind of guy to settle down and have some romance with someone expectin' twins. I'm fat and you feel sorry for me."

"What's your excuse then? Why are you allowed to feel that way about me, but I can't feel the same damn way?"

"Because you're you."

I was feeling offended. Maybe I deserved it, but I knew this wasn't like anything else I felt before. "The thing is, a friend of mine told me that she knew love from lust because when she pictured herself without that person she didn't want to go on. You see, I've questioned these feelin's for a while now, so I sat back and thought about your theory. When you went into that hospital, I dropped everything to get to you. I didn't want anything to happen to you or the twins. Imagining losing any of you was Hell. It was the worst feelin' I've ever experienced. I know you worked things out with my brother and I'm not obligated to take responsibility for them, but what if I want to? What if I want to be their father?"

"You're talkin' crazy, Shayne. You can't just sign up for a lifetime of raising someone else's children. It doesn't work that way."

I grabbed both of her hands and looked directly into her beautiful blue eyes. "Ash, I can't promise what will happen with us, but I want to be the father to these children. I want them to be mine. They've got my blood runnin' through their veins. I'll never abandon them, I promise you that."

She started getting herself into an emotional fit. Tears ran down her eyes, while snot ran out of her nose. I got up and grabbed her the tissues, then came back and pulled her into my arms. "You don't know what you're sayin'."

I held her close to me and kissed her head. "You're the first woman that I never wanted to sleep with. Bein' with you was never about gettin' you into bed. That's when I knew it was real. I wanted to be with you, without ever kissin' you. It's not about sex or playin' head games. I want somethin' with you that I've never shared with anyone else. I've seen you at your worst and still thought you were gorgeous. I get that we promised it would never happen between us, but it did anyway. I want a chance, Ash. Just give me a chance. Please?"

Ashley cried herself to sleep, never responding to my pleas. I knew she was scared, so was I. We were sailing through a storm and bound to sink, but wanted to take the chance anyway. I didn't know if I'd changed, or even if I could, but I wanted to. I wanted to do whatever it took to keep her and those babies from walking out of my life.

I may not have seen it happening, because it was slow and unexpected, but I wouldn't change it. I was in love with Ashley, even if she was carrying my brother's children and still carried around feelings for my cousin. The family was going to hate me even more, but I didn't care. For the first time, in a very long time, I felt happy. I had something to look forward to. She'd become my best friend and so much more.

I finally understood what I'd taken from Lacey with my lies. I finally realized what it felt like to fear losing the one you loved.

We may not have ended up together, but she taught me how to love and I'd never forget that. Losing Lacey finally made sense, as I woke up still holding Ashley in my arms.

She greeted me with a smile and one word that changed everything. "Okay."

Our story was just starting out. We had a lot of explaining to do, but for now, we weren't leaving this bed, or each other's arms.

Lacey

I felt like I was dreaming.

It was hard, sitting in his apartment and waiting for everyone to leave, so we could be alone. I think they sensed what was going on between us. As happy as I was to have him back, I didn't want his mother getting mad at me for hogging him to myself.

Joey saw the last of the company out and held his arm out to help me off of the couch. "As much as I like seein' you in this, I think we need to get you out of this dress."

He pulled me into his bedroom, kissing me the whole way. I hoped up into his arms and let him carry me to the bed. He leaned down, letting me fall on the mattress. Joey reached around, unzipping the dress. I got on my knees and held up my arms so he could pull it off of me. His shirt was the next thing to disappear. I tugged it over his head. We were so eager to be together that we began taking off our own clothes. I needed to be naked and feeling his skin touching mine.

"Slow down, Lace. We've got all night. His body was on top of mine and I was devouring him in kisses. I was smelling him, licking him and sucking on his skin, as if he were a craving that I had to have.

I dug my nails into his back and didn't let up. My mouth wanted to savor every inch of him.

He flipped us over and I sat up, grinding my naked pussy against him. Joey reached down and ran his finger in between my folds, pulling it back up to his mouth and sucking on it. "As sweet as I remembered."

I moaned and threw my head back, trying to control the chills he was giving me already. He held my thighs and let me dry hump him as if we were fucking. I reached up and pinched my nipples, before bringing one finger up and gathering some saliva off of my tongue. Then I rubbed it over my hardened nipple, getting it shiny and wet. Joey licked my lips as he watched me. He took one of my hands and placed it between my legs. I knew what he wanted and I happily obliged by rubbing my clit. My body rocked as he grabbed my nipple and sucked it into his mouth. I clung to his head with my free hand, holding his hair as my body bucked. I was so wet, so turned on already that I'd made myself cum.

He grabbed my hand and put it to my lips. I eagerly sucked up my own juices, watching him watching me. My pussy was throbbing for more and I began to touch myself there again, but he grabbed my hand and batted it away.

He held onto my waist and lifted me up, where my pussy was directly in his face. I sat on my knees and watched him dive in, lapping up my lips and sucking them hard. He teased my clit with his tongue. I threw my head back and squeezed my nipple again. He continued sucking in my clit then releasing. It was driving me wild with desire. When his thumb came into play, too, I knew what he wanted.

"Show me how much you missed me, Lace. Show me what I do to you."

He rubbed it hard, applying a circular pattern to my swollen bud. It was already sensitive from moments ago when I'd had my first orgasm. This time would be stronger. I could already feel it happening. He moved his thumb swiftly, applying the necessary pressure for me to explode in passion.

I let go, feeling the gush of euphoria pouring out of me. Joey ran his chin stubble over it, soaking it up. He groaned and licked my soaked lips, before lightly smacking it. My body shuttered again and I flipped over, falling onto the bed next to him.

After wiping his face, he climbed on top of me, kissing up my neck and sucking on my ear. "Tell me you love me."

"I do, Joey. I love you so much it hurts. I can't believe you're here with me."

He stopped kissing me and looked in my eyes. "This is where I belong. Get that through your head. I'm not goin' anywhere, and neither are you."

He took my breath away, first with his words, and then as he slowly entered me. He was fully erect, but my body accepted all of him. I gasped as he thrust himself in and out. The walls of my pussy responded and tightened each time. Our lips met and our tongues collided together. I felt like we were floating on a sexual high that I never wanted to come down from.

My legs wrapped around his back and we sat up, still attached. I kept my arms there clinging to him with everything I had. Our bodies slammed together and the harder we went the better it felt. Sweat ran down his forehead, but he stayed at the same pace.

We continued colliding together, absorbing each other's emotions, while giving ourselves to one another. I'd never felt so complete, so loved. He was everything to me and maybe it was wrong for me to feel that way about someone, but it was true.

Our time apart had only intensified our connection. Nothing was slow or romantic about what we were doing, but it was still mind-blowing.

Joey tightened and I watched him finally letting go.

We had all the time in the world for a repeat, but I wasn't about to let him go, not ever again.

Our lips met as we embraced. "It's good to have you home."

"It's funny you said it like that. How would you feel about livin' here with me? You'd be able to see Sky and sleep next to me every night."

I didn't let him keep talking. My lips were on his immediately. "I wasn't planning on ever leaving you again."

We were both adults and I could make my own decisions. Living with Joey was something that I didn't have to think about. Now that I had him back, there was no way I could be anywhere else.

The End

Want to know Joey's side of this romance? His novella, Reform Me, will out in January 2014.